The Firebird in Russian folklore is a fiery, illuminated bird; magical, iconic, coveted. Its feathers continue to glow when removed, and a single feather, it is said, can light up a room. Some who claim to have seen the Firebird say it even has glowing eyes. The Firebird is often the object of a quest. In one famous tale, the Firebird needs to be captured to prevent it from stealing the king's golden apples, a fruit bestowing youth and strength on those who partake of the fruit. But in other stories, the Firebird has another mission: it is always flying over the earth providing hope to any who may need it. In modern times and in the West, the Firebird has become part of world culture. In Igor Stravinsky's ballet *The Firebird*, it is a creature half-woman and half-bird, and the ballerina's role is considered by many to be the most demanding in the history of ballet.

The Overlook Press in the U.S. and Gerald Duckworth in the UK, in adopting the Firebird as the logo for its expanding Ardis publishing program, consider that this magical, glowing creature—in legend come to Russia from a faraway land—will play a role in bringing Russia and its literature closer to readers everywhere.

Today I Wrote Nothing

The Selected Writings of Daniil Kharms

Edited and translated from the Russian by

Matvei Yankelevich

ARDIS PUBLISHERS
NEW YORK, NY

This edition published in the United States and the United Kingdom in 2009 by
Ardis Publishers, an imprint of Peter Mayer Publishers, Inc.

NEW YORK:
The Overlook Press
Peter Mayer Publishers, Inc.
141 Wooster Street
New York, NY 10012
www.overlookpress.com
For bulk and special sales, please contact sales@overlookny.com

LONDON:
Gerald Duckworth Publishers Ltd.
90-93 Cowcross Street
London EC1M 6BF
www.ducknet.co.uk
info@duckworth-publishers.co.uk

English translation copyright © 2007, 2009 by Matvei Yankelevich

Cataloging-in-Publication Data is available from the Library of Congress

Book design and type formatting by Bernard Schleifer
Manufactured in the United States of America
ISBN 978-1-59020-042-1 US
ISBN 978-0-7156-3771-5 UK
5 7 9 10 8 6

Go to **www.ardisbooks.com** to read or download the latest Ardis catalog.

CONTENTS

Contents

ACKNOWLEDGMENTS

I WOULD LIKE TO THANK the editors of literary journals who encouraged my translation of Daniil Kharms and opened their pages to some of the works contained in the present volume: Vincent Standley of *3rd Bed*, Natasha Randall and Brigid Hughes at *A Public Space*, John Sakkis for *Bombay Gin*, Brandon Shimoda of *CutBank*, Cynthia Conrad and David Todd of *Dirigible*, Macgregor Card of *The Germ*, Gian Lombardo of *key satch(el)*, Paul Hoover of *New American Writing*, Zachary Schomburg of *Octopus*, Joanna Yas of *Open City*, Daniel Feinberg of *Soft Targets*, and Liz Lisle of *Watchword*. I am grateful to Northwestern University Press for permitting us to revisit some of the pieces originally published in *OBERIU: An Anthology of Russian Absurdism* (2006).

I would like to thank everyone at Overlook for taking a chance on Kharms and for all their support, and particularly my editors Alex Young and Aaron Schlechter, and designer Bernard Schleifer.

I am indebted to my co-translators, who lighted paths that had been obscured by solitary thinking: Ilya Bernstein, Simona Schneider (who is in turn grateful for the help of Rachel Schneider and Victor Persik), and in particular Eugene Ostashevsky, who generously shared his insights into Kharms's work, enriched my commentary on the text, and generally advised me throughout the process of shaping this collection; his wisdom and poetic skill are indispensible to the promulgation of OBERIU writing in this country.

Special thanks are due to Simona Schneider and Katya Klistorina for rooting around in the Kharms archives; to Evgeniya Ostroukhova for her aid in glossing the names of Kharms's characters; and to Lee Norton for his scrupulous copyediting.

Over the years, I have discussed these translations with people close to me who have been willing to lend an editorial ear or field questions about the Russian language and the Russia of Kharms's time. I would like to name them here: Elena Bonner, Tatiana Yankelevich, Inna Giter (who helped me draft a few of the translations), Efrem Yankelevich, and Anna Moschovakis, whose encouragement, poetic ear, and astute edits I could not have done without.

I am also grateful to the generous scholars, teachers, and colleagues who, whether through their textual or interpretive work on Kharms, or with insights from other fields, or by way of personal support, enlightening conversation and shared excitement aided me in this undertaking throughout the years: Jon Barlow, Lydia Chukovskaya, Katerina Clark, Vladimir Earl, Thomas Epstein, Anna Gerasimova, Daniel Gerould, Tomáš Glanc, Michael Goldman, Giulia Greppi, Mikhail Iampolski, Kornelija Icin, Jean-Philippe Jaccard, Alexander Kobrinskii, Ilya Kukuj, Lena Lencek, Mikhail Meilach, Tatiana Nikolskaya, Aleksandr Skidan, Raisa Solovyeva, Dmitry Tokarev, Andrei Ustinov, Julija Valieva, and especially Branislav Jakovljevic. My deepest thanks to Susanne Fusso, my adviser in the early stages of this project at Wesleyan University. I would like to acknowledge the Ford Foundation for a grant that propelled my studies of Daniil Kharms and whose moneys I scrounged to make my first pilgrimage to Kharms's archives at the Russian National Library (formerly the Saltykov-Schedrin Public Library) in St. Petersburg, where the staff in the manuscript department deserves our gratitude.

Lastly, I would like to dedicate this translation to the memory of my father, Efrem Yankelevich.

INTRODUCTION
THE REAL KHARMS

And then I realized that I am the world.
But the world—is not me.
Although at the same time I am the world.

—from "The Werld" by Daniil Kharms

WRITING THE WORLD

IN THE AUTUMN OF 1937, Daniil Kharms wrote in his diaries: "I am interested only in nonsense; only in that which has no practical meaning. Life interests me only in its most absurd manifestations." The words I translate here as "nonsense," *chush'*, and "absurd," *nelepy*, have, in Russian, a less technical ring. *Chush'* means nonsense in the most everyday sense—baloney, a bunch of crap, rubbish, something that happens by chance, something seemingly meaningless. And the adjective *nelepy* can mean "awkward," "out of place," or "ridiculous," as well as "absurd."

Kharms's commitment to nonsense, to *chush'*, did not wane even in the bleakest of times. The journal entry quoted above dates from the height of Stalin's purges, during what is sometimes referred to as the Great Terror, which was also a period of dire hunger and poverty for the writer. And yet he is reiterating here, almost verbatim, a pronouncement he made about five years earlier in a list of his likes and dislikes recorded during conversations with his close friends.[1]

It is tempting to take Kharms at his word and view him through the prism of the absurd. What word could better describe a petty argument between two grown men that ends with one of them beating the other to death with a cucumber, as in Kharms's story "What They Sell in Stores Nowadays"? Indeed, much has been made of Kharms's "absurdism," a label that has been generously sprinkled throughout both scholarly and popular discussions of the collaborators in the OBERIU, the avant-garde collective to which Kharms belonged. It has become almost a commonplace that these writers, and Kharms in particular, are unwitting predecessors of the European "Theatre of the Absurd." But there are important differences between Kharms and "absurdist literature," a term which is itself ill-defined and overplayed.

For one thing, in Kharms's world, absurd life is real life. Transcendent, noumenal reality can be glimpsed only in the oddest objects, in the most awkward gestures and the most senseless events. The "events" he describes are simultaneously completely normal, even banal, and outside the norm. They are by turn everyday incidents—as in his story "The Meeting," in which two people simply cross paths in the city—and otherworldly interventions in our daily affairs, as with the appearance of a wish-granting fairy in a hotel restaurant in the story "On Equalibrium" or the raising of the dead in his novella, *The Old Woman*. It is precisely in these manifestations of nonsense that the artificial logic of civilization (the deterministic logic of scientific progress, the perception of human time as a teleological continuum, the materialist ideology of Stalinism) is made vulnerable to the illogic of something at its base inexplicable, infinite, and immeasurable: the Real.

There are, of course, points of contact between Kharms and the post-war existential thinkers who sought to define the absurd, to employ it as a philosophical category. As Albert Camus describes it in *The Myth of Sisyphus*, the absurd is not particular to an event or an object and can be seen only through a prism of comparison—something outside the norm must be compared to the norm in order for its absurdity to become evident—and therefore the absurd is a "schism" born in the "collision" of two objects.[2]

In the charter manifesto of the OBERIU, or Union of Real Art, which Kharms and his friends founded in 1928, Kharms's poetics are described in terms of the collision of words and objects. Kharms experimented with such collisions in order to cleanse words of their "normal" meanings and to imbue objects with a sense of ontological being beyond their practical functions and uses. By these means, Kharms endeavored to create an "objective," non-representational writing, much like the abstract art of the Russian avant garde which he so admired.

The effect achieved by collision is "beautiful as the chance encounter, on an operating table, of a sewing machine and an umbrella," to quote Lautreamont's famous line, which the Surrealists claimed as their artistic dictum. The phrase "chance encounter" may work beautifully to describe the narrative mechanism behind many of Kharms's miniature stories, or "events," but Kharms himself would not have used the word "beautiful" to describe that encounter. For him, art is neither "beautiful" nor "ugly" but, rather, "correct" or "incorrect," "right" or "wrong." A work of art has to exist in the world as an object, as real as the sun, grass, a rock, water, and so on. It must also possess a "slight error"[3]—in other words, to be "right" it has to be a little bit wrong, a tad strange, and thereby truly real. Art, for Kharms, has an "independent existence."

In a letter to his friend, the actress Klavdia Pugacheva, Kharms wrote of bringing the world into order, at which point "Art appeared":

> Now my task is to establish the correct order. [. . .] When I write poems, what seems to me to be most important is not the idea, not the content, and not the foggy concept of "quality," but something even more foggy and incomprehensible to the rationalistic mind, but comprehensible to me and, I hope, to you as well, Klavdia Vasilyevna. It is the cleanliness of order.
>
> This cleanliness is the same in the sun, in the grass, in man, and in poems. True art stands in rank with the first reality, it creates the world and is its first reflection. It is necessarily real. [. . .]

For Kharms, the poem must—through the "clean" or correct order of its words—itself become an object in the world that is capable of doing something that changes the world.

> It isn't just words or thoughts printed on paper, it is a thing as real as a crystal inkwell standing in front of me on the table. It seems that these verses have become a thing, and one can take them off the page and throw them at a window, and the window would break. That's what words can do![4]

The American Objectivist poet Louis Zukofsky also strove for a poetry which was "an order of words that exists as another created thing in the world." The often quoted postulation of William Carlos Williams—"no ideas but in things"—also echoes Kharms's view of the world. It seems that Kharms embraced Kazimir Malevich's theory of non-representational, "non-objective" art, and then transformed that avant-garde impulse for abstraction into an equally idealistic art of ideas *as* objects, close in spirit to the American Objectivist project.

When Kharms writes that the poem can be thrown at a window, he is not creating a metaphor (to the OBERIU, metaphor was a rusty remnant of the old literature). Kharms believes that the ideal poem actually breaks glass; once again, two objects collide. Kharms's poem-object exists not only as "another created thing in the world," but also as a thing that does something. The written word goes beyond "thing-ness" and becomes an action. If the poem can break the window, if words (as in spells and prayers) can work miracles, and if words create the world, then something is *happening*. Writing becomes an *event*: The act of writing is an act in the world, a destructive gesture—like throwing the poem at the window—that opens the world up to the possibility of new connections, new objects, new events. For Kharms, the performance of writing is deeply connected to the performance of life: Even his manner of dress and public behavior become part of the larger work of "making" his life as one would make art.[5] The destruction of previously established connections between words and their meanings, things and their functions, and events and their causes is a prerequisite for the establishment of connections more truthful, more real.

The literary scholar Mikhail Iampolski has written that Kharms and the OBERIU writers reoriented the emphasis of the avant garde "from the social reality to a semiotic reality," the reality of signs. "Everything that the earlier avant garde employed for the magical transformation of reality is used by Kharms for the 'deconstruction' of the very concept of 'reality' or for the criticism of the mimetic functions of literature."[6] The OBERIU's major contribution to the Russian avant garde, argues Iampolski, was irony—something which the utopian arts movements of the early twentieth century had necessarily lacked.

"Before them, avant-garde art, despite the joyful antics of the Futurists, was serious to the core."[7] In truth, Kharms's critique does not require him to "throw the classics overboard,"[8] but rather to use them in a way they hadn't been used before: in one of Kharms's mini-plays, Pushkin literally trips over Gogol, and Gogol in turn trips over Pushkin. The establishment of ironic distance permits Kharms to reinvent prose as meta-prose: He parodies narrative structures and undresses the mimetic function of art. Birth, love, heroism, violence, and death are made senseless through slapstick. The major tools of Kharms's short prose works are digression and interruption; with these he attempts to save literature from its enslavement to progress.

Though his playful humor is apparent, Kharms also had a religious sense of responsibility for words.[9] He threw nothing away; if it was written, he'd have to live with it. Instead, he crossed out many texts in blue or red pencil and sometimes even labeled them in the margins— some "so-so," others simply "awful" or "wrong." He seemed convinced that he would answer for them before a higher authority than Soviet censorship or the political police. Kharms wrote in his diary:

> I was most happy when pen and paper were taken from me and I was forbidden from doing anything. I had no anxiety about doing nothing by my own fault, my conscience was clear, and I was happy. This was when I was in prison.

Otherwise Kharms was distraught when he couldn't write—his prayers for inspiration (some of which are collected in this edition) and his depressive diary entries correlate to the period of increasing hunger and material destitution in the late 1930s. Ironically, however, many of his stories seem to hatch straight out of writer's block. *The Old Woman* is only one example among many: The narrator tries to write about a miracle worker but succeeds only in writing one line, "The miracle worker was tall." The hero of the narrator's ill-fated story is, in turn, a miracle worker who refuses to work any miracles and passively submits to his own demise. Sometimes this psychological inability to write is translated into the loss of physical ability which prematurely ends many a story, as in "The Artist and His Watch": "I'd write some more but the inkwell's gone missing somewhere." In a text called "Something About Pushkin," the writer can't decide who it is he wants to write about and thrashes back and forth until he gives up in frustration: "Yet, after Gogol, it's a shame to have to write about Pushkin. But you can't write anything about Gogol. So I'd rather not write anything about anyone." Still other times, the end comes with the exasperated loss of the subject—as in "Blue Notebook #10," the story of the redheaded man of whom Kharms concludes "we don't even know who we're talking about. We'd better not talk about him any more." These are gestures that Kharms elevates to radical technique.

The subject of a story may shift over and over due to lack of sustained interest, insufficient information, or loss of memory. For example, in the circus-like narrative frenzy of "Sinfonia #2," the narrator turns from one character to another in lightning succession:

> But it's not that easy to tell you about Anna Ignatyevna. First of all, I know nothing about her, and second of all, I fell off my chair just now and forgot what I was going to tell you about. Better, I'll tell you about myself.

Logical connections are thrown out, chance seeks revenge on received order, fables lose their didactic morals, violence begets violence with neither motive nor authorial reprimand, and magic and nonsense prevail over reason. Kharms uses the language of sequence and logic only to undermine it:

> The incident was really quite typical, but still curious, for thanks to me Marina Petrovna went completely bald, like the palm of your hand. It happened like this: One day I came over to see Marina Petrovna and, bang!, she went bald. And that's all.

Language subjects the world to reason, dividing it into what Kharms and his philosopher friend Yakov Druskin liked to call "this" and "that." What is between "this" and "that"? is a question Kharms seeks to answer in many of his comic-philosophical sketches and pseudo-tracts. The real world, after all, is not "this" or "that," nor is it simply the sum of its parts. Rather, it can be found in the obstruction that exists between two linguistic (and therefore arbitrary) poles, in the point of collision between "this" and "that."

The Moscow philosopher Valery Podoroga calls the OBERIU gesture "transgressive":

> Directed at the objects, bodies, and events of the world, the OBERIU gesture does not return to the one who makes it. After it has broken into the world, the world changes its face, it is no longer the same world. That is why the OBERIU gesture is always destructive. The object is extricated by this gesture from its everyday surroundings and at that moment it loses its stable forms of existence.[10]

This gesture, Podoroga says, asserts itself as an event that lasts as long as we keep reading. In the moment that this eventful gesture throws itself at the world, the writer sees the world "with naked eyes" in order to experience the liminal space between "this" and "that" and encounter the world in an impossible, nonsensical way—without mediation.

But where is the "I" in this confrontation with the world that culminates in total identification? Does the writer disappear in the gesture? Is this liminal space located on the brink of obliteration? In his pseudo-treatise called "The Werld," Kharms comes to that very brink: "And I'm the world. But the world's not me. And I'm the world. And after that I didn't think anything more."

The toggling between unity and disjunction—the "shimmering" of the world (to use OBERIU poet Alexander Vvedensky's image)— is a recurring trope of Kharms's writing. It attests to his deeply dichotomous attitude toward foundational tenets of avant-garde aesthetics: the whole-hearted belief in universal language, speed and flux, the collective subconscious, and 360-degree vision on one hand, and— on the other—the plunge into collage, disjuncture, and broken lines and narratives, in light of the loss of a stable world. The interminable back and forth of the narrator's dilemma in "The Werld" is interrupted by the loss of thought, or of the ability to think. Here, as in many of his best works, Kharms tests the waters of oblivion and then dives into negation, perhaps knowing that nothingness and infinity are one and the same.

THE LIFE OF A MAN IN THE WIND[11]

If you believe him, Daniil Kharms was born twice. The first time, they pushed him back in. Then again, maybe he was never born at all. And this is in some sense closer to the truth. Perhaps it's most accurate to admit, as Kharms himself did, about the redheaded man, "We don't even know who we're talking about."

On the other hand, the world agrees that someone with the name Daniil Ivanovich Yuvachev was born in 1905 in St. Petersburg. Precisely what day in December depends on which calendar you go by, the Julian (which they used back then) or the Gregorian, which was adopted in Russia soon after the October 1917 revolution.

His father, Ivan Pavlovich Yuvachev, had been a *narodovolets*, a member of The People's Will (*Narodnaya Volya*), a revolutionary organization that succeeded on its eighth attempt to assassinate the tsar, Alexander II, and later had a go at Alexander III. The police cracked down on the organization (with popular support) and arrested many of its key members. Ivan Yuvachev was one of the defendants in the Trial of the Fourteen in 1884, during which he was convicted of terrorist activities, and sentenced to fifteen years of hard labor. He served the first four at the Peter and Paul Fortress on the Neva River in St. Petersburg and upriver at the infamous Schlusselburg Fortress on Lake Ladoga, north of Petersburg, along with his fellow *narodovolets* Alexander Ulyanov, Lenin's brother, who was hanged within its walls. This notorious prison for political dissenters (the anarchist Mikhail Bakunin among them) caused Yuvachev to undergo a religious transformation or, by some accounts, a mental breakdown. Yuvachev declined an offer of transfer to a monastery and served eight more years of forced labor on the far-eastern peninsula of Sakhalin. He returned to civilian life a Tolstoyan pacifist, a writer (he would publish two memoirs and several mystical-religious tracts), and something of an ascetic.

Legend has it that Ivan Yuvachev predicted the day of his son's birth. He telephoned his wife, Nadezhda Kolyubakina, from Leo Tolstoy's estate and insisted that a son would be born on the 30th of December (old style), and that he would be called Daniil (the Russian version of Daniel) after Ivan Yuvachev's favorite Biblical visionary. "I have spoken," he yelled into the receiver. And so it was.

Daniil's parents' were by no means rich, though his mother was from an aristocratic family. In the pre-revolutionary years, she was the director of a shelter for women who had done time in the camps; her husband got a job with the government as a financial inspector and was often away on business. Despite his parents' modest employment, Daniil enjoyed an upper-class education. At an early age, he displayed an excellent ear for music and a knack for drawing and acting. He was enrolled in the prestigious Peterschule, where classes were conducted in German. Though the memoirs of his friends attest to his fluent knowledge of German and English, his attendance is rumored to have been poor. He was transfered to the old Mariinsky Gymnasium (where his aunt was the director) in Detskoe Selo outside Petersburg, which by that time had been renamed Petrograd. In 1924, he enrolled in a technical college, where he made a short-lived attempt to study engineering. Although he abandoned his studies before the year was out, Daniil enjoyed saying he was an inventor.

That same year, Petrograd acquired a new name, Leningrad, and Daniil Yuvachev literally became Daniil Kharms (pronounced with a hard "h") when he penned the pseudonym into his passport. The name appears to derive from the English "charm" and/or "harm" reflecting a boyhood interest in magic[12]; its Germanic aspect may also have appealed to the young Daniil, whose schooling had led early on to a predilection for all things German. Of course, the name's resemblance to that of Sherlock Holmes—one of Karms's idols—is not coincidental. Whatever its provenance, this was to be the failed engineer's most lasting invention.

As a young man, Kharms memorized poems by a variety of contemporary poets—from the symbolist Alexander Blok to the visionary *zaum* (trans-sense) poet Velimir Khlebnikov. He had taken an interest in the Futurist legacy and joined a sound-poetry club led by Alexander Tufanov, an older poet who considered himself the keeper of Khlebnikov's flame. In Tufanov's circle, Kharms met the young but already confident Vvedensky, and they established a friendship that would change both their lives. Vvedensky was attending classes taught by the likes of Mikhail Matiushin and Igor Terentiev—artists and writers associated with Futurism—at the new State Institute for Art and Culture (GINKhUK), which was, until the later 1920s, a safe haven for avant-garde artists in the transitional period of Soviet culture.

Kharms embraced Futurism and its outgrowths as laid out by his idols—Kazimir Malevich, Khlebnikov, and Terentiev, among others— and quickly identified himself with what was seen as "Leftist Art."[13] The workshops taught by the older avant-garde generation were still pervaded by a sense of millenarianism and utopian mission: Matiushin, for example, led the ZorVed faction, which prized 360-degree vision and taught young artists to "see with the backs of their heads." The painter Pavel Filonov also taught his personal blend of cubist and futurist methods at GINKhUK, and his students would later become close to Kharms's circle; some even illustrated the children's books of Kharms and Vvedensky.

Kharms quickly absorbed all the new ideas in the artistic air at that time, and these served as a springboard for his idiosyncratic aesthetic theories centered around fragmentation, disruption, and the autonomy of art from logical thought, practicality, and everyday meanings.

In the mid-1920s, Kharms and Vvedensky joined with other young writers and theatre artists to form an experimental theatre group called Radix (which rehearsed with Malevich's permission in an unheated auditorium at GINKhUK). After several experimental rehearsals (rumor has it that their creative process involved various intoxicants and hallucinogens), the production dissolved around the time of Malevich's removal from the post of director and the dispersion of the Institute.

Kharms, however, was resolved to be avant-garde, and the best way he knew how was to found some kind of movement, in the tradition of the artistic unions of the past that he admired. He craved attention, and even more, still yearned to organize his companions into allegiances with prominent avant-garde artists and critics. He sought alliances with writers published in New LEF (Mayakovsky's magazine), with popular but increasingly alienated Formalist critics and linguists, and with artists such as Malevich, Kharms's favorite painter. Malevich apparently agreed to cooperate, saying "I am an old troublemaker, and you're young troublemakers. Let's see what happens."[14]

Kharms dreamed of an anthology (to be called *Archimedes' Bath*, after one of his own poems) that would include his and Vvedensky's poetry alongside creative works by their mentors and critical writings from the Russian Formalists. If Kharms had his way, all his favorite radical artists would unite under the banner of a newly invigorated movement to be known as the "Left Wing of the Arts." He was catching the end of a wave that had suddenly become dangerous, as even the word "Left," once a signal of progressive political allegiance, was now under serious scrutiny, with its echoes of Trotsky, NEP, and armchair liberalism.

It was in this changing world, a time Katerina Clark has diagnosed as the period of intense centralization of Soviet Culture and the cultural marginalization of Leningrad's previously important avant garde,[15] that a group of like-minded young artists with Kharms at the helm came to found a multifaceted avant-garde collective. At meetings, which took place in members' apartments, the young artists often deliberated on a name for the group and spoke of who should be included. They had gone through a series of monikers, the last of which had been "Academy of Leftist Classics," when Nikolai Baksakov,[16] the rather daring director of the Leningrad House of Print (the union hall of the city's printers), invited the group to perform as part of a series of presentations of "new artistic movements," under the condition that the group's name omit any mention of the word "leftist."

The group settled on a name that stuck: OBERIU, a nonsense word that, with some tweaking, would stand for what translates as the Union of Real Art, or the Association for Real Art.[17] Kharms drafted a little mandala-like emblem in his notebook that might have served as the OBERIU's brand logo: a six-sided star inside a hexagon inside a circle, with the word REAL placed beneath it in Roman letters. The OBERIU's manifesto was printed in the club's program. Though the group had already changed its name to this veiled and foreign-sounding acronym, their debut on January 24, 1928 went under the title "Three Left Hours."[18]

The show began with the reading of the manifesto and segued into the "literary section," which included poetry by Kharms, Vvedensky,

Nikolai Zabolotsky, Konstantin Vaginov, and Igor Bakhterev. Other attractions included clowns, acrobats, a "classical" dancer, a play, a jazz band, a magic show, and a screening of the made-to-shock montage called *Film Number One: The Meat-grinder* (since lost). They topped off the event with a public debate, a format very much in vogue at the time. At the heart of the evening was Kharms's newly written play, *Elizabeth Bam*,[19] which brought to the stage many of the theoretical premises of the OBERIU's theatrical mission, as stated in its manifesto, and derived in large part from their earlier experiments as Radix. Based loosely around a circular plot (Elizabeth Bam is accused of murder by her alleged victim), the action seems often autonomous, unmotivated by any psychology or cause-and-effect structure. In addition, the play's scripted *zaum*-songs and rhythmic movements created a highly stylized environment. Each "bit" was to be played in a different theatrical register, ranging—as Kharms noted in his copy of the script—from "realistic comedy" (in the style of the Moscow Art Theatre's Chekhov productions) to "absurdly comic-naive," to "solemn melodrama with undertones of Radix." Kharms's theater lifted up the autonomous theatrical act—the "bit"—against the structure of plot, psychological motivation, and dramatic trajectory.

Though *Elizabeth Bam* was shown only once, the OBERIU went on to present similar "theatricalized evenings" in venues ranging from university auditoriums to dormitories and prisons for about two and a half years. These often tumultuous spectacles earned the OBERIU some notoriety and much bad press. It's no surprise that the press turned against this late avant-garde buffoonery rather quickly—after all, these were serious times; the building of socialism, and careers, was at stake.

During the height of the OBERIU's public performances, Kharms had no luck publishing his poetry but found himself writing for children, a seemingly strange profession for a childless avant-gardist who often proclaimed an extreme dislike of children in his diaries and stories. Presumably enlisted by the State Children's Publishing House (under the editorship of well-known children's author Samuil Marshak) because of their taste for nonsense and humor, a number of the *oberiuty* began writing for the children's magazines *Hedgehog* [*Ezh*] and, later, *Siskin* [*Chizh*]. Several went on to publish whole children's books, such as Kharms's *Ivan Ivanych Samovar* and *A Million* (ostensibly about the

Pioneers, a newly formed Soviet youth organization, this poem was really a humorous counting game). These booklets were often illustrated by similarly disenfranchised artists from among the students of the older avant garde, direct descendants of the studios of Malevich and Filonov. Translation and writing for children were important sources of income for many writers in the Soviet period who were not accepted by (or refused to submit to) the new Soviet cultural mainstream and the dogmatic aesthetics of Socialist Realism. Kharms's poems and stories for children (including his version of Wilhelm Busch's German classic *Max und Moritz*) were popular in his day, and some even became classics, while his work "for adults" went unknown—neglected, if not actively suppressed.

His earlier Futurist-style verse, with elements of *zaum*, abstract sound poetry, and Russian peasant folk-song, now shifted towards a poetics centered on the "collision of objects," in which words shed themselves of the everyday and soared toward their "fifth meanings," which were infinitely more real than those to which the mundane world wanted to tie them. (In his introduction to a comprehensive edition of OBERIU poetry, Mikhail Meilakh noted that the interests of the OBERIU poets "were relocated from the sphere of *zaum* phonetics toward the sphere of *zaum* semantics."[20]) Finding inspiration in nonsense, Kharms played with rhyme and syntax, plot and narrative, and any literary convention at which he could poke fun.

By the late 1920s, Kharms was a fixture in artistic salons. His first wife, Esther Rusakova, sister of composer Paul Marcel and sister-in-law of famous anarchist and revolutionary Victor Serge, brought Kharms into the fold of the upper echelons of Leningrad's cultural life, and connections through fellow *oberiuty* made Kharms welcome at literary salons and circles (from Mikhail Kuzmin's to Kornei Chukovsky's), and many artists' studios. Kharms attended meetings of the Bakhtin circle as well as lectures of the Formalists. He was even involved, if peripherally, in the movement for opera reform, writing a libretto to be set to music by maverick composer Dmitri Shostakovich, but the project never materialized.[21] And though his eccentricities may have caused him to be laughed at by a good number of his contemporaries, he seems to have had an "in" with almost every crowd.

Public displays of decadent and purposefully alogical behavior earned Kharms a reputation in Leningrad cultural circles. It was hard not to notice this tall and striking man parading down the main boulevards, dressed as a tweedy English dandy complete with hunting cap and calabash pipe. He had by now completely assumed a role of his own creation, and though he used a plethora of other pseudonyms in his writings, to most people he *was* Kharms—a name which, whatever its etymology, suited the self-styled aristocrat and die-hard avant-gardist. Rumors, some of which were later elevated to the status of legend, circulated about his unusual behavior. He brought his own silverware, stamped with noble insignias, to proletarian pubs. He was prone to interrupt the flow of foot traffic on Nevsky Prospect by suddenly taking a prostrate position on the pavement, then, after a crowd had gathered around to see what was the matter, getting up and walking away as though nothing had happened. He kept a large machine at home, which he made of found scrap. When asked what it did, Kharms would retort, "Nothing. It's just a machine."

On stage at OBERIU performances, backed by banners reading "Art is a cupboard!" and "We are not cakes!" in the midst of the burlesque chaos—clowns, magic tricks, jazz, mechanical dancing—he read his poems proudly from atop a large armoire. When he was booed and hissed (which happened often enough), he became haughty, impatient, and volatile. On one such occasion, responding to an audience that wouldn't settle down, he blew up—"Comrades, I will not perform in stables and brothels!"—and left the building. Because the reading was sponsored by the Writer's Union—and its members tended to take things personally—Kharms was reprimanded; later he was stripped of his membership for not keeping up with his dues.

By the late 1920s, Leningrad was no longer a safe space for the *oberiuty's* brand of idiosyncratic public performance. The avant garde had lost its powerful place in the hierarchy of Soviet culture. Kharms's aim of unhinging art from the everyday—and turning life into art—was incompatible with the prevailing ideology. Soviet authorities, who had become increasingly hostile toward the avant garde, were already planning to put a stop to the OBERIU's activities. Following a slew of derogatory statements in the press (where the group's members were called "reactionary jugglers" and "literary hooligans" and their poetry was labeled counter-revolutionary), the former futurist Nikolai Aseev outed them in a speech to the Writer's Union, saying that their "poetic practice is far from the issues involved with building socialism." At the end of 1931, just about the time of the publication of Aseev's speech, Kharms and several of his friends were arrested and charged with anti-Soviet activities in the field of children's literature.

The police deemed Kharms's writing for children anti-Soviet because of its absurd logic and its refusal to preach materialist Soviet values. In the course of interrogations, Kharms basically agreed that his work for children was written with the explicit intent of distancing his young readers from reality. Kharms confessed that he "consciously renounced contemporary reality," admitting that his philosophy was "deeply hostile to the present." The utilitarian ideology of Soviet Russia and, arguably, the technologically oriented thrust of modernity were anathema to Kharms's world view. This stance does not suggest, however, a wholesale rejection by Kharms of the Russian avant garde, which had also become suspicious of the new world order, as can be seen in the imperative inscribed by Kazimir Malevich in a copy of *God Is Not Cast Down*, which he gifted to Kharms in 1928: "Go and stop progress."

After a short time in exile (in the small Russian city of Kursk), Kharms returned to Leningrad with a somewhat broken spirit. He no longer had access to venues where he could perform his work. As the dogma of Socialist Realism took hold of the arts, he also found it increasingly difficult to publish even his work for children, which was his sole source of income. Kharms became ever more destitute over the next decade. He wrote, as the Russians say, for the desk drawer, sharing his writings with his second wife, Marina Malich, and with a small group of friends, often referred to by contemporary literary historians as the *chinari*[22]—a title Kharms and Vvedensky had given themselves in the years preceding the formation of the OBERIU—who met privately to discuss philosophy, music, mathematics, and literature. He met often with artists and fellow writers, and also enjoyed the company of "natural thinkers," men living on the margins or even on the streets, whose unusual ideas and manner of behavior Kharms found exciting precisely because they were out of sync with the norm.

"Only miracle interests me, as a break in the physical structure of the world," Kharms wrote in a diary entry in 1939. Kharms continued to embrace idiosyncratic behavior, developing—apparently on purpose—a tic, an involuntary gesture somewhat like a seizure or a hiccup. A friend later recalled that "Kharms not-quite-hiccuped, not-quite-snorted . . . For a number of reasons Daniil Ivanovich thought it helpful to develop a few oddities in himself."[23] Like the interruptions in his stories, Kharms's self-inflicted tic brought the independent moment into the foreground and broke up the regular flow of time. It seems that this was just one more way that Kharms sought to avoid a "mechanized" life: Surprise and unpredictability created, in the otherwise dull continuum, a "slight error"—something critically important to Kharms's aesthetic theory and which, by extension, he applied to the real world.

As war loomed over Europe, Kharms feared being drafted and may have purposefully performed, as Marina Malich recalls in her memoir, a subtle act for the medical review which released him from duty on psychological grounds.[24] But after the Germans crossed the Soviet border, Stalin's police rounded up most everyone with a political record as a precaution, reasoning that such people may put themselves in service to the enemy.

And so Kharms was picked up by the NKVD on a fine August morning in 1941. Fearing the forced labor of the camps as much, if not more, than the front, Kharms may have simulated mental illness again. On the other hand, he didn't have to lie or pretend to make the police interrogators think he was crazy: While he denied having committed any act against the Soviet government, he was forthcoming about his theories of "slight error," about his belief in miracles, and his desire to shield his thoughts from others by means of wearing a cap or kerchief. Of course, the interrogators couldn't help but notice his unnerving tic. But in the end, the art that had become his life did not save Daniil Kharms. He was subjected to investigations by a medical panel, which determined (after interrogations and tests, including a spinal tap) that Kharms was psychologically unfit and suggested a sentence of forced treatment in the psychiatric ward of the prison hospital. After some bureaucratic delays, he was transferred to the prison's psychiatric ward, where no actual treatment occurred.[25] The blockade of Leningrad had begun[26] (it would last 900 days), and the prison guards had little to eat themselves, never mind feeding the inmates. Kharms died in his cell on February 2, 1942. Or was it Daniil Yuvachev who died that day?

TRIPPING OVER KHARMS

In the popular imagination, inside and particularly outside Russia, Kharms is easily becoming assimilated as another symbol of the artist as victim of Soviet totalitarianism, discovered and recovered after the fall of the Iron Curtain.[27] The trend of pushing Kharms as a counter-cultural prose writer battling dark forces in dark times with absurdist humor is pervasive in scholarly works, student and amateur theatrical productions, and informal commentary on Web sites and blogs; it is even hinted at in the somber overtones of the title of the first book to showcase Kharms in English translation, *The Man in the Black Coat*.[28]

Indeed, Kharms's writing fell victim to the shift in official aesthetics away from the avant garde and "Leftist" art and toward mandated Socialist Realism. It was the politically motivated Soviet press, writers who wanted to be accepted in the new order, and the KGB's precursors that dismantled the OBERIU. Kharms couldn't publish anything other than his writing and translations for children, and even those sources of income became scarce as his editors got deeper into trouble with Soviet censors. Kharms's notebooks from the years 1936 to 1941 detail his impoverishment, and the effect of hunger on his relationship with his wife and on his writing. In his desperation, Kharms alternately begs God to inspire him and to destroy him.

Kharms himself was a political victim: He was arrested three times, all on Stalin's watch—first in 1931 as a member of an "anti-Soviet group of children's writers," as the NKVD was building a bigger case against the editors of the state publishing house that employed him; then briefly under pretense of some shady black-marketeering in 1935 (the charges were dropped); and finally in 1941, after Nazi Germany had begun its invasion of the Soviet Union and all previously convicted political wrong-doers were swept up in Leningrad and across the country as probable turncoats.

There is much truth to the narrative of Kharms's victimhood at the hands of the Soviet regime. However, because of the power of the trope, Kharms's writing is often forced into political paradigms, thus making it possible to read his stories and even poems as parables of totalitarianism, comments on the violence of power and the absurdity of Soviet life. "It is the environment in which he wrote, that is the most striking thing of all," claims the British translator Neil Cornwell.[29]

This is in part why it has been so easy for the West to embrace the idea of Kharms as a proto-absurdist, as having something in common with the theatre of the absurd, and to read his work as a social allegory in the manner of Ionesco's *Rhinoceros*. Cornwell paints him as a "black miniaturist" while comparing him to Beckett (with whom, as Dmitry Tokarev shows in his extensive monograph, a deep comparison is fruitful and uncovers some key differences[30]). The *Village Voice* online, in a piece on the culture of the new Russia, calls Daniel [sic] Kharms "the preeminent poet of Russia's Absurdist tradition."[31] The claim that there is an "Absurdist tradition" in Russia runs close to revisionism, and at best is an attempt to apply a generic label to that which is unfamiliar or hard to pin down. When the same author claims that Kharms belonged to an "Absurdist school" (which was in no way the case), we might recall that Beckett and Ionesco didn't quite like Martin Esslin's "Theatre of the Absurd" label either. But Kharms and his "school" are not around to complain; their writings didn't reach the West until long after most of them were dead.[32] The domestication may be pardonable, but it's not subtle. To quote the *Village Voice* writer on the OBERIU poets, "Their shit is hilarious. But it got them killed." We stumble on (or over) this kind of oversimplification again and again in our culture's popularization of difficult writers who lived in difficult times.[33]

In fact, Kharms consistently denies us our desire to draw any moral conclusions from his work. "What big cucumbers they sell in stores nowadays!" the writer exclaims after one of his characters beats another to death with an oversize cuke. A series of events in which one character after another meets an accidental or senseless demise concludes with the lamentation: "All good people, but they don't know how to hold their ground." In another story, Kharms's Aesopian crow, having spilled its coffee beans, simply goes back "on its four, or to be precise, on its five legs to its lousy house." Every fable ends with a false moral, or none at all.

The problem with glossing Kharms's texts as social or political allegories is the belief—implicit in the approach of such readings—that they function mimetically, or as "coded" messages decrying Soviet life.[34] If the form of Kharms's texts is judged to be subversive (with regard to tradition), the content is often seen as politically subversive. Moreover, we risk falling into the same paradigm as did the NKVD detectives who interrogated Kharms: For them the poem (and especially *zaum*) was a "code" behind which they saw an anti-Soviet idea being cleverly disseminated by the poet. Anyone considered a counter-revolutionary by Stalin's police becomes a revolutionary hero for us.

The supposition that poetry is a kind of code or that writing is a facade for some concealed "inner meaning" may lead us to false conclusions in the case of Kharms. His texts confront the desire to interpret head on. Interpretation becomes synonymous with looking beyond and behind the text to get into the author's mind by any means necessary. (The deeply ingrained and often lauded interpretive inclination begins to resemble the spinal tap employed by the NKVD doctors after Kharms told them as much as they needed to know to come to the same conclusion about the state of his mental health.)

Take for example Kharms's story about a father and daughter who keep dying, getting buried, and coming back to life. The story ends on a tangent about the neighbors who go out to a movie and never come back. Such an ending may be read as code or double-speak: The chance disappearance of the neighbors is easily associated with political terror. But such an interpretation assumes agency and a causal world, whereas Kharms tries consistently to deny and parody both agency and causality, even in the very same story. For Kharms, cause-and-effect paradigms force the world into materialist parameters. We risk making a kind of translation into more accessible terms—it is easier to "understand" if the car is equivalent to a Black Maria, because nothing happens for no reason. By imposing a logical reading, this "translation" does violence to Kharms, for whom chance itself is a transcendent category; error and accident, the very glue of the universe, constitute manifestations in this world of the miraculous, which is otherwise hidden in some parallel dimension behind or beyond mundane reality.

Kharms's earliest statements of his poetics and the main tenets of the OBERIU manifesto emphasize that it is precisely art's domain to operate outside these rules of logic, to create access, to poke holes in the fabric between our world and the other. In one of Kharms's most eerie texts ("How I Was Visited by Messengers"), the angels or shades that he believed would visit us now and then from another dimension seem to enter the protagonist's room when the clock has stopped. Though their presence is felt, they can't be identified in the mundane objects in the room. They are absent and present simultaneously. The "messengers" constitute a kind of interruption, common to many of Kharms's stories, which changes the structure of the world, permitting something out of the ordinary—or even miraculous—to occur.[35] The clock begins ticking again when they've gone; mechanized life returns with their departure.

Kharms makes us aware of our own mechanization, our own ruts, our weakness for unthinkingly, following predetermined patterns of action and perception that limit our confrontation with the world, blinding us to differences, to the "slight error." If I, as an editor, provide the most accessible context in my introduction to a foreign writer— "artist writing under Stalin" or "absurdist writer in a repressive society" —I am upholding (and upheld by) a generalization that has become commonplace in the 20th century, that the true artist fights against totalitarian control. Unfortunately, in the current marketplace, where translations of little-known writers are all but ignored, commentators faced with a limited word-count may be justified in thinking that the best they can do is devise a few catch phrases that help place the unfamiliar author into a familiar paradigm.

If I emphasize "Blue Notebook #10" in this introduction, it is because this short text has often been put to the above purpose, offered up as an example of how Kharms deals a blow of dark (or "absurdist") humor to the oppressive totalitarianism of Stalin's Russia:

> There was a redheaded man who had no eyes or ears. He didn't have hair either, so he was called a redhead arbitrarily.
>
> He couldn't talk because he had no mouth. He didn't have a nose either.
>
> He didn't even have arms or legs. He had no stomach, he had no back, no spine, and he didn't have any insides at all. There was nothing!

So, we don't even know who we're talking about.
We'd better not talk about him any more.

Any sudden disappearance of a man is easily equated with political repression, and specifically with Stalin's purges. But this reading is prompted solely by the fact that the piece was written in late-1930s Russia. While I am not advocating reading the piece apart from or against its historical context, I am arguing for a fuller view of that context, a context that did not consist only—or even primarily—of Stalin and politics. The prevalence of the "Stalin reading" is a result of our (American) blindness to anything else, to all those aspects of life in Soviet Russia that the official culture and the "cult of personality" succeeded in overshadowing. After all, it wasn't all Stalin all the time.

The fuller view is not something we can access easily, but it begins with some very basic questions: What was Kharms reading? What were people talking about in artistic and scientific circles? What music was being played?

In fact, the story of the redheaded man can be read many ways, the political dimension being only one of them. Any critique of the limitations of language ("We don't know who we're talking about") can be seen as a political statement, but it is also a hermeneutic one, and a critique of narrative traditions, of literature itself ("We'd better not talk about him any more"). "Blue Notebook #10" investigates, through language, language's own pitfalls. The narrative begins like any other but abruptly, precipitously declines into silence, what Iampolski has called "oblivion."

Kharms first wrote this particular story in a blue notebook, placing it tenth among a variety of other texts (stories, poems, aphorisms, diary entries). A year or so later, he copied it out of the blue notebook into another notebook, placing it first in a collection he called *Sluchai* which translates variously as "incidents," "chance occurrences," "cases," or "events." Here he named the piece according to the notebook and position it had been in previously: "Blue Notebook #10." (Though they differ only slightly, both versions appear in this volume.) But what is the incident or event in "Blue Notebook #10"? What happens? Is the man "disappeared" or did he ever exist in the first place? Perhaps he just came into being in (or during) the act of writing itself. There is an "arbitrary" event—creation, coming into being, perhaps akin to the writer's inspiration. But the man made solely of words doesn't actually possess any physical attributes: They disappear, or are negated, as soon as they appear in language: "he had no mouth. He didn't have a nose, either." Here, absence is pitted against presence, lack against fullness. As the attributes are withdrawn, they glimmer briefly—appearing, disappearing.

The English verb *to have*, which connotes ownership or possession—as in "he had no mouth"—is analogous in usage to the Russian verb Kharms uses, but is not nearly an equivalent. It is the verb *byt'* (to be) that corresponds to the English construction, and which Kharms uses with the negative *ne* throughout. The most literal translation of this common Russian construction would be: *there was no mouth being*—so that *being* is foregrounded, even with or through *non-being*.

Still, it would be too hasty to say that "Blue Notebook #10" is about nothing. Rather, it is about being about nothing. Because if this story is not really about anything, if the subject vanishes or was never clearly there to begin with, then it must be about the writing itself, about the act, performance, and especially the event of writing. (The title of the piece itself hints at this interpretation—the story is not titled "The Redheaded Man," for example.) Kharms performs his writing, and the text is a trace of that performance—one that involves the movement (or gesture) away from the subject, toward annihilation and oblivion. There is still something left for the reader, though everything has been taken away. It is not the same as a blank page or an empty stage. Rather, it is a stage that holds on to the shimmering traces of an event, of something having happened, or almost happened. Kharms gestures at something barely perceptible, a shadow of existence—a ghostly presence, almost invisible. His writing moves toward silence—toward the impossibility of writing, toward self-negation and oblivion, in which being is revealed.

Specific comparisons with what we already know are no doubt helpful in understanding a foreign author. In the case of Kharms, what we have is a kind of explosion of trajectories that link so many avant-garde trends that we begin to get lost in a forest of symbols. Kharms's influences themselves unite modes of thinking usually seen in some opposition. His equal respect for the Symbolist lyric poet Blok and for the Futurist visionary Khlebnikov bears out this point. The underlying occultism of Russian Symbolism and the idea of the poet as demiurgic creator are as embedded in Kharms's work as Russian Futurist and Formalist claims for the self-sufficient "word as such." His voracious reading of occult literature is well documented, as is his interest in mathematics (especially Kantor and theories of infinity) and his familiarity with contemporary philosophy. An avid list-maker, Kharms enjoyed cataloging his idols. The lists of his favorite writers usually included the strange pleiade of Gogol, Pushkin, Goethe, Kozma Prutkov,[36] Gustav Meyerink (author of *The Golem*, one of Kharms's favorite books), Lewis Carroll and Knut Hamsun.

Though "published" in the 1960s and 1970s only in suppressed *samizdat* and foreign editions with very limited circulation inside Russia, Kharms's literary output seems to have contributed significantly—albeit posthumously—to the Russian post-modern arts of the latter Soviet period. He lurks in the background of Moscow Conceptualism (in the work of Ilya Kabakov and D.A. Prigov), the Sots Art movement, Leningrad bohemian subculture (from the Hellenukty group headed by Kharms scholar Vladimir Earl to the Mit'ki artists who compiled anecdotes attributed to Kharms), and even Russian rock outfits like Aquarium, Kino, and Grazhdanskaya Oborona. In the late 1980s Kharms's work began to appear in mainstream publications, and soon a variety of new private publishing houses was cashing in on the "discovery" of Kharms with a barrage of books. The almost yearly Kharms Festivals in Petersburg, organized by alternative theaters and visual artists and harvesting significant media coverage, attest to his cult status.

Kharms has been compared to many of the 20th century writers and thinkers who collectively define for us the most audacious, ambitious experiments in modern writing and thought. At a cursory glance, and even in their apparent disarray, the papers left behind by Daniil Kharms conjure a world in which readers may glimpse inklings of Beckett, Camus, and Ionesco. It is even more striking to hear echoes in Kharms's work of near contemporaries, whose work never reached him: Franz Kafka, Bruno Schulz, Kurt Schwitters (and the whole of Dada[37]), Robert Walser, Stanisław Witkiewicz, and—though Kharms disliked the French —Artaud, Breton, Blanchot, Daumal, and Duchamp (with whom he shares a predilection for invention, mathematics, and chance). I would also include in this list the Belgian artists Magritte and Michaux; philosophers such as Heidegger and Wittgenstein[38]; and American modernists like Gertrude Stein, William Carlos Williams, and Laura Riding. Appreciators of American post-modern writing—the tragicomic meta-fictions of Donald Barthelme, the "ontological" hysterics of Richard Foreman, the brutal "sudden" fiction of Diane Williams, the stark minimalism of Lydia Davis, or the phantasmagoric prose-poetry of Russell Edson—will also find in Kharms a somewhat familiar taste.

Despite his obvious relevance to the history of avant-garde writing, I hope that Kharms will not be completely domesticated, that he will always remain somewhat strange to us, that he will remain Daniil Kharms. Perhaps the variety of his creations selected for the present volume will give his readers a good many reasons to avoid the generalizations and simplifications that would boil him down to a pre-existing common denominator, be it Absurdism or political allegory.

And, in spite of any impressive list of recommendations, Kharms will, I sincerely hope, always stay in the margins of modern literature, slightly out of reach of the omnivorous canon.[39] When literature gets too self-important, he's just outside, pointing at it mockingly from the street with his pipe, even giving it a good thrashing now and then, and sometimes making it disappear altogether.

"A VERY STRANGE TRANSLATION!"

Nowadays, translation in America is increasingly like Kharms's red-headed man: not to be talked about. A translator's introduction such as this can offer one of the only opportunities to say a few words on an element of literary production that has been almost "disappeared" by our assimilation of certain foreign writers and a book-review culture that often pretends that the translation *is* the original, obscuring the translator's presence as much as possible. Despite the emergence of translation studies as a vibrant academic field and the plethora of writing about translation that seeks to remedy this problem, in the cultural mainstream translation is still deemed secondary, subservient to the "source" text, and, paradoxically, is often unnoticed in its role as mediator between reader and author.[40]

It is a tricky affair to translate a writer who suffered from and, to a great extent, embraced marginality.[41] It would be no less than a travesty to translate Kharms into an idiom of "great books" or literary "discoveries" and to smooth out the inconsistencies and "mistakes" that make him a subversive writer, evading easy categorization. Translation often goes hand in hand with selection, and here I was charged not only with translating but also with selecting from Kharms's work, thus increasing the risk that I might paint a skewed picture of the writer. (For example, due to the limits of space and of my own abilities, I could not include in this selection examples of Kharms's longer, hybrid verse-plays, which I hope shall be made available in translation in future editions.[42]) Even categorizing the various texts as either short prose or journal entries, poems or plays, fiction or philosophy is a pitfall; Kharms crosses these categories with emphatic purpose. Thus, in gathering for the fourth section a variety of texts which Kharms had not clearly marked as part of any series or groups, I have placed them in simple chronological order, thinking this the lesser of evils.

In contrast to Kharms, who wrote most of the texts translated here without hope (or preparation) for publication, I have not translated "for the desk-drawer." I therefore have a different intention from the author's, and that is to relay to a wider readership the effect that his writing has on me, in Russian. As a bilingual speaker I cannot know whether or not a Russian text has the same effect on me as it would on a monolingual Russian speaker. As far as I can discern, however, Kharms's writing does have a specific effect (and intends to) on the Russian language, and on language in general. I have tried more than one approach (especially with the poems) to recreate some of that effect—not on the English speaking audience, but on the English language itself.

I have been reading Kharms—for pleasure, for study, as a would-be director, and as a translator—for over a decade (much longer if you count the illustrated *Ivan Ivanych Samovar* of my childhood). As Kharms has grown on me and become a favorite author, he has also had an overwhelming influence on the way I have thought about and executed these (and other) translations. Much is done intuitively in the ephemeral event of translation, but here my intuition (shaped by, and sometimes against, the present cultural ear) is altered or improved by

the ideas and forms Kharms himself presents to me. Here is Kharms's
own take on translation:

> Translations of different books make me squeamish. Various and
> sundry and, from time to time, even interesting stuff is described in them.
> At times it is written about interesting people, sometimes about events, and
> other times simply of this or that insignificant incident. But it happens that
> sometimes you read it and can't understand what it is you read about. It
> happens like that, too. And then you come across such translations that are
> impossible to read. What strange letters; some are okay but others are such
> that you can't tell what they signify. Once I saw a translation in which not
> one letter was familiar. Some kind of squiggles. For a long time I turned
> the translation this way and that. A very strange translation![43]

Similarly, the present volume of translations is not transparent in
that it cannot claim to be Kharms. It is not a pane of glass through
which you will see Kharms as he really is, or "as if" he were an English-
language writer. I should add that Kharms's texts do most of the work of
creating opacity, fighting against the mimetic function, battling mean-
ing, and parrying interpretive attacks. Partly for this reason, I present
Kharms's texts as close to the manuscript form as is possible in a trade
edition, retaining his signatures and dates and marginal markings as
much as a typeset collection will allow, to at least acknowledge that these
writings were performed only once—what we have here are records of
that performance, though I hope that something of that original per-
formance comes to life again as the new reader encounters it.

Strangely, the more painstaking the work, the more attention paid to
the original, the less "fluent," it seems to me, the translation becomes—
the more strange. But Kharms is here, as much as I know him, and every-
thing I know about him is here in my words—with the important excep-
tion that, were I Kharms, I would have crossed out this introduction,
foregone the footnotes, and perhaps placed a red "X" over much of the
rest of the book as well. In this respect, I have resisted the seductive (yet
perhaps more "correct") temptation of keeping my mouth shut.

—MATVEI YANKELEVICH
August 2007, Brooklyn and South Kortright, NY

NOTES

1. Leonid Lipavsky, "Razgovory" ["Conversations"], *Logos*, no. 4 (1993), pp. 7-88. The *chinari*, as they are referred to in recent criticism, were a small group of friends who met in the early- to mid-1930s to discuss philosophy, mathematics, art, music, and literature. The conversations recorded from 1933 to 1934 at these meetings, included the following participants: Yakov Druskin, Daniil Kharms, Leonid Lipavsky, Tamara Lipavsky, Nikolai Oleinikov, Alexander Vvedensky, Nikolai Zabolotsky.

2. Dmitry Tokarev discusses the relation of Camus' category of the absurd to Kharms and the OBERIU in his monograph, *Kurs na budshee: Absurd kak kategoriia teksta u Daniila Kharmsa i Semyuelia Bekketa* [*Worstward, Ho!: The Absurd as Textual Category in the Work of Daniil Kharms and Samuel Beckett*] (Moscow: Novoe Literatur-noe Obozrenie, 2002).

3. Kharms and Druskin used the term "slight error," or the Latin "peccatum parvum," to speak of a special property or law at the foundation of the equilibrium of all creation. For an explication of this term and for an image of the emblem Kharms created bearing the inscription "Quaedam aequilibritas cum pecatto parvo," see Branislav Jakovljevic's excellent new study *Daniil Kharms: Writing and the Event* (Chicago: Northwestern University Press, 2009).

4. Letter to K. V. Pugacheva, October 16, 1933, in Daniil Kharms (A.A. Alexandrov, ed.), *Polet v nebesa* [*Flight to the skies*] (Leningrad: Sovetskii pisatel', 1991) pp. 482-485.

5. Yakov Druskin reported that in the late 1920s, Alexander Vvedensky said of his friend "that Kharms doesn't create art, but is himself art." (Yakov Druskin, "Kharms," in Daniil Kharms, *O iavleniiah i sushchestvovaniiah* [*On Phenomena and Existences*], Dmitry Tokarev, ed., (St. Petersburg: Azbuka, 1999), pg. 363.)

6. Mikhail Iampolski, *Bespamiatstvo kak istok* [*Oblivion as Source*] (Moscow: Novoe Literaturnoe Obozrenie, 1998), pp. 370-371.

7. Iampolski, ibid., 372.

8. In their manifesto "A Slap in the Face of the Public Taste," the Russian Futurists famously called for the classics to be thrown overboard, off the ship of progress.

9. For an analysis of Kharms's writings in connection to religion and negative theology in particular, see: Neil Carrick, *Daniil Kharms, theologian of the absurd* (Birmingham, UK: University of Birmingham, Dept. of Russian Language and Literature, 1998).

10. V. A. Podoroga, "K voprosu o mercanii mira: Beseda s V. A. Podorogoj." ["Towards the question of the shimmering of the world: A conversation with V. A. Podoroga"], *Logos*, no. 4 (1993), pp. 139-150.

11. "The Life of a Man in the Wind" is the title of one of Kharms's longer early poems, dated November 1928. The protagonist of the poem is a horseman, an archetypical figure prominent in OBERIU poetry, whom Kharms identifies in several poems with his poetic idol, Velimir Khlebnikov.

12. When writing this pseudonym in Roman letters, Daniil transliterated it as

"Charms," following the prevailing German (and French) transliteration of the hard Russian "H" (the Russian letter "X").

13. Katerina Clark, in her informative study of the Petersburg avant garde, notes that "in the years immediately following the Revolution, Russian Futurists [. . .] preferred to be called 'left artists'" (*Petersburg, Crucible of the Cultural Revolution* (Cambridge and London: Harvard University Press, 1995) pg. 36).

14. Malevich's words have a double meaning: "troublemaker" in Russian [*bezobraznik*] also means "non-objective artist."

15. Clark, ibid.

16. Baksakov was arrested in 1931 at Kharms's apartment not long before Kharms's first arrest.

17. For more information in English about the history of the OBERIU, see: Graham Roberts, *The Last Soviet Avant-Garde—OBERIU: Fact, Fiction, Metafiction* (Cambridge: Cambridge University Press, 1997).

18. In Russian, the colloquial meanings of "left" are "illegal" or "extraneous." Although the title of the show was ambiguous, it could still be understood that the evening would consist of three hours of *leftist* art.

19. English translations of Daniil Kharms's early masterpiece *Elizabeth Bam* can be found in the following editions: George Gibian (tr., ed.), *The Man in the Black Coat; Russia's Lost Literature of the Absurd* (Evanston: Northwestern University Press, 1987); and Daniil Kharms, Neil Cornwell (ed. & tr.), *Incidences* (London: Serpent's Tail, 1993).

20. Mikhail Meilakh, ed., *Poety Gruppy "OBERIU" [Poets of the OBERIU Group]* (St. Petersburg: Sovetskii Pisatel' (Biblioteka Poeta), 1994), pg. 57.

21. Clark, ibid., pg. 232.

22. For information about the *chinari* group, their relation and overlap with the *oberiuts*, and the complex derivation of the group's name itself, see Eugene Ostashevsky's introduction to *OBERIU: An Anthology of Russian Absurdism* (Evanston, IL: Northwestern University Press, 2006). The *Anthology* also contains numerous examples in English translation of the work of writers belonging to Kharms's circle, as well as more of Kharms's own writing. For an in-depth discussion of the philosophy, and philosophical influences, of the *chinari* group, see Jean Philippe-Jaccard's ground-breaking dissertation and subsequent monograph, *Daniil Kharms and the End of the Russian Avant Garde*, available both in French—*Daniil Harms et la fin de l'avant-garde russe* (Bern: Peter Lang, Slavica Helvetica 39, 1991)—and in Russian: *Daniil Kharms i konec russkogo avangarda* (St. Petersburg: Akademicheskij Proekt, 1995).

23. V.N. Petrov, (A.A. Alexandrov, ed.) "Materialy o Daniile Kharmse i stikhi ego v fonde V.N. Petrova" in *Ezhegodnik rukopisnogo otdela Pushkinskogo doma na 1990 god*, (Saint Petersburg: Pushkinskii Dom, 1993).

24. Marina Malich (with Vladimir Glotzer), *Moi Muzh Daniil Kharms [My Husband Daniil Kharms]* (Moscow: BSG-Press, 2000).

25. NKVD Case File #2196-1941.

26. Legend has it that Kharms had predicted that the first bomb to hit Leningrad would fall on his house, and he was only slightly wrong: It fell on the building next door.

27. Internet hits, via Google, of Web pages that contain both Kharms *and* Stalin—in Roman characters—account for about 10% of the total finds for "Kharms."

28. The first book-length publication of English translations of OBERIU writing was: George Gibian (ed., tr.), *Russia's Lost Literature of the Absurd; A Literary Discovery; Selected Works of Daniil Kharms and Alexander Vvedensky* (Ithaca and London: Cornell University Press, 1971; Norton Library, 1974). The same book was re-published as: George Gibian, *The Man in the Black Coat; Russia's Lost Literature of the Absurd* (Evanston: Northwestern University Press, 1987).

29. Daniil Kharms, Neil Cornwell (ed. & tr.), *Incidences* (London: Serpent's Tail, 1993) pp. 1-13.

30. See note #2 for citation of Dmitry Tokarev's study.

31. http://www.villagevoice.com/blogs/unamericanactivities/archives/2005/06/tits_and_class.php

32. Igor Bakhterev, one of the youngest original members of the OBERIU, lived into the 1980s.

33. In a turn of Anglophone domestication, Kharms's first name appears as "Daniel" on many internet sites and weblogs. Approximately one fifth of web entries for Kharms make this unnecessary "translation." At the time of the writing of this introduction, Google counted 10,700 instances of "Daniel" to 40,200 mentions of "Daniil." The same trend can be seen in some Western publications of Kharms, both in periodical print and on-line, even in high-brow literary journals; see, for example: Daniel Kharms, translated by Dinara Georgeoliani and Mark Halperin, *Kenyon Review*, Volume XXI, 3/4 (Summer /Fall 1999). In such cases it seems that the translators or the editors, or both, have deemed it the path of least resistance to Anglicize Kharms's "strange" name just as his foreignness is made accessible by references to the Soviet context.

34. A comment posted on a poetry site in regard to Kharms's poem "Song" reads: "An original form created by twisting and tearing at a traditional one. In the 1930s Russian poets were often writing in code because of the cultural dictatorship. I think that Kharms is writing here about the resilience of the Russian people and their ability to survive the Stalin dictatorship and still defend their land" (http://oldpoetry.com/opoem/45169-Daniil-Ivanovich-Kharms-A-Song).

35. Kharms's textual stutters and hiccups are the very fabric of his writing. Compare the interruption of the "messengers" to Kharms's narrative techniques on the level of plot (for example, the darkly farcical appearance of the police at the door of the two unconsummated lovers in "An Interference," the intrusion of the janitor's news in "Holiday," the baby's broken jaw in "Sonnet," the shawl in "Tumbling Old Women"). On the level of structure, we see interruption such as that caused by missing inkwells ("The Artist and His Watch"), and repetition, as in the recurring interference of "Knock!" or the interminable tripping over each other of "Pushkin and Gogol." The mechanical and basically vaudevillian circular structure of "The Carpenter Kushakov"—slipping on the ice, getting a bandage, slipping on the ice again, etc.—ends in a complete loss of identity: the carpenter's neighbors fail to recognize him and refuse to let him into the apartment.

36. Kozma Prutkov was a fictional author (really a parody of a writer) created in the mid-19th century by the team of the Brothers Zhemchuzhnikov and A. K. Tolstoy. Under

this name they published a variety of purposefully stupid verse, plays, aphorisms, and fables that made fun of romantic pretensions and the petty bureaucrats in the era of Nicholas I.

37. Scholarship about the OBERIU's connection to Dada includes a complete monograph, in Croatian: Anica Vlasic-Anic, *Harms i dadaizam*, (Zagreb: Hrvatsko filolosko drustvo, 1997). Two short papers of my own, which sketch out some preliminary comparisons of Kharms and Duchamp, appear in two collections of the proceedings of conferences, held in Belgrade and in Petersburg, devoted to Kharms's 100th birthday. Kharms and Dada is also the theme of the 2003 edition of *Kharmsizdat*—a publication of the Petersburg book-arts group of the same name. (Founded by Mikhail Karasik, Kharmsizdat also organizes the semi-annual "Kharms-Festival.")

38. Mikhail Iampolski's book on Kharms is perhaps the most weighty consideration of Kharms's work from the point of view of philosophy. Iampolski discusses Kharms in the context of philosophers including Bergson, Emerson, Florensky, Gadamer, Heidegger, Husserl, Kierkegaard, A.F. Losev, N.O. Lossky, Kant, Shpet, and many others (see note #6 above for the citation.) Also, Graham Roberts discusses the OBERIU writers in connection to Western philosophers in *The Last Soviet Avant-Garde* (see note #17 for citation).

39. The very impossibility of fully reproducing Kharms's notebooks and scraps of paper, with their intricate, playful, sometimes hieroglyphic or cypher-like writings and drawings (and writings as drawings), makes this marginal oeuvre a challenge to the standardizing mechanism of assimilation.

40. The view of translation as a second-rate, derivative form of writing prevails in Western discourse on the subject since sometime around the 17th century. (See, for example, excerpts from John Dryden's prefaces to several of his translations in Rainer Schulte and John Biguenet, *Theories of Translation* (Chicago: Chicago University Press, 1992), pp. 17-31.) The lowly status of translation is reflected in standard book publishing practices and in modern copyright law; see: Lawrence Venutti, *The Translator's Invisibility* (London: Routledge, 1995). It is perhaps because of our desire to think of the translation as a transparency—a clear window through which we see the meaning of the original—that we lose sight of the obvious impossibility of a one-to-one correspondence and take for granted the presence of the translator and the choices and praxis involved in the task.

41. In a paper given at an international conference in Belgrade marking a hundred years since Kharms's birth, the Italian scholar Rosanna Giaquinta writes: "Kharms and Vvedensky were stripped of their voices, becoming 'marginal figures,' and left isolated from their own culture and their own epoch; therefore they continue to hold an unstable position, are continuously on the edge." (Collected in *Stoletie Daniila Kharmsa* [*A Century of Daniil Kharms*], Aleksaner Kobrinskii, ed. (St. Petersburg: IPC SPGUTD, 2005).)

42. Three important examples of Kharms's longer verse-plays, which can be better described as hybrid works of prose and poetry with dialogs in a play format, and which form an important part of Kharms's oeuvre, are available in English translation: "Lapa"—in *PAJ: A Journal of Performance and Art*, no. 68, (May 2001)—and "The Story of Sdygr Appr" and "The Measure of Things," both in *OBERIU: An Anthology of Russian Absurdism* (see note #22 for citation).

43. Daniil Kharms (Anna Gerasimova, ed.), *Menya Nazyvajut Kapucinom* [*They Call Me the Capuchin*] (Moscow: Karavento & Pikment, 1993) pg. 238.

NOTE ON THE TEXT

I N MEDIATING BETWEEN the idiosyncratic look of Kharms's manuscripts, never prepared for publication in his lifetime, and the rules and regulations of the printed book, I have made certain compromises toward legibility, while trying to maintain some peculiarities of the original, more chaotic format, as well as meaningful instances of Kharms's non-standard, personalized orthography.

To make things simple, I have chosen to use a fairly phonetic and intuitive system for rendering the Russian names that appear in the book into the Roman alphabet, rather than forcing the reader to learn the more complex transliteration standards used in scholarly editions. If I've done my job well, the English-language reader will be able to sound out the Russian names and come close to the Russian pronunciation with relative ease.

Because Kharms often dated and signed his manuscripts, I have elected to keep many of those markings present here; they are in italics. In the interests of the reader, I have included (in parentheses) the dates that have been ascribed by scholars to those pieces which Kharms did not date; sometimes these are approximations or educated guesses, and sometimes indisputably supported by evidence from his notebooks and manuscripts. To retain the visual rhythm of the two "cycles" or notebooks given here in their entirety (*Events* and *The Blue Notebook*), the ascribed dates for pieces in those collections have been relegated to the commentary at the end of the book. Explanatory notes, descriptions of relevant marginalia found in the manuscripts, and other potentially useful information have likewise been placed at the back of the book, so as not to clutter each page with footnotes. There the reader will also find a glossary of character names, place names, and historical figures that populate Kharms's written world.

Some of the titles appear in brackets—these are editorially imposed titles that have stuck to certain works of Kharms through a chain of previous Russian publications. It would be unfair to the reader to omit these posthumously added titles; the brackets merely serve to acknowledge that those works were left untitled by the author.

In the cases where I have worked side-by-side with another translator (or group of translators), their names appear at the end of those works. In all other cases (including quotations from the Russian critical literature on Kharms) the translations are my own.

EVENTS

To Marina Vladimirovna Malich

BLUE NOTEBOOK #10

There was a redheaded man who had no eyes or ears. He didn't have hair either, so he was called a redhead arbitrarily.

He couldn't talk because he had no mouth. He didn't have a nose either.

He didn't even have arms or legs. He had no stomach, he had no back, no spine, and he didn't have any insides at all. There was nothing! So, we don't even know who we're talking about.

We'd better not talk about him any more.

EVENTS

One day Orlov stuffed himself with mashed peas and died. Krylov, having heard the news, also died. And Spiridonov died regardless. And Sprirdonov's wife fell from the cupboard and also died. And the Spiridonov children drowned in a pond. Spiridonov's grandmother took to the bottle and wandered the highways. And Mikhailov stopped combing his hair and came down with mange. And Kruglov sketched a lady holding a whip and went mad. And Perekhryostov received four hundred rubles wired over the telegraph and was so uppity about it that he was forced to leave his job.

All good people but they don't know how to hold their ground.

TUMBLING OLD WOMEN

Because of her excessive curiosity, one old woman tumbled out of her window, fell and shattered to pieces.

Another old woman leaned out to look at the one who'd shattered but, out of excessive curiosity, also tumbled out of her window, fell and shattered to pieces.

Then a third old woman tumbled from her window, and a fourth, and a fifth.

When the sixth old woman tumbled out of her window, I got sick of watching them and walked over to the Maltsev Market where, they say, a blind man had been given a knit shawl.

SONNET

A peculiar thing happened to me: I suddenly forgot what comes first—7 or 8?

I set off to ask my neighbors what their thoughts were on the matter.

How great was their surprise—and mine, too—when they suddenly realized that they also could not recall the counting order. 1, 2, 3, 4, 5 and 6 they remember, but what comes next they've forgotten.

We all went down to the commercial store called "Gastronom" that's on the corner of Znamenskaya and Basseynaya Streets, and asked the cashier there about our incomprehension. Smiling a sad smile, the cashier extracted a small hammer from her mouth, and twitched her nose slightly. She said, "In my opinion seven comes after eight, but only when eight comes after seven."

We thanked the cashier and in utter joy ran out of the store. But after we had pondered deeply the cashier's words grief came over us again, for it seemed that not a word of hers made any sense to us.

What was there to do? We went to the Summer Garden and began counting the trees there. But when we reached the number 6 we stopped counting and began to argue: some thought seven was next in the order, others—8.

We would have argued very long, but, luckily, just then somebody's child toppled off a park bench and broke both of its jaws. This distracted us from the argument.

After that everyone went home.

PETROV AND MOSKITOV

PETROV:
> Hey, Moskitov!
> Let's catch mosquitoes!

MOSKITOV:
> No way, I'm not ready for that;
> Let's better catch cats.

AN OPTICAL ILLUSION

Semyon Semyonovich, having put on his spectacles, looks at a pine tree and this is what he sees: In the pine tree sits a man showing him his fist.

Semyon Semyonovich, taking off his spectacles, looks at the pine and sees that no one is sitting in the tree.

Semyon Semyonovich, putting on his spectacles, looks at the pine tree and again he sees that a man is sitting in the tree, showing him his fist.

Semyon Semyonovich, taking off his spectacles, again sees that there is no one sitting in the pine tree.

Semyon Semyonovich, putting his spectacles on again, looks at the pine tree, and, as previously, he sees that in the pine tree sits a man showing him his fist.

Semyon Semyonovich does not wish to believe this phenomenon and deems this phenomenon an optical illusion.

PUSHKIN AND GOGOL

GOGOL (*falls onto the stage from behind the curtains and lies still*).

PUSHKIN (*walks out, trips on Gogol and falls*): What the devil! Could it be Gogol!

GOGOL (*getting up*): What a filthy, no-good . . . ! Won't let you alone. (*Walks, trips on Pushkin and falls.*) Could it really be Pushkin I tripped on!

PUSHKIN (*getting up*): Not a moment's peace! (*Walks, trips on Gogol and falls.*) What the devil! It couldn't be—Gogol again!

GOGOL (*getting up*): Always something going wrong! (*Walks, trips on Pushkin and falls.*) What filthy, no-good . . . ! On Pushkin again!

PUSHKIN (*getting up*): Foolery! Foolery all over the place! (*Walks, trips over Gogol and falls.*) What the devil! Gogol again!

GOGOL (*getting up*): This is mockery, through and through! (*Walks, trips on Pushkin and falls.*) Pushkin again!

PUSHKIN (*getting up*): What the devil! Truly the devil! (*Walks, trips on Pushkin and falls.*) On Gogol!

GOGOL (*getting up*): Filthy good-for-nothings! (*Walks, trips over Pushkin and falls.*) On Pushkin!

PUSHKIN (*getting up*): What the devil! (*Walks, trips over Gogol and falls behind the curtains.*) Gogol!

GOGOL *(getting up)*: Filthy good-for-nothings! *(Walks off stage.)*

From offstage the voice of Gogol is heard:
"Pushkin!"

CURTAIN.

THE CARPENTER KUSHAKOV

There once lived a carpenter and his name was Kushakov.

One day he walked out of his house and went to a kiosk to buy some carpenter's glue.

It was during a thaw, and the streets were very slippery.

The carpenter took a few steps, slipped, fell and busted his head.

"Oh well," said the carpenter, got up and went to a drugstore, bought a bandage and taped up his head.

But when he walked out onto the street and took a few steps, he slipped again, fell and busted his nose.

"Phooey," said the carpenter, went to the drugstore, bought a bandage, and taped up his nose with it.

Then he went outside again, slipped again, fell and busted his cheek.

He had to go to the drugstore again and tape up his cheek with a bandage.

"Listen here," said the pharmacist to the carpenter. "You fall and bust yourself up so often that I'd advise you to buy a few extra bandages."

"No," said the carpenter, "no more falling!"

But when he went outside he slipped again, fell and busted his chin.

"Lousy ice!" screamed the carpenter and took off for the drugstore.

"See now," said the pharmacist, "you've gone and fallen again."

"No!" screamed the carpenter. "I don't want to hear it! Quick, give me the bandage!"

The pharmacist gave him the bandage; the carpenter taped up his chin and ran home.

But at home they didn't recognize him and wouldn't let him into the apartment.

"I'm the carpenter Kushakov!" screamed the carpenter.

"Tell us about it!" came the reply from inside the apartment, and they locked the door with the hook and the chain.

The carpenter Kushakov stood awhile on the landing, spat and went outside.

THE TRUNK

A man with a long, skinny neck crawled into a trunk, closed the cover behind him and began to suffocate.

"Now," said the man with the long, skinny neck, suffocating, "I'm suffocating in this trunk because I have a long, skinny neck. The cover of the trunk is closed and isn't letting any air in here. I'll continue suffocating, but I won't open the trunk anyway. Gradually, I'll start dying. I will see the battle of life and death. The battle that will occur will be unnatural, with even odds, because naturally death is victorious, while life, doomed to die, vainly battles its enemy, not giving up its useless hope to the very last minute. In this same battle, which will take place presently, life will know the method of its victory—for that life would have to force me to open the cover of the trunk. Let's see who wins. Only it stinks of mothballs. If life wins out, I'll sprinkle tobacco on my clothes instead . . . Now it's begun: I can no longer breathe. It's clear, I'm done for! There's no salvation for me now! And my head is devoid of any elevated thoughts. I'm suffocating! . . .

"Oh no! What's this? Something just happened, but I can't figure out what exactly. I saw something, or heard something . . .

"Oh no! Again something's happened. Oh my god! There's nothing to breathe. I think I'm dying . . .

"And what's all this supposed to be? Why am I singing? I think my neck hurts . . . But where's the trunk? Why do I see all the things in my room? Can it be that I'm lying on the floor?! But where's the trunk gone?"

The man with the long, skinny neck got up off the floor and looked around. The trunk was not around. Strung up on the chairs and on the bed were the things that had been taken out of the trunk, but the trunk was nowhere to be seen.

The man with the long, skinny neck said:

"That means that life defeated death by a method unknown to me."

AN INCIDENT INVOLVING PETRAKOV

So, once Petrakov wanted to go to sleep but, lying down, missed his bed. He hit the floor so hard he lay there unable to get up.

So Petrakov mustered his remaining strength and got on his hands and knees. But his strength abandoned him and he fell on his stomach again, and he just lies there.

Petrakov lay on the floor about five hours. At first he just lay there, but then he fell asleep.

Sleep refreshed Petrakov's strength. He woke up invigorated, got up, walked around the room and cautiously lay down on the bed. "Well," he thought, "now I'll get some sleep." But now he's not feeling very sleepy. So Petrakov keeps turning in his bed and can't fall asleep.

And that's it, more or less.

FIGHT STORY

Alexei Alexeyevich squashed Andrei Karlovich beneath him and, having pummeled his face, let him go.

Andrei Karlovich turned pale with rage, threw himself at Alexei Alexeyevich, and hit him in the teeth.

Alexei Alexeyevich, surprised by such a quick attack, fell to the floor. Then Andrei Karlovich straddled him, took his dentures out of his mouth and so thoroughly worked over Alexei Alexeyevich with them that the latter rose from the floor with a mutilated face and a torn nostril. With his hands over his face, Alexei Alexeyevich ran away.

Meanwhile, Andrei Karlovich wiped down his dentures, inserted them into his mouth, clicked his teeth together, looked around and, catching no glimpse of Alexei Alexeyevich, went looking for him.

A DREAM

Kalugin fell asleep and had a dream: He's sitting in some bushes and a policeman is walking by.

Kalugin woke up, scratched around his mouth, and fell asleep again, and again he had a dream: He's walking by the bushes, and in the bushes sits a policeman, hiding.

Kalugin woke up, placed a newspaper under his head to keep his drool from drowning the pillow, and fell asleep again. And again he had a dream: He's sitting in the bushes and a policeman is walking by.

Kalugin woke up, changed the newspaper, lay down and fell asleep. And when he fell asleep he had the dream again: He's walking by the bushes and in the bushes sits a policeman.

Kalugin woke up and decided not to go to sleep again, but he fell asleep right away and had a dream: He's sitting behind the policeman and a bush is walking by.

Kalugin screamed and thrashed in his bed, but now he couldn't wake up.

Kalugin slept four days and four nights in a row, and on the fifth day he woke up so skinny that he had to tie his boots to his legs with twine so they wouldn't slip off. They didn't recognize him at the bakery where he always bought millet bread and they slipped him half-rye. The sanitary commission, making its rounds from apartment to apartment, set eyes on Kalugin and, deeming him unsanitary, ordered the co-op management to throw him out with the trash.

Kalugin was folded in half and they threw him out, like trash.

THE MATHEMATICIAN
AND ANDREI SEMYONOVICH

MATHEMATICIAN (*removing a sphere from his head*):
I removed a sphere from my head.
I removed a sphere from my head.
I removed a sphere from my head.
I removed a sphere from my head.

ANDREI SEMYONOVICH:
Put it back.
Put it back.
Put it back.
Put it back.

MATHEMATICIAN:
No, I won't put it back!
No, I won't put it back!
No, I won't put it back!
No, I won't put it back!

ANDREI SEMYONOVICH:
Well then don't.
Well then don't.
Well then don't.

MATHEMATICIAN:
Well I won't put it back!
Well I won't put it back!
Well I won't put it back!

ANDREI SEMYONOVICH:
Well alright then.
Well alright then.
Well alright then.

MATHEMATICIAN:
So I won!
So I won!
So I won!

ANDREI SEMYONOVICH:
Alright, you won, now calm down!

MATHEMATICIAN:
No, I won't calm down!
No, I won't calm down!
No, I won't calm down!

ANDREI SEMYONOVICH:
You may be a mathematician, but, the truth is, you're not too smart.

MATHEMATICIAN:
No, I'm smart and I know a whole lot!
No, I'm smart and I know a whole lot!
No, I'm smart and I know a whole lot!

ANDREI SEMYONOVICH:
A whole lot, but it's all crap.

MATHEMATICIAN:
No, it's not crap!
No, it's not crap!
No, it's not crap!

ANDREI SEMYONOVICH:
I'm sick and tired of squabbling with you.

MATHEMATICIAN:
No, you're not sick and tired!
No, you're not sick and tired!
No, you're not sick and tired!

Andrei Semyonovich waves his hand in frustration and exits. After standing there a minute, the Mathematician follows after Andrei Semyonovich.

CURTAIN.

THE YOUNG MAN WHO SURPRISED
THE WATCHMAN

"Son of a gun," said the watchman as he examined a fly. "Turns out that if you swab it with carpenter's glue, it looks like it'll meet its end. What a story! Just plain glue!"

"Hey you, old monster!" a young man in yellow gloves called out to the watchman.

The watchman didn't get it right away that he was being addressed and kept looking at the fly.

"Isn't somebody talking to you?" yelled the young man, "you jerk!"

The watchman crushed the fly with a finger and without turning around to face the young man said:

"What are you yelling for, you filthy pig? I heard you twice the first time. Don't have to yell."

The young man dusted off his trousers with his gloves and asked in a delicate voice:

"Tell me, gramps, which way is it to the sky?"

The watchman took a good look at the young man, squinted one eye, and squinted the other, then scratched his beard and looked at the young man again and said:

"Well, don't waste your time here, go on by."

"Excuse me," said the young man, "it's just that I'm on urgent business. There's already a room prepared for me."

"Alright," said the watchman, "show me the ticket."

"I don't have a ticket. They said that I'd be let through without one," said the young man, peering straight at the watchman's face.

"Son of a gun!" said the watchman.

"So what do you say?" asked the young man. "You'll let me through?"

"Alright, alright," said the watchman. "Go ahead."

"But how do I get there? Which way?" asked the young man. "I don't know the way there."

"Where are you going?" asked the watchman, making a stern face.

The young man cupped his palm to his mouth and said very quietly: "To the sky!"

The watchman leaned forward, shifted his right foot for a firmer stance, fixed his stare on the young man and said gruffly:

"What are you up to? Trying to make a fool of me?"

The young man smiled, lifted his yellow-gloved hand, waved it over his head and vanished.

The watchman sniffed at the air. The air smelled of burnt feathers.

"Son of a gun!" said the watchman. He opened up his coat, scratched his belly, spat at the spot where the young man had stood and slowly went back to his booth.

FOUR ILLUSTRATIONS OF HOW A NEW IDEA DUMBFOUNDS A PERSON WHO IS NOT PREPARED FOR IT

I

WRITER: I am a writer.
READER: I think you are s _ _ t!

(The writer stands still for a few minutes, shocked by this new idea, and falls dead as a doornail.)

II

ARTIST: I am an artist.
WORKER: And I think you are s _ _ t!

*(Right then the artist turned pale as canvas,
And shook like a blade of grass,
And, unexpectedly, he passed away.
He is carried out.)*

III

COMPOSER: I am a composer.
VANYA RUBLEV: And I think you are ——.

*(Breathing heavily, the composer drops on the spot.
He is, unexpectedly, carried out.)*

IV

CHEMIST: I am a chemist.
PHYSICIST: And I think you are ——.

(The chemist said not a single word more and collapsed heavily onto the floor.)

LOSSES

Andrei Andreyevich Myasov bought a wick at the market and carried it home.

On the way home Andrei Andreyevich lost the wick and went into a store to buy a quarter-pound of Poltava salami. Then Andrei Andreyevich stopped into the milk union and bought a bottle of buttermilk, then he drank a small mug of bread beer at the kiosk and got in line for a newspaper. The line was pretty long and Andrei Andreyevich stood in the line for over twenty minutes, but just as he was approaching the newspaper salesman, the newspapers sold out from right under his nose.

Andrei Andreyevich hesitated a while and started homeward. On the way he lost the buttermilk and popped into a bakery where he bought a French boule, but lost the Poltava salami.

Then Andrei Andreyevich went straight home, but on the way he fell, lost the French boule and broke his pince-nez.

Andrei Andreyevich arrived at home in a foul mood and went straight to bed. But he couldn't get to sleep for a long time, and when he did fall asleep he had a dream: He had lost his toothbrush and had to brush his teeth with some kind of candlestick.

MAKAROV AND PETERSEN
#3

MAKAROV: Here, in this book, it is written of our desires and about the fulfillment of our desires. Read this book and you will understand how vain our desires are. You will likewise understand how easy it is to fulfill the desires of another and how difficult it is to fulfill a desire of your own.

PETERSEN: What's with the solemn tone? That's the way Indian chiefs talk.

MAKAROV: This book is such that it is necessary to speak of it loftily. I take off my hat just thinking about it.

PETERSEN: And do you wash your hands before touching this book?

MAKAROV: Yes, one's hands must also be washed.

PETERSEN: You should wash your feet, too, just in case.

MAKAROV: That is not clever. Moreover, it's rude.

PETERSEN: So what's this book all about?

MAKAROV: The name of this book is mysterious . . .

PETERSEN: Hee-hee-hee!

MAKAROV: The name of this book is **MALGIL**.

(Petersen vanishes.)

MAKAROV: Lord! What is this? Petersen!

PETERSEN'S VOICE: What happened? Makarov! Where am I?

MAKAROV: Where are you? I can't see you!

PETERSEN'S VOICE: And where are you? I can't see you either! What's with these spheres?

MAKAROV: What do I do? Petersen, can you hear me?

PETERSEN'S VOICE: I can hear you! But what happened? And what are these spheres?

MAKAROV: Can you move?

PETERSEN'S VOICE: Makarov! Do you see the spheres?

MAKAROV: What spheres?

PETERSEN'S VOICE: Let go! . . . Let me go! . . . Makarov! . . .

(Silence. Makarov stands in awe, then he grabs the book and opens it.)

MAKAROV *(reading)*: ". . . Gradually man loses his shape and turns into a sphere. And, having become a sphere, he loses all his desires."

CURTAIN.

LYNCH LAW

Petrov gets on his horse and, addressing the crowd, delivers a speech about what would happen if, in place of the public garden, they'd build an American skyscraper. The crowd listens and, it seems, agrees. Petrov writes something down in his notebook. A man of medium height emerges from the crowd and asks Petrov what he wrote down in his notebook. Petrov replies that it concerns himself alone. The man of medium height presses him. Words are exchanged and discord begins. The crowd takes the side of the man of medium height, and Petrov, saving his life, drives his horse on and disappears around the bend. The crowd panics and, having no other victim, grabs the man of medium height and tears off his head. The torn-off head rolls down the street and gets stuck in the hatch of a sewer drain. The crowd, having satisfied its passions, disperses.

THE MEETING

Now, one day, a man went to work, and on the way he met another man, who, having bought a loaf of Polish bread, was heading back home where he came from.

And that's it, more or less.

AN UNSUCCESSFUL PLAY

Petrakov-Gorbunov comes out on stage, tries to say something, but hiccups. He begins to feel sick. He leaves.

Enter Pritykin.

PRITYKIN: His honor, Petrakov-Gorbunov, asked me to excu . . . (*Begins to vomit and runs away.*)

Enter Makarov.

MAKAROV: Egor Pritykin . . . (*Makarov vomits. He runs away.*)

Enter Serpukhov.

SERPUKHOV: So as not to . . . (*He vomits and runs away.*)

Enter Kurova.

KUROVA: I would be . . . (*She vomits and runs away.*)

Enter Little Girl, running.

LITTLE GIRL: Daddy asked me to tell all of you that the theater is closing. All of us are getting sick!

CURTAIN.

KNOCK!

Summer. A writing desk. A door to the right. A picture on the wall. A horse is drawn on the picture, and in the horse's mouth, a gypsy. Olga Petrovna is splitting wood. Every time she strikes the wood, the pince-nez falls from Olga Petrovna's nose. Evdokim Osipovich sits in an armchair, smoking.

OLGA PETROVNA *(drives the wood splitter into the log, which, however, doesn't split a bit).*

EVDOKIM OSIPOVICH: Knock!

OLGA PETROVNA *(putting on her pince-nez, strikes the log).*

EVDOKIM OSIPOVICH: Knock!

OLGA PETROVNA *(putting on her pince-nez, strikes the log).*

EVDOKIM OSIPOVICH: Knock!

OLGA PETROVNA *(putting on her pince-nez, strikes the log).*

EVDOKIM OSIPOVICH: Knock!

OLGA PETROVNA *(putting on her pince-nez):* Evdokim Osipovich! I beg you, do not utter that word, "knock."

EVDOKIM OSIPOVICH: Okay, okay.

OLGA PETROVNA *(strikes the log with the splitter).*

EVDOKIM OSIPOVICH: Knock!

OLGA PETROVNA *(putting on her pince-nez):* Evdokim Osipovich! You promised me you wouldn't say that "knock" word!

EVDOKIM OSIPOVICH: Okay, okay, Olga Petrovna! I won't do it again.

OLGA PETROVNA *(strikes the log with the splitter).*

EVDOKIM OSIPOVICH: Knock!

OLGA PETROVNA (*putting on her pince-nez*): This is preposterous! A grown elderly man who doesn't understand a simple human request!

EVDOKIM OSIPOVICH: Olga Petrovna! You can continue your work without worry. I will no longer hinder you.

OLGA PETROVNA: Evdokim Osipovich! I'm begging you, I'm really begging you—let me at least split this one log.

EVDOKIM OSIPOVICH: Of course, go right ahead, split away!

OLGA PETROVNA (*strikes the log with the splitter*).

EVDOKIM OSIPOVICH: Knock!

Olga Petrovna drops the wood splitter and opens her mouth but is unable to say a word. Evdokim Osipovich gets up from his armchair, gives Olga Petrovna a once-over and slowly exits. Olga Petrovna stands motionless with her mouth open, looking at Evdokim Osipovich as he moves into the distance. The curtain descends slowly.

WHAT THEY SELL IN STORES
NOWADAYS

Koratygin came to see Tikakeyev but did not find him at home.

Meanwhile, Tikakeyev was at the store buying sugar, meat and cucumbers. Koratygin milled around in Tikakeyev's doorway and was about ready to write him a note when he saw Tikakeyev himself, carrying a plastic satchel in his hands. Koratygin saw Tikakeyev and yelled:

"And I've been waiting here for a whole hour!"

"That's not true," said Tikakeyev, "I've only been out 25 minutes."

"Well, that I don't know," said Koratygin, "but I've been here an hour, that much I do know."

"Don't lie," said Tikakeyev. "It's shameful."

"My good sir," said Koratygin, "you should use some discretion in choosing your words."

"I think . . . ," started Tikakeyev, but Koratygin interrupted:

"If you think . . . ," he said, but then Tikakeyev interrupted Koratygin, saying:

"You're one to talk!"

These words so enraged Koratygin that he pinched one nostril with his finger and blew his other nostril at Tikakeyev.

Then Tikakeyev snatched the biggest cucumber from his satchel and hit Koratygin over the head.

Koratygin clasped his hands to his head, fell over and died.

What big cucumbers they sell in stores nowadays!

MASHKIN KILLED KOSHKIN

Comrade Koshkin danced around Comrade Mashkin.

Com. Mashkin followed Com. Koshkin with his eyes.

Com. Koshkin waved his arms in an insulting way and made disgusting contortions with his legs.

Com. Mashkin furrowed his brow.

Com. Koshkin wiggled his belly and added a stomp with his right foot.

Com. Mashkin let out a yelp and threw himself at Com. Koshkin.

Com. Koshkin tried to flee, but he tripped and was caught up with by Com. Mashkin.

Com. Mashkin punched Com. Koshkin in the head.

Com. Koshkin yelped and dropped to his hands and knees.

Com. Mashkin whopped Com. Koshkin with a kick under the stomach and punched him once more in the back of the head.

Com. Koshkin sprawled out on the floor and died.

Mashkin killed Koshkin.

SLEEP MOCKS A MAN

Markov took off his boots and, sighing, lay down on the couch. He wanted to sleep, but as soon as he closed his eyes, his desire to sleep instantly vanished. Markov would open his eyes and grope for a book. But drowsiness would come over him again and, without reaching the book, Markov would lie back down and close his eyes again. But just as his eyes closed, sleep would drift away from him again, and his consciousness would become so clear that Markov could solve algebraic equations with two variables in his head.

For a long time Markov suffered in this way, not knowing what he should do: to sleep or to be wakeful? Finally, suffering all he could stand and growing to loathe himself and his room, Markov put on his coat and hat, and, with cane in hand, went out into the street. The fresh air calmed Markov. He felt at peace in his soul and a desire came upon him to return to his room.

Upon entering his room, he felt a pleasant exhaustion in his body and wanted to sleep. But as soon as he lay down on the couch and closed his eyes, his drowsiness instantly evaporated.

At wit's end, Markov sprung from the couch and without hat or coat rushed off in the direction of the Tavrichesky Garden.

THE HUNTERS

Six people went hunting, but only four returned.
You see, two of them did not come back.
Oknov, Kozlov, Struchkov, and Motylkov returned safely, but Shyrokov
and Kablukov died on the hunt.

Oknov was sad all day, didn't even want to talk to anybody. Kozlov was
unrelenting in following Oknov and pestering him with all sorts of questions,
which drove Oknov to the highest degree of aggravation.

KOZLOV: Like a smoke?

OKNOV: No.

KOZLOV: Would you like me to bring you that thingy over
there?

OKNOV: No.

KOZLOV: How about I tell you a funny story?

OKNOV: No.

KOZLOV: Well, you want to have a drink? I've got some tea and
cognac right here.

OKNOV: It's not enough that I just smashed you over the head
with this here rock—I'm also going to tear your leg off.

STRUCHKOV AND MOTYLKOV: What are you doing?
What are you doing?

KOZLOV: Get me off the ground!

MOTYLKOV: Don't you worry, the wound will heal.

KOZLOV: Where's Oknov?

OKNOV *(tearing Kozlov's leg off)*: I'm here, not too far off!

KOZLOV: Oh! Mother of God! Sa-a-ave me!

STRUCHKOV AND MOTYLKOV: Don't tell me he tore off
his leg.

STRUCHKOV: That's treachery!

OKNOV: What-what?

STRUCHKOV: ... Echery.

OKNOV: Hu-u-uh?

STRUCHKOV: N ... n ... nothing.

KOZLOV: How will I get home?

MOTYLKOV: Don't you worry. We'll fix a stick to it.

STRUCHKOV: Can you stand on one leg?

KOZLOV: Yeah, but not too well.

STRUCHKOV: Well, we'll just have to prop you up.

OKNOV: Let me at him!

STRUCHKOV: Oh, no, you'd better go!

OKNOV: No, let me through! .. Let me! .. Let .... - - - - - - That's what I wanted to do!

STRUCHKOV AND MOTYLKOV: How terrible!

OKNOV: Ha-ha-ha!

MOTYLKOV: And where's Kozlov?

STRUCHKOV: He crawled under the bushes!

MOTYLKOV: Kozlov, you here?

KOZLOV: Sha-sha...!

MOTYLKOV: Now see what he's come to!

STRUCHKOV: What'll we do with him?

MOTYLKOV: Now there's nothing we can do. I think we just have to smother him. Kozlov! Hey, Kozlov? You hear me?

KOZLOV: Oh, I hear you, but not so well.

MOTYLKOV: Don't grieve, my friend. We'll just smother you. Hold still now! .. Right ... right ... right ...

STRUCHKOV: Here, just a little more! That's it, that's it, that's it! Come on, one more time ... Well, that's done it!

MOTYLKOV: That's done it!

OKNOV: God bless!

AN EPISODE FROM HISTORY

For V.N. Petrov

Ivan Ivanovich Susanin (that same historical figure that laid his life down for the tsar and, as a result, was later celebrated in Glinka's opera) once stopped into a Russian tavern and, sitting down to a table, demanded a steak. While the tavern keeper was frying the steak, Ivan Ivanovich nipped his beard with his teeth and fell into thought, as was his habit.

Thirty-five notches of time passed, and the tavern keeper brought Ivan Ivanovich the steak on a round wooden board. Ivan Ivanovich was hungry and, in keeping with the times, grabbed the steak with his hands and started eating it. But, in his haste to quell his hunger, Ivan Ivanovich attacked the steak so greedily that he forgot to take his beard out of his mouth and ate the steak with a chunk of his beard.

And that's when an awful thing happened. Before fifteen notches of time had passed, powerful seizures began in Ivan Ivanovich's stomach. Ivan Ivanovich sprung from the table and dashed for the yard. The tavern keeper had tried to shout to Ivan Ivanovich, "Behold, how your beard is tattered." But Ivan Ivanovich ran out to the yard paying no mind.

Then the boyar Kovshegub, who was sitting in a corner of the tavern drinking wort, banged his fist on the table and shouted, "What man is this?" And the tavern keeper, bowing low, replied to the boyar, "That is our patriot, Ivan Ivanovich Susanin." "So it is!" said the boyar, dredging his wort.

"Would it please you to try the fish?" asked the tavern keeper.

"Go to hell in a bucket!" shouted the boyar and launched the pitcher at the tavern keeper. The pitcher whistled by the tavern keeper's head, flew out through the window into the yard where Ivan Ivanovich was sitting with his legs spread-eagle, and walloped him in the teeth. Ivan Ivanovich grabbed his cheek with one hand and slumped onto his side.

Just then from the shed on the right came Karp running at a clip. Jumping over a trough where a pig lay among the slop, he ran with a yelp toward the gates. The tavern keeper poked his head out of the tavern to have a look. "What are you yelling for?" he asked Karp. But Karp said nothing in reply and ran off.

The tavern keeper went out into the yard and saw Susanin lying motionless on the ground. The tavern keeper stepped closer and looked him in the face. Susanin stared intently at the tavern keeper. "You alive?" asked the tavern keeper. "Alive I am, jus' fearful I may get hit again with some other thing." "No," said the tavern keeper, "do not fear. 'Twas the boyar Kovshegub nearly killed you, but now he is left." "Well glory be to You, God!" said Ivan Susanin, lifting himself up from the ground. "I'm a brave man, but I don't like to put my life on the line jus' cuz. That's why I humbled myself to the ground and waited to see what was coming. Anything more and I would have crawled on my stomach all the way to the Yeldyrin settlement . . . Lookit—my cheek's all swollen. Good father! It took off half my beard!" "You had it like that before," said the tavern keeper. "What do you mean, before?" shouted Susanin the patriot. "What, you think I would walk around with a tattered beard?" "You did," said the tavern keeper. "You old ragamuffin," muttered Ivan Susanin. The tavern keeper squinted his eyes, and winding up, pummeled Susanin across the ear with all his might. The patriot Susanin crumpled to the ground and lay still. "Take that! Ragamuffin yourself!" said the tavern keeper and retired to the tavern. Susanin lay on the ground for several notches of time listening, but having heard nothing suspicious, lifted his head cautiously and looked around. There was no one in the yard, except for the pig that had tumbled out of the trough and was now lolling in a filthy puddle. Glancing around, Ivan Susanin crept up to the gates. Luckily, the gates were unlocked and the patriot Ivan Susanin, writhing on the ground like a worm, crawled in the direction of the Yeldyrin settlement.

And so ends an episode from the life of the famous historical figure who lay his life down for the tsar and, as a result, was later celebrated in Glinka's opera.

1939

FEDYA DAVIDOVICH

Fedya had been sneaking up to the butter dish for a long time now, and, finally, catching the moment when his wife bent down to clip off a toenail, took all the butter out of the butter dish in one quick motion and shoved it in his mouth. Closing the butter dish Fedya accidentally clinked the cover. His wife straightened up abruptly and, seeing the empty butter dish, pointed at it with the scissors, and said sternly:

"There's no butter in the butter dish. Where is it?"

Fedya got a surprised look in his eyes and, stretching out his neck, peeked into the butter dish.

"That butter is in your mouth," said his wife, pointing the scissors at Fedya.

Fedya shook his head negatively.

"A-ha," said his wife. "You keep silent and shake your head because your mouth is filled with butter."

Fedya bulged his eyes and waved his arms at his wife as if to say, "Why really, really, nothing of the sort." But his wife said:

"You're lying. Open your mouth."

"Mmm," said Fedya.

"Open your mouth," repeated his wife.

Fedya spread out his fingers and started to moo as if to say, "Oh yes, I completely forgot, I'll be right back." He stood up, intending to leave the room.

"Halt!" yelled his wife.

But Fedya increased his speed and disappeared out the door. His wife rushed after him but stopped near the door because she was naked and, looking this way, could not go out into the corridor where the other tenants of the apartment walked.

"He's gone," said his wife, sitting down on the couch. "What a devil!"

Having come through the hallway to the door on which hung the sign

"Entrance Categorically Forbidden"

Fedya opened this door and entered the room.

The room Fedya entered was long and narrow, with a window curtained with newspapers. On the right side of the room, near the wall, stood a dirty, broken sofa, and near the window—a table made of a wooden board supported on one end by the night-stand and on the other by a chair back. On the wall to his left hung a double shelf on which lay something nondescript. There was nothing else in the room —not counting the man with the pale-green face lying on the sofa. The man was dressed in a long and torn brown frock and black nankeen pants, out of which stuck two freshly washed unshod feet. This person was not asleep, and he stared at his guest.

Fedya bowed, scuffed his foot across the floor and, having taken the butter out of his mouth with his finger, showed it to the man on the sofa.

"One and a half," said the owner of the room, without changing his position.

"That's not much," said Fedya.

"It's enough," said the owner of the room.

"Well, fine," said Fedya, and taking the butter off his finger placed it on the shelf.

"Come for the money tomorrow morning," said the host.

"Oh no, what's this now!" yelped Fedya. "I need it now. And it's only one-and-a-half rubles . . ."

"Get out," said the host dryly. Fedya ran out of the room on tiptoe, carefully closing the door behind him.

1939

ANEGDOTES FROM THE LIFE OF PUSHKIN

1

Pushkin was a poet and was always writing something. Once Zhukovsky caught him at his writing and loudly exclaimed:

"Well, ain't you a scribbler!"

From then on Pushkin took a great liking to Zhukovsky and began calling him, friendly-like, simply Zhukov.

2

As we well know, Pushkin could never grow a beard. Pushkin was tormented by this and always envied Zakharin, whose beard, contrary to Pushkin's, grew quite decently. "His grows and mine doesn't," Pushkin used to mutter, pointing his long nails at Zakharin. And every time he was right.

3

Once Petrushevsky broke his watch and sent for Pushkin. Pushkin came in, looked over Petrushevsky's watch and placed it back on the chair. "What do you say, brother Pushkin?" asked Petrushevsky. "No go," said Pushkin.

4

When Pushkin broke his legs, he got around on wheels. His friends liked to tease Pushkin by grabbing at these wheels. Pushkin grew angry with his friends and wrote abusive poems about them. He called these poems "erpigarms."

5

Pushkin spent the summer of 1829 in the country. He would wake up early in the morning, drink a jug of fresh milk and then run down to the river to bathe. Having bathed in the river, Pushkin would lie down in the grass and sleep till lunchtime. After lunch, Pushkin would nap in the hammock. Upon meeting stinky peasants Pushkin would nod to them and hold his nose with his fingers. And the stinky peasants would crumple their hats and say, "that's aw-right."

6

Pushkin liked to throw rocks. He'd see some rocks and, right away, he'd start throwing them. Sometimes he would fly into such a rage that he'd stand there all red in the face, waving his arms, throwing rocks—something awful!

7

Pushkin had four sons and all of them idiots. One didn't even know how to sit on a chair and was always falling off. Pushkin himself was not so great at sitting on chairs. As it often happened—simply sidesplitting—they're all sitting at the table. At one end, Pushkin keeps falling off his chair—at the other end, his son is doing the same. You'd laugh like it was the end of the world!

THE BEGINNING OF A
VERY FINE SUMMER'S DAY
A Symphony

As soon as the cock crowed, Timofey jumped out of a window onto the roof and scared the daylights out of everyone who was out on the street at the time. The peasant Khariton paused, picked up a stone, and hurled it at Timofey. Timofey disappeared somewhere. "Isn't he clever!" cried the human herd, and someone by the name of Zubov took a running start and slammed his head against a wall with everything he had. "Ho!" cried a woman with a cold sore. But Komarov gave her a knick-knack-paddywhack and the woman ran away moaning into the nearest courtyard. Fetelyushin was walking by, chuckling to himself. Komarov walked up to him and said, "Hey, lard ass!" and hit Fetelyushin in the stomach. Fetelyushin leaned against the wall and started to hiccup. Nearby a big-nosed broad was beating her baby with a tub. Meanwhile, a young chubby mom rubbed her cute little girl's face into a brick wall. A small dog squirmed on the sidewalk with one of its thin legs broken. A little boy was eating filth from a spittoon. A long line for sugar formed in front of the dry goods store. The women argued loudly, shoving each other with their baskets. The peasant Khariton, drunk on methyl, stood in front of the women with his pants undone declaiming filthy words.

And so began a fine summer's day.

PAKIN AND RAKUKIN

"Don't get all snorty with me, you hear!" said Pakin to Rakukin.

Rakukin scrunched up his nose and looked at Pakin malevolently.

"What are you staring at? Don't you recognize me?" said Pakin.

Rakukin chewed his lips and, turning away on his swivel chair with indignation, looked in the opposite direction. Pakin drummed his fingers awhile on his knee and said:

"What a fool! I really should smash him on the back of the head with a folder."

Rakukin got up and started to walk out of the room, but Pakin quickly jumped to his feet, caught up to Rakukin and said:

"Wait a minute! Where are you running off to? You'd better sit down and I'll show you something."

Rakukin stopped and surveyed Pakin skeptically.

"You don't believe me?" asked Pakin.

"I believe you," said Rakukin.

"Then sit down over here, in this here chair," said Pakin.

And Rakukin sat back down in his swivel chair.

"Now what?" said Pakin, "just sitting in that chair like a dummy?"

Rakukin moved his feet around and started blinking his eyes very quickly.

"Don't you wink at me," said Pakin.

Rakukin stopped blinking and, hunching over, pulled his head into his shoulders.

"Sit straight," said Pakin.

Still hunched over, Rakukin bulged his stomach and stretched his neck out.

"Heh," said Pakin, "how I'd like to slap you in the muzzle!"

Rakukin hiccuped, puffed up his cheeks and then cautiously let the air out through his nostrils.

"Don't you dare snort!" said Pakin to Rakukin.

Rakukin stretched his neck out even further and his eyes went blink-blink again.

Pakin said:

"If you don't immediately stop blinking, Rakukin, I'll kick you in the boobs."

In order not to blink, Rakukin screwed up his jaw and stretched his neck out even further, tipping his head back.

"Ugh, you look absolutely vile," said Pakin. "A mug like a chicken's, and his neck is blue. Nasty!"

Meanwhile, Rakukin's head was tipping further and further back and finally, losing tension, collapsed onto his back.

"What the hell!" exclaimed Pakin. "What kind of dirty trick is that?"

If one were to look at Rakukin from Pakin's perspective, one would think that Rakukin was sitting there without a head at all. His Adam's apple stuck straight up. One couldn't help thinking that it was Rakukin's nose.

"Hey, Rakukin!" said Pakin.

Rakukin was silent.

"Rakukin!" repeated Pakin.

Rakukin made no reply and continued to sit there without moving an inch.

"That's it," said Pakin. "Rakukin's croaked."

Pakin crossed himself and tip-toed out of the room.

In about fourteen minutes, a little soul crawled out of Rakukin's body and cast an evil glance at the spot where, not long ago, sat Pakin. But then, from behind the armoire appeared the tall figure of the angel of death and, taking Rakukin's soul by the hand, led it away through walls and buildings. Rakukin's soul ran after the angel of death, turning back with a malevolent look every so often. Then the angel of death picked up the pace and Rakukin's soul, skipping and stumbling, vanished in the distance past a turn in the road.

THE OLD WOMAN

And between them occurs the following conversation.
—*Hamsun*

In the courtyard stands an old woman holding in her hands a clock. I walk past the old woman, stop and ask her: "What time is it?"

"Take a look," says the old woman.

I look and see that the clock has no hands.

"There are no hands there," I say.

The old woman looks at the clock face and says to me:

"It's quarter to three."

"So, that's how it is? Thanks very much," I say and leave.

The old woman yells something at my back, but I walk on without looking around. I go out onto the street and walk on the sunny side. The spring sun is very pleasant. I walk on, squinting and smoking my pipe. On the corner of Sadovaya I happen upon Sakerdon Mikhailovich walking towards me. We greet each other, stop and talk for a long while. I get bored of standing out on the street and invite Sakerdon Mikhailovich into a cellar. We drink vodka, chasing it with hard-boiled eggs and sprats, then say our goodbyes, and I go on alone.

Then I suddenly remember that I've forgotten to turn off the electric stove at home. I'm very upset. I turn around and walk home. The day began so well, and already the first bad turn. I should not have gone outside.

I come home, take off my jacket, take my watch out of my vest pocket and hang it up on the nail; then I lock the door and lie down on the sofa. I'll lie here and try to fall asleep.

From the street I can hear the unpleasant screams of little boys. I lie there dreaming up tortures for them. Most of all I like the idea of afflicting them with tetanus so that they'd suddenly stop moving. Their parents drag them back to their respective homes. They lie in their little beds and can't even eat, because their mouths don't open. They are nourished artificially. After a week the tetanus goes away, but the children are so weak that they still have to be confined to their beds for a whole month more. Then, bit by bit, they begin to recover, but I afflict them with a second bout of tetanus and they all expire.

I lie on the sofa with my eyes open and can't fall asleep. I recall the old woman with the clock that I saw today in the yard, and it pleases me that her clock had no hands. Just the other day at the pawn shop I saw the most hideous kitchen clock and the hands were made in the form of a knife and a fork.

My God! but I haven't yet turned off the electric stove! I jump up and turn it off, then lie down again on the sofa and try to fall asleep. I close my eyes. I'm not sleepy. In the window the spring sun shines right down on me. I get hot. I get up and sit down in the armchair by the window.

Now I'm sleepy, but I will not sleep. I will take paper and pen and I will write. I sense an awful strength within me. I thought everything over yesterday already. It will be a story about a miracle worker who lives in our time and does not work miracles. He knows he is a miracle worker and could create any sort of miracle, but he does not do it. He is evicted from his apartment—he knows that were he to just wave a finger the apartment would stay his, but he does not do it; he timidly vacates his apartment and lives outside of town in a shed. He can turn this old shed into a wonderful brick house, but he does not do it; he continues to live in the shed and in the end he dies, not having worked a single miracle in all his life.

I sit and wring my hands with joy. Sakerdon Mikhailovich will explode with envy. He thinks that I'm no longer capable of writing a thing of genius. Quickly, quickly, to work! Away with any sleep and laziness! I will write for eighteen hours straight!

I shiver all over with anticipation. I can't figure out what I should do: I needed to take pen and paper, but I grabbed various objects, not at all the ones that I needed. I ran about the room from the window to the desk, from the desk to the stove, from the stove to the desk again, and then to the couch and again to the window. I couldn't breathe from the fire that raged in my chest. It's only five o'clock yet. The whole day is ahead, and the evening, and all of the night.

I stand in the middle of room. What am I thinking? It's already twenty past five. I have to write. I push the little table up to the window and sit down at it. In front of me is the graph paper; in my hand, the pen.

My heart is still pounding too hard and my hand shakes. I wait to settle down. I put down the pen and fill my pipe. The sun is shining right in my eyes; I squint and light my pipe.

Now a crow flies past the window. I look out the window and see a man on the sidewalk with a mechanical leg. He's knocking loudly with his leg and his cane.

"So . . ." I say to myself as I continue looking out the window.

The sun hides behind the chimney of the apartment house standing opposite. The shadow cast by the chimney runs along the roof then flies across the street and falls across my face. I ought to take advantage of this shadow and write a few words about the miracle worker. I grab the pen and write:

The miracle worker was tall.

I can't write anything more. I sit until the moment I start experiencing hunger. Then I stand up and go over to the small cupboard where my provisions are kept. I feel around in there but find nothing. A cube of sugar and nothing more.

Someone's knocking at the door.

"Who is it?"

No one answers me. I open the door and before me I see the old woman who this morning was standing in the courtyard with the clock. I'm very surprised and can't say a thing.

"And here I am," says the old woman and walks into my room.

I stand at the door and don't know what to do—boot her out or, on the contrary, offer her a seat? But the old woman walks over to my armchair by the window and sits down herself.

"Close the door, and lock it," the old woman tells me.

I close and lock the door.

"Get down on your knees," says the old woman.

And I get down on my knees.

But here I begin to understand the complete awkwardness of my situation. Why am I standing on my knees before some old woman? And why is this old woman in my room sitting in my favorite chair? Why did I not throw this old woman out?

"Listen up," I say, "what right do you have giving orders in my room, and moreover ordering me around? I have no desire to stand on my knees."

"And you don't have to," says the old woman. "Now you must lie down on your stomach and stick your face in the floor."

I instantly fulfill her command.

Directly in front of me I see precisely drafted squares. Pain in my shoulder and in my right hip forces me to change my position. I was lying face down; now with great difficulty I get up onto my knees. All my members had fallen asleep; they bend poorly. I look around and see myself in my room standing on my knees in the middle of the floor. Consciousness and memory slowly come back to me. I look around the room again and see that on the chair by the window someone is sitting. It's not very light in the room, probably because it's white nights. My gaze is fixed. My God! Can it really be the old woman sitting in my armchair still? I crane my neck and look. Yes, of course, it's the old woman, and she's dropped her head onto her chest. She must have fallen asleep. I get up and, limping, approach her. The old woman's head droops on her chest, her arms hang by the sides of the chair. I want to grab this old woman and push her out the door.

"Listen to me," I say, "you are in my room. I need to work. I'm asking you to leave."

The old woman doesn't budge. I bend down and peer into the old woman's face. Her mouth is slightly open and jutting out of her mouth are the false teeth that must have come loose. And suddenly everything becomes clear to me: The old woman is dead.

A terrible feeling of irritation overtakes me. What for did the old woman die in my room? I can't stand dead people. And now fuss over this carrion, go talk to the janitor and the building super and explain to them why this old woman turned up at my place. I look at the old woman with loathing. But what if, maybe, she's not dead? I feel her forehead. It's cold. Her hand also. Well, what am I to do?

I light up my pipe and sit down on the sofa. A mad anger swells up inside me.

"What a scumbag!" I say out loud.

The dead old woman sits like a sack in my armchair. The teeth jut out of her mouth. She resembles a dead horse.

"A disgusting scene," I say, but I can't cover the old woman with a newspaper because who knows what might happen under a newspaper.

Behind the wall I can hear movement: That's my neighbor getting up, a train engine driver. That's just what I need, for him to sniff out that I've got a dead old woman sitting in my room! I listen closely to the steps of my neighbor. What's taking him so long? It's already half past five! It's long time for him to be going. Oh my God! He's fixing to have tea! I can hear the primus stove making noise behind the wall. Ack, if that cursed engine driver would just hurry up and leave!

I pull my legs up onto the sofa and lie there. Eight minutes go by, but the neighbor's tea still isn't ready and the primus stove is hissing. I close my eyes and nap.

I dream that my neighbor has gone and I go out, at the same time as he, onto the landing and slam the door with the spring lock behind me. I don't have a key and I can't get back into the apartment. I have to buzz and wake the rest of the tenants, and that's real bad. I stand on the landing thinking what I should do, and suddenly I notice that I have no hands. I tilt my head to get a better look if I have hands or not, and I see that on one side instead of a hand a table knife juts out, and on the other side, a fork.

"There now," I say to Sakerdon Mikhailovich, who's sitting for some reason right nearby on a folding chair. "You see," I say to him, "what kind of hands I've got."

But Sakerdon Mikhailovich sits silently, and I realize that it's not the real Sakerdon Mikhailovich, but a clay one.

Then I wake up and it dawns on me that I'm lying in my room on the sofa and that at the window in the armchair is the dead old woman.

I quickly turn my head towards her. The old woman is not in the armchair. I gaze at the empty armchair and I am filled with wild joy.

That means it was all a dream. Only, where did it begin? Did the old woman come into my room yesterday evening? Perhaps that was also a dream? I came back home yesterday because I'd forgotten to turn off the electric stove. But maybe that was also a dream? Either way, how great is it that there is no dead old woman in my room and I don't have to go to the building super and fuss with the corpse!

But wait, how long have I been asleep? I looked at the clock—half past nine, must be morning.

God! What doesn't happen in dreams!

I dropped my feet down off the sofa about to stand up, when suddenly I saw the dead old woman lying on the floor behind the table by the chair. She was lying there face up and the dentures that had fallen out of her mouth bit into her nostril with one tooth. The arms were turned under the torso and were not visible, and bony legs in white, dirty wool stockings stuck out from under her hiked-up skirt.

"Scumbag!" I yelled and, running up to the old woman, kicked her in the chin with my boot.

Her dentures flew off into the corner. I wanted to hit the old woman a second time, but hesitated to leave marks on the body, or else they'd later decide that it was me who killed her.

I backed away from the old woman, sat down on the sofa and lit up my pipe. About twenty minutes passed like that. Now it was clear to me that no matter what, the case would be transferred to criminal investigation and the pea brain detective would charge me with murder. The situation was turning out to be serious, and then there was the boot to the chin on top of it all.

I walked up to the old woman again, bent down and started examining her face. There was a small dark spot on the chin. No, they couldn't raise a stink about that. So what? Maybe the old woman banged herself on something or other while she was still alive? I calm down a little and start to pace the room, smoking my pipe and mulling over my situation.

I'm walking around and around the room, and I start feeling my hunger more and more. I even start shivering from hunger. Again I fumble around in the little cupboard where my provisions are kept, but find nothing except for the piece of sugar.

I take out my wallet and count the money. Eleven rubles. That means I can buy myself some ham and bread and there'll still be some left over for tobacco.

I straighten my tie which had gotten beaten out of shape over the course of the night. I take my watch, put on my jacket, walk out into the hall, thoroughly lock the door to my room, put the key in my pocket and walk outside. First I must eat, then my thoughts will be clearer and I will undertake some kind of action with this carrion.

On the way to the store I get this idea: Why not drop in on Sakerdon Mikhailovich and tell him everything, maybe together we can come up with something sooner. But right away I reject this idea because some things must be done alone, without witnesses.

There was no ham at the store so I bought myself half a kilogram of sausage links. There was no tobacco either. From the store I went straight to the bakery.

At the bakery there was a big crowd and a long line formed for the cashier. I made a face but got in line anyway. The line moved very slowly and then stopped completely because some sort of scene had occurred at the cash register.

I made a face as though I knew nothing about it and gazed into the back of a young little lady who was standing in line ahead of me. The young little lady was obviously very curious: She craned her little neck right and left and once a minute she would get up on her tippy-toes to get a better look at what was going on at the register. Finally she turned to me and asked:

"Do you know what's going on over there?"

"Sorry, I don't," I said as dryly as possible.

The little lady spun around in all directions and finally again addressed me:

"Do you think you could go and find out what's going on over there?"

"I'm sorry, I'm not in the least interested," said I, even more dryly.

"It doesn't interest you?" exclaimed the little lady. "But you're being held up in the line because of it too."

I did not reply and only bowed slightly. The little lady looked me over carefully.

"Of course it's not a man's business to stand in line for bread," she said. "I feel bad for you—you have to stand here. You must be a bachelor?"

"Yes, I'm a bachelor!" I replied, a bit confused, but continuing by inertia to answer rather dryly and with that bowing slightly.

Once more the little lady looked me over from head to toe and suddenly, stretching her finger out toward my sleeve, said:

"How about I buy what you need and you wait for me outside."

I was at a complete loss.

"I'm grateful to you," I said. "It's very kind of you, but, really, I could do it myself."

"No, no," said the little lady, "go on outside. What were you going to buy?"

"You see," said I, "I was going to buy half a kilo of black bread, but only the form-baked loaf, the one that's cheaper. I like it better."

"Well, there now, that's good," said the little lady. "And now on your way. I'll buy it and we'll settle up after."

And she even pushed me a little under the elbow.

I walk out of the bakery and stand right by the door. The spring sun shines right in my face. I light up my pipe. What a kind little lady! It's so rare nowadays. I stand there squinting from the sunlight, smoking my pipe, and think about the kind little lady. She does have light brown eyes. Simply marvelous how nice looking she is!

"You smoke a pipe?" I hear a voice near me. The kind little lady extends the bread to me.

"Oh, I'm eternally grateful to you," I say, taking the bread.

"And you smoke a pipe! I like that terribly," says the kind little lady.

And between us occurs the following conversation:

SHE: I take it you go for bread yourself?

I: Not only for bread; I buy everything for myself.

SHE: And where do you dine?

I: Ordinarily I cook dinner for myself. And sometimes I eat at the pub.

SHE: You like beer?

I: No, I like vodka better.

SHE: I like vodka too.

I: You like vodka? How excellent! I would like to have a drink together with you sometime.

SHE: And I too would like to drink vodka with you.

I: I'm sorry, but can I ask you about one thing?

SHE (*blushing heavily*): Of course, ask away.

I: Alright, I'll ask you. Do you believe in God?

SHE (*surprised*): In God? Yes, of course.

I: And what would you say if we were to buy some vodka now and go to my place. I live not far from here.

SHE (*keenly*): Well then, I accept.

I: Then let's go.

We walk into a store and I buy half a liter of vodka. I don't have any more money, only some measly change. We're talking about different things all the time, and I suddenly remember that in my room, on the floor, is a dead old woman.

I look back at my new acquaintance—she's standing at a counter and looking at jars of jam. I carefully make my way to the door and exit the store. Just then there's a tram stopping right across from the store. I jump into the tram, not even looking at the number. I get off at Mikhailovskaya Street and walk to Sakerdon Mikhailovich's. In my hand a bottle of vodka, sausage links and bread.

Sakerdon Mikhailovich himself opened the doors for me. He was in a robe thrown over his bare body, in Russian boots with the tops cut off and a fur hat with ear flaps, but the earflaps were pulled up and tied in a bow on top.

"A pleasure," said Sakerdon Mikhailovich, seeing me there.

"Have I torn you away from your work?" I asked.

"No, no," said Sakerdon Mikhailovich. "I wasn't doing anything, just sitting on the floor."

"You see," I said to Sakerdon Mikhailovich, "I've come to you with vodka and chasers. If you have nothing against it, let's have a drink."

"Very good," said Sakerdon Mikhailovich. "You should come in."

We walked through to his room. I uncorked the bottle of vodka and Sakerdon Mikhailovich placed two shot glasses on the table and a plate of boiled meat.

"I've got some sausage links here," said I. "So how are we going to eat them—raw, or should we boil them?"

"We'll put them on to boil," said Sakerdon Mikhailovich, "and while they're boiling, we'll drink the vodka with boiled meat. It's from a soup—excellent boiled meat!"

Sakerdon Mikhailovich placed a small pot on the kerosene stove, and we sat down to drink vodka.

"Drinking vodka is healthy," said Sakerdon Mikhailovich, filling the glasses. "Mechnikov wrote that vodka is healthier than bread and bread is just straw that rots in our stomachs."

"Your health!" I said, clinking glasses with Sakerdon Mikhailovich. We drank and chased it down with boiled meat.

"Tastes good," said Sakerdon Mikhailovich. But at that moment something made an abrupt cracking noise in the room.

"What's that?" I asked.

We sat silently and listened. Suddenly it cracked once more. Sakerdon Mikhailovich jumped out of his chair and, running up to the window, tore down the curtain.

"What are you doing," I screamed.

But, without a reply, Sakerdon Mikhailovich threw himself toward the kerosene stove, grabbed the pot with the curtain and placed it on the floor.

"Damn it!" said Sakerdon Mikhailovich. "I forgot to pour water in the pot, and the pot's enamel, and now the enamel's popped off."

"Now I get it," I said, nodding my head.

We sat down to the table again.

"Damn them," said Sakerdon Mikhailovich, "we'll eat the sausages raw."

"I'm terribly hungry," I said.

"Eat," said Sakerdon Mikhailovich, pushing the sausages towards me.

"In fact, the last time I ate was yesterday, with you, in that cellar, and since then I haven't yet eaten anything," I said.

"Yes, yes, yes," said Sakerdon Mikhailovich.

"I was writing all that time," I said.

"Damn it!" Sakerdon Mikhailovich raised his voice in an exaggerated way. "It's such a pleasure to see a genius before me."

"Sure it is," I said.

"And did you unload a heap?" asked Sakerdon Mikhailovich.

"Yes," I said, "I marred an abyss of paper."

"To the genius of our days," said Sakerdon Mikhailovich lifting his glass.

We drank. Sakerdon Mikhailovich ate the boiled meat, and I ate the sausages. Having eaten four sausages, I lit up my pipe and said:

"You know, I came to you escaping pursuit."

"And who was pursuing you?" asked Sakerdon Mikhailovich.

"A lady," I said. But since Sakerdon Mikhailovich didn't put any questions to me and only silently poured vodka into our glasses, I continued:

"I made her acquaintance at the bakery and fell in love straight away."

"Good looking?" asked Sakerdon Mikhailovich.

"Yes," I said. "My type."

We drank, and I continued:

"She agreed to go to my place to drink vodka. We stopped into a store, but I was forced to quietly slip out of the store."

"Not enough money?" asked Sakerdon Mikhailovich.

"No, I had just enough money," I said, "but I remembered that I couldn't let her into my room."

"What, did you have another lady in your room?" asked Sakerdon Mikhailovich.

"Yes, if you like, there is another lady in my room," I said, smiling. "Now I can't let anyone in my room."

"Marry her. And you'll have me over for dinner," said Sakerdon Mikhailovich.

"No," I said, snorting with laughter. "I will not marry that lady."

"Well, then marry the other one, the one from the bakery," said Sakerdon Mikhailovich.

"Why are you so eager to marry me off?" I said.

"And why not?" said Sakerdon Mikhailovich filling our glasses. "To your success."

We drank. It seems the vodka was beginning to take its effect on us. Sakerdon Mikhailovich took off his fur hat with the earmuffs and tossed it onto the bed. I stood up and walked around the room already feeling slightly dizzy.

"What's your attitude toward dead people?" I asked Sakerdon Mikhailovich.

"Absolutely negative," said Sakerdon Mikhailovich. "I'm afraid of them."

"Yeah, I can't stand dead people either," I said. "Were I to bump into a dead person, and if he wasn't a relative, I'd probably kick him."

"One shouldn't kick dead people," said Sakerdon Mikhailovich.

"I would give him a boot right in the muzzle," I said. "I just can't stand dead people and children."

"Yeah, children are disgusting," Sakerdon Mikhailovich agreed.

"In your opinion, what's worse—dead people or children?" I asked.

"Children, I'd say, are worse. They get in the way more often. You have to admit, dead people don't barge into our lives like that," said Sakerdon Mikhailovich.

"They *do* barge in!" I yelled and quickly shut up.

Sakerdon Mikhailovich scrutinized me closely.

"Some more vodka?" he asked.

"No," I said, but getting a hold of myself added, "No, thank you, I don't want anymore." I walk over and sit down at the table again. For some time we stay silent.

"I want to ask you a question," I say, finally. "Do you believe in God?"

A perpendicular wrinkle appears on Sakerdon Mikhailovich's forehead and he says:

"There exist impolite actions. It is impolite to ask a man to loan you fifty rubles if you saw that he just put two hundred in his pocket. It's his business whether to give you the money or to decline, and the most convenient and pleasant way to decline is to lie that you have none. You've seen that this man has the money and thereby you have stripped him of the opportunity to simply and pleasantly decline. You have stripped him of his right to choose, and that's rotten. It is an impolite and tactless act. And to ask a person 'Do you believe in God?' is also an impolite and tactless act."

"Well," I said, "there's no comparison."

"And I'm not comparing," said Sakerdon Mikhailovich.

"Well alright," I said, "let's drop it. Only forgive me for asking you such an impolite and tactless question."

"Please," said Sakerdon Mikhailovich. "After all, I simply declined to answer you."

"I, too, would not have answered," I said, "but for a different reason."

"And what would that be?" asked Sakerdon Mikhailovich indifferently.

"You see," I said, "in my opinion, there are no believers or non-believers. There are only those who want to believe and those who do not want to believe."

"So those who do not want to believe already believe in something?" said Sakerdon Mikhailovich. "And those who want to believe already believe in nothing?"

"That may be," I said. "I don't know."

"And what is it that they believe or do not believe in? In God?" asked Sakerdon Mikhailovich.

"No," I said, "in immortality."

"Then why did you ask me whether I believed in God?"

"Simply because to ask 'Do you believe in immortality?' sounds stupid somehow," I said to Sakerdon Mikhailovich and stood up.

"Are you—leaving?" Sakerdon Mikhailovich asked me.

"Yes," I said. "It's time."

"But what about the vodka?" asked Sakerdon Mikhailovich. "There's just enough left for but a glass each."

"Well, let's finish it," I said.

We drank the vodka and chased it with what was left of the boiled meat.

"And now I must go," I said.

"Goodbye," said Sakerdon Mikhailovich, walking me from the kitchen to the stairs. "Thank you for the refreshments."

"I thank *you*," I said. "Goodbye."

And I went.

Left alone, Sakerdon Mikhailovich cleared the table, threw the empty vodka bottle on top of the cupboard, put his fur hat with the earflaps back on his head and sat down on the floor by the window. Sakerdon Mikhailovich laid his hands behind his back where they were not to be seen. And from underneath his hiked-up robe protruded bare bony legs shod in Russian boots with their tops cut off.

I walked down Nevsky submerged in my thoughts. I should go right away to the building super and tell him everything. And after I've finished with the old woman I will stand by the bakery day in and day out until I see that nice little lady. After all, I owe her 48 kopeks for the bread. I have an excellent excuse to search for her. The vodka was still having its effect and it seemed that everything was coming together nice and easy.

On the Fontanka I approached a kiosk and with the leftover change I drank a large mug of bread beer. The bread beer was bad and sour, and I walked on with a vile taste in my mouth.

On the corner of Liteinaya some drunk staggered and pushed me. It's a good thing that I don't have a revolver—I would have killed him right on the spot.

I must have walked all the way home with an angry scowl on my face. In any case, almost everyone I passed turned to look at me.

I walked into the building super's office. On the desk sat a squat, dirty, pug-nosed, cross-eyed and fair-headed girl, rubbing her lips with rouge and gazing into a compact mirror.

"And where's the super?" I asked.

The girl was silent, still rubbing her lips.

"Where's the super?" I repeated in a sharp voice.

"Tomorrow, not today," answered the dirty, pug-nosed, cross-eyed and fair-headed girl.

I walked out onto the street. On the opposite side walked a cripple on a mechanical leg knocking loudly with his leg and his stick. Six little boys ran after the cripple, mocking his gait.

I turned into my vestibule and started climbing the stairs. On the second floor I stopped—a disgusting thought went through my head:

The old woman must have begun to decompose. I hadn't closed the windows and they say that with open windows dead people decompose more quickly. Utter stupidity! And that damned super won't be in till tomorrow! I stood there several minutes in indecision and climbed onward.

I stopped again at the door to my apartment. Maybe I should go down to the bakery and wait for that sweet little lady? I would plead with her to let me stay at her place for two or three nights. But then I remember that she's already bought bread today, and that means she won't be going to the bakery. And, anyway, nothing would come of it.

I unlocked the door and walked into the hallway. At the end of the hallway a light was on and Marya Vasilyevna, holding some sort of rag in her hand, was rubbing it with another rag. Seeing me, Marya Vasilyevna shouted:

"An owd man was wooking fow you!"

"What old man?"

"I dunno," Marya Vasilyevna answered.

"When was it?" I asked.

"Awso dunno," said Marya Vasilyevna.

"Was it you who talked to the old man?" I asked Marya Vasilyevna.

"I," answered Marya Vasilyevna.

"So how is it that you don't know when?" I said.

"Two hows o' so ago," said Marya Vasilyevna.

"And what did this old man look like?" I asked.

"Awso dunno," said Marya Vasilyevna and went away into the kitchen.

I went to my room.

"And what if," I thought, "the old woman's vanished? I'll walk into the room and the old woman's gone. My God! Are there really no miracles?"

I unlocked the door and slowly pushed it ajar. Maybe I only imagined it, but the sickeningly sweet smell of decay wafted in my face. I peeked around the slightly opened door and for a moment was frozen to the spot. The old woman was on all fours slowly crawling toward me.

With a shout I slammed the door, turned the key and jumped back against the wall opposite the door.

Marya Vasilyevna appeared in the hallway.

"D'you caw fow me?" she asked.

I was shaking so bad that I couldn't answer and only shook my head no. Marya Vasilyevna came closer.

"You wuh tawking to someone," she said.

Again I shook my head no.

"Cwazy," said Marya Vasilyevna and walked back into the kitchen, looking back at me several times on her way.

"Can't stand here like this. Can't stand here like this," I repeated in my thoughts. The phrase came together somewhere inside me. I chanted it until it made it all the way to my consciousness.

"Yes, I can't stand here like this," I said to myself, but continued standing there like I was paralyzed. Something awful had happened, but ahead of me there was something that had to be done that was perhaps even more awful than what had already happened. A whirlwind spun my thoughts around in circles and I could see only the wrathful eyes of the dead old woman as she slowly crawled toward me on all fours.

Burst into the room and shatter the old woman's skull. That's what must be done! I even searched around with my eyes and was content upon noticing a croquet mallet that had for no known reason and for many years been standing in the corner of the hallway. Grab the mallet, burst into the room, and slam..!

The shivers had not yet passed. I stood with shoulders raised from the inner chill. My thoughts raced, got tangled, and returned to their starting point, then raced again, gaining new ground, while I stood listening intently to my thoughts and was as if standing apart from them, as if I were not their captain.

"Dead people," my own thoughts were explaining to me, "are a no-good lot. It's wrong to call them deceased, because they are, rather, un-deceased. They have to be watched, and carefully. Ask any watchman at the mortuary. Why do you think he's been posted there? For one thing only—to keep watch so that the dead people don't crawl away. There have been, in this regard, some curious cases. One dead man, while the watchman was at the public baths on executive orders, crawled out of the mortuary and into the disinfection chamber, and there he ate a bunch of linens. The sanitation crew gave him an excellent thrashing, but they had to pay for the ruined linen out of their own pockets. And another dead man crawled into the maternity ward and scared everyone to the point that one of the mothers-to-be man-ufactured a premature miscarriage and the dead man threw himself onto the ejected fetus and, chewing loudly, set to consuming it. And when one nurse struck the dead man on the back with a wooden stool he bit the brave nurse in the leg and she was infected with corpse poi-son and died soon thereafter. So, dead people—a no-good lot. You can't let down your guard."

"Stop!" I said to my own thoughts. "You are talking nonsense! Dead people are immobile!"

"Alright," my own thoughts said to me, "then go in your room, where there is, as you say, an immobile dead person."

A surprising stubbornness spoke up inside me.

"I will!" I said with confidence to my own thoughts.

"Try it!" my own thoughts mocked me.

This mockery infuriated me once and for all. I grabbed the cro-quet mallet and rushed to the door.

"Wait!" my own thoughts shouted to me. But I had already turned the key and thrown the door wide open.

The old woman lay by the threshold with her face to the floor.

With the croquet mallet raised, I stood at the ready. The old woman didn't budge.

My shivers subsided, and my thoughts flowed bright and clear. I was the captain of them.

"First things first: Close the door!" I commanded myself.

I took the key out of the outer side of the door and inserted it on the inside. I did this with my left hand while in my right I held the cro-quet mallet and did not let the old woman out of my sight the whole time. I locked the door and, cautiously stepping over the old woman, walked out into the middle of the room.

"Now I'm going to get even with you," I said. I had come up with a plan, the kind that murderers in crime novels and newspaper stories regularly resort to: I wanted simply to hide the old woman in a suit-case, take her outside the city and dump her in a swamp. I knew one such place.

The suitcase was under the sofa. I dragged it out and opened it. In it were various odd items: several books, an old felt hat, and torn linens. I laid all this out on the sofa.

At that moment the apartment door slammed and it seemed to me that the old woman shuddered.

Momentarily I jumped up and grabbed the croquet mallet.

The old woman is lying still. I stand there listening. It's the engine driver come back; I hear him walking in his room. Now he's walking down the corridor into the kitchen. It would be no good if Marya Vasilyevna tells him of my crazy behavior. Damn it all! I should walk down the hallway and calm them with my appearance.

Again I stepped over the old woman. I set the mallet down right by the door so that upon my return without even entering the room I could have the mallet in my hands, and I walked out into the hallway. Voices carried from the kitchen, but I couldn't make out the words. I closed the door to my room part way and went cautiously to the kitchen—I wanted to know what Marya Vasilyevna and the mechanic were talking about. I walked quickly down the hallway but slowed my pace as I got nearer the kitchen. The mechanic was talking; it seemed he was speaking of something that happened to him at work.

I walked in. The mechanic stood talking with a towel in his hands and Marya Vasilyevna sat listening on a stool. Catching sight of me, the mechanic waved.

"Hello, hello, Matvei Philipovich," I said to him as I passed on my way to the bathroom. So far everything was calm. Marya Vasilyevna had gotten used to my peculiarities and might already have forgotten this most recent case.

Suddenly it occurred to me: I didn't lock the door. And what if the old woman crawls out of the room?

I rushed back, but caught myself in time and, in order not to scare the tenants, I walked through the kitchen at an even pace.

Marya Vasilyevna was knocking on the kitchen table with her finger, saying to the mechanic:

"Excewent! Now that's excewent! I would've whistwed too!"

My heart froze as I walked out into the hallway and, now almost running, went off to my room.

Outside everything was calm. I walked up to the door and opened it just enough to look inside. The old woman was lying calmly as before with her face to the floor. The croquet mallet stood by the door where I'd left it. I took it, walked into the room and locked the door behind me. The room certainly smelled of a corpse. I stepped over the old woman, walked over to the window and sat down in the armchair. I hope this odor, still faint but already unbearable, doesn't make me sick. I lit my pipe. I felt nauseous and there was a slight pain in my stomach.

What am I sitting here for? I need to act, quickly, before this old woman goes completely rancid. In any case, she must be stuffed into the suitcase with caution, because that's exactly the moment she could bite my finger. And then to die of an infection from a corpse—no thank you!

"Aha!" I suddenly exclaimed. "I'm quite interested—what will you bite me with? Aren't those your little teeth way over there!"

I bent over in the armchair and looked into the corner on the far side of the window, where, by my calculations, the old woman's false teeth should have been. But the false teeth were not there.

I wondered: Maybe the old woman was crawling around my room looking for her teeth? And maybe she even found them and put them back in her mouth?

I took the croquet mallet and used it to poke around in the corner. No, the dentures were gone. Then I took a heavy flannel sheet from a drawer and walked over to the old woman. I held the croquet mallet in my right hand at the ready, and in my left hand I held the flannel sheet.

The dead old woman aroused in me a mixture of squeamishness and fear. I lifted up her head with the mallet—her mouth was open, her eyes rolled upwards, a large dark stain spread across the whole of her chin where I had kicked her with my boot. I looked into the old woman's mouth—no, she had not found her false teeth. I let go of her head. It dropped and banged against the floor.

I spread the flannel sheet across the floor and pulled it right up to the old woman. Then with my foot and the croquet mallet I turned the old woman over to her left and onto her back. Now the old woman was lying on the sheet. The old woman's legs were bent at the knees and her fists pressed against her shoulders. It seemed that the old woman, lying on her back like a cat, was getting ready to defend herself against an eagle that was attacking her. Quickly, be gone with this carrion!

I wrapped the old woman in the thick sheet and lifted her into my arms. She turned out to be lighter than I thought. I let her down into the suitcase and tried closing the lid. Here I expected some difficulties, but the lid closed with relative ease. I snapped in the locks of the suitcase and straightened up.

The suitcase stood before me looking perfectly respectable as if inside it were books and linens. I took it by the handle and tried lifting it. It was, of course, heavy, but not too much so—I could no doubt carry it to the tram.

I looked at my watch: twenty past five. That's good. I sat down in the armchair to have a rest and finish smoking my pipe.

The sausages that I ate today were definitely not so good, because my stomach ached more and more. And maybe it was because I ate them raw? Yet again, maybe my stomach ache was purely my nerves.

I sit and smoke. And minute after minute goes by.

The spring sun shines in the window and I squint from its rays. Now it hides behind the chimney of the apartment house standing opposite, and the shadow cast by the chimney runs along the roof then flies across the street and falls across my face. I recall how yesterday at this exact time I sat writing my story. Here it is—the graph paper, and an inscription made in a fine hand: "The miracle worker was tall."

I looked out the window. A cripple walked down the street on a mechanical leg knocking loudly with his leg and his stick. Two workers and with them an old woman guffawed, holding their sides, at the cripple's funny gait.

I stood up. It's time! Time to be on my way! Time to take the old woman to the swamp! I also need to borrow money from the train engineer.

I went out into the hallway and walked up to his door.

"Matvei Philipovich, are you at home?" I asked.

"I'm home," answered the engineer.

"Then, forgive me, Matvei Philipovich, are you not flush with money? I'll be paid the day after tomorrow. You wouldn't be able to lend me thirty rubles, would you?"

"I would," said the mechanic. And I could hear his keys clanging as he unlocked some kind of box. Then he opened the door and stretched out a new thirty-ruble bill.

"Many thanks, Matvei Philipovich," I said.

"It's nothing, it's nothing," said the mechanic.

I shoved the money in my pocket and returned to my room. The suitcase stood serenely in the same place.

"Well, now to get on my way, with haste," I said to myself.

I took the suitcase and walked out of the room.

Marya Vasilyevna saw me with the suitcase and shouted:

"Where to?"

"My aunt's place," I said.

"You be gone wong?" asked Marya Vasilyevna.

"No," I said. "I just need to bring some things to my aunt's. I'll be back, maybe even tonight."

I went out into the street. I got to the tram without a hitch, carrying the suitcase now in my right hand, now in my left.

I climbed into the tram from the front landing of the last car and started waving to the conductor so that she'd come over and receive payment for the luggage and the ticket. I didn't want to pass along my only thirty-ruble bill through the whole tram, and I couldn't bring myself to leave the suitcase and go to the conductor myself. The conductor came over to me at the landing and announced that she didn't have change. I was forced to get off at the very first stop.

I stood there stewing and waited for the next tram. My stomach ached and my legs faintly quivered.

And suddenly I saw my sweet little lady—she was crossing the street, not looking in my direction.

I grabbed the suitcase and ran after her. I didn't know her name so I couldn't call out to her. The suitcase was a terrible hindrance—I held it in front of me with both hands, pushing it forward with my knees and stomach. The sweet little lady walked quite quickly and I had a feeling that I wouldn't be able to catch up to her. I was drenched with sweat and exhaustion. The sweet little lady turned into an alleyway. When I made it to the corner she was nowhere to be seen.

"Damn old woman!" I hissed, throwing the suitcase on the ground.

The sleeves of my jacket were soaked through with sweat and clung to my arms. I sat down on the suitcase and, taking out a handkerchief, wiped my neck and face. Two boys stopped in front of me and began looking me over. I made a calm face and gazed intently at the nearest gateway as if I were waiting for someone. The boys whispered to each other and pointed their fingers at me. Wild malice choked me. Oh, that I could afflict tetanus on them all!

And all because of these lousy kids I get up, lift the suitcase, walk over to the gateway and peer inside. I make a surprised face, get out my watch and shrug my shoulders. The boys watch me from afar. Again I shrug my shoulders and look into the gateway. "How strange," I say out loud. I take the suitcase and drag it to the tram stop.

I arrive at the train station at five to seven. I get a round trip ticket to Foxes Nose and board the train.

Apart from myself in the train car there are two people. One of them is clearly a worker—he's tired, with his cap pulled over his eyes he's gone to sleep. The other one, still a young man, is dressed like a village dandy: He's got a pink Russian collar shirt under his sports coat and a curly tuft of hair sticks out from under his cap. He's smoking a cigarette stuck in a bright-green plastic cigarette holder.

I put the suitcase between the benches and take a seat. I've got such spasms in my stomach that I clench my fists to avoid howling from the pain.

On the platform two policemen lead a civilian to the police station. He walks with his hands behind his back and his head down.

The train starts to move. I look at my watch—ten minutes past eight.

What a pleasure it will be to dump this old woman in the swamp! Pity I forgot to take a stick with me as the old woman might need a push.

The dandy with the pink collar shirt eyes me insolently. I turn my back to him and look out the window.

Terrible pangs attack my stomach—I clench my teeth and my fists and tense my legs.

We pass Lanskaya and New Village. There's the golden top of the Buddhist pagoda, shining, and a glimpse of the sea.

But now I jump up and, forgetting everything around me, run in short steps to the bathroom. A dreadful wave sways and spins my consciousness . . .

The train slows its pace. We are approaching Lakhta. I sit still, trying not to move so that they don't chase me out of the bathroom at the stop.

"Why won't it hurry up and move! Hurry up and move!"

The train jerks to a start and I close my eyes in blissful pleasure. Oh, these minutes can be as sweet as moments of love! All my powers are in play; but I know that a frightening decline will follow.

The train stops again. It's Olgino. And again this torture!

But now these are false urges. A cold sweat emerges on my forehead and a slight chill flutters around my heart. I get up and stand there for some time with my head pressed against the wall. The train is moving and the rocking of the train car is very pleasant.

I gather all my strength and stagger out of the bathroom.

The train car is empty. The worker and the dandy in the pink shirt must have gotten off at Lakhta or Olgino. Slowly, I walk over to my window.

And suddenly I stop and look ahead with a dull stare. The suitcase is no longer there where I left it. I must have mistaken the window. I jump to the next window. No suitcase. I jump backward and forward, I run the length of the car in both directions, looking under the bench seats, but the suitcase is nowhere to be found.

There's no doubt about it. Of course, while I was in the bathroom, the suitcase was stolen. That could have been foreseen!

I sit on the bench, my eyes bulging, and for some reason I remember how the enamel cracked, popping off the burning hot pan at Sakerdon Mikhailovich's.

"What's happened?" I ask myself. "Now who'll believe me that I didn't murder the old woman? I'll be apprehended this very day, here, or in the city at the train station, like that civilian walking with his head down."

I walk out onto the landing of the train car. The train is approaching Foxes Nose. The white posts that border the road are flashing by. The train slows to a stop. The steps of my train car don't reach the ground. I jump down and walk to the station house. There's another half-hour before the train back to the city.

I walk into a little wood. There are some short mulberry bushes—nobody will see me behind them. I set out in their direction.

A large green caterpillar crawls along the ground. I get down on my knees and touch it with my fingers. It folds up its strong, sinewy body in one direction and then the other.

I look around. No one can see me. A light shudder runs up my back.

I bow my head low and quietly speak:

"In the name of the Father and the Son and the Holy Spirit, now and forever. Amen." . . . .
. . . .
. . . .

At this point I temporarily end my manuscript in the belief that it has drawn on long enough.

End of May and first half of June, 1939

THE BLUE
NOTEBOOK

For the scrapbook:

I once saw a fly and a bedbug get into a fight. It was so frightening that I ran out into the street and ran as far as I could.

The same thing goes for the scrapbook: Do some dirty thing and then it's too late.

Aug. 23, 1936
Kharms

1.

My opinion of traveling is succinct: When traveling, do not go too far or else you might see something that will even be impossible to forget. And if anything settles in the memory too stubbornly, a person first starts to feel uneasy, and then it gets quite difficult to keep up the vivacity of the soul.

2.

So, for instance: One watchmaker, Comrade Badaev, could not forget a phrase he heard once long ago: "If the sky were crooked, it wouldn't make it any lower." Comrade Badaev didn't really get this saying, it irritated him, he found it unreasonable, even lacking any kind of sense, malignant even, because its claim was obviously incorrect (Comrade Badaev felt that a knowledgeable physicist could say something regarding "the height of the sky," and would question the expression "the sky is crooked." Were this phrase to get to Pearlman, Comrade Badaev was certain, Pearlman would tear its meaning to shreds, the way a young pup tears up house slippers), and obviously antagonistic to the normal pattern of European thought. If indeed the claim contained in this saying were true, then it was too unimportant and worthless to speak of. And in any case, hearing this phrase just once, one ought right away to forget it. But he couldn't make that happen: Comrade Badaev constantly remembered this phrase and suffered greatly.

3.

It is healthy for a person to know only that which he is supposed to. I can offer the following incident as an example: One person knew a little more and another a bit less than they were supposed to know. And what happened? The one that knew a bit less got rich, and the one that knew a little more lived his whole life with simply adequate means.

4.

Since ancient times people have wondered about what was smart and what was stupid. In that regard I remember this incident: When my aunt gave me a writing desk as a gift, I said to myself: "Well now I'll sit down at this desk and the first thought I come up with at this desk will be especially smart." But I could not come up with an especially smart thought. Then I said to myself: "Okay. I wasn't able to come up with an especially smart thought, so I'll come up with an especially stupid one." But I couldn't come up with an especially stupid thought either.

5.

Everything that's extreme is difficult. The middle parts are done more easily. The very center requires no effort at all. The center is equal to equilibrium. There's no fight in it.

6.

Is it necessary to get out of equilibrium?

7.

While traveling, do not give yourself over to daydreams, but fantasize and pay attention to everything, even the insignificant details.

8.

When sitting in place do not kick your feet.

9.

Any old wisdom is good if somebody has understood it. A wisdom that hasn't been understood may get covered in dust.

10.

There lived a redheaded man who had no eyes or ears. He didn't have hair either, so he was called a redhead arbitrarily. He couldn't talk because he had no mouth. He had no nose either. He didn't even have arms or legs. He had no stomach, he had no back, he had no spine, and he had no innards at all. He didn't have anything. So we don't even know who we're talking about. It's better that we don't talk about him any more.

January 7, 1937

11.

One grandma had only four teeth in her mouth. Three teeth on top, and one on the bottom. This grandma couldn't chew with these teeth. Truly speaking, they were useless to her. And so grandma decided to pull out all her teeth and insert a corkscrew in her lower gums and miniscule pliers on top. Grandma drank ink, ate beets, and cleaned her ears out with matches. Grandma had four rabbits. Three rabbits on top, and one on the bottom. Grandma used to catch rabbits with her bare hands and put them in little cages. The rabbits cried and scratched their ears with their hind legs. The rabbits drank ink and ate beets. Sha-ha-ha! The rabbits drank ink and ate beets!

12.

A certain Panteley hit Ivan with his heel.
A certain Ivan hit Natalya with a wheel.
A certain Natalya hit Semyon with a muzzle.
A certain Semyon hit Seliphan with a washbasin.
A certain Seliphan hit Nikita with an over-shirt.
A certain Nikita hit Roman with a board.
A certain Roman hit Tatiana with a shovel.
A certain Tatiana hit Elena with a pitcher.
And a fight broke out.
Elena beat Tatiana with a fence.
Tatiana beat Roman with a mattress.
Roman beat Nikita with a suitcase.
Nikita beat Seliphan with a serving tray.
Seliphan beat Semyon with his bare hands.
Semyon spit into Natalya's ears.
Natalya bit Ivan's fingers.
Ivan kicked Panteley with his heel.
Ack, we thought, good people fighting each other.

13.

One little girl said: "gvya."
Another little girl said: "hphy."
A third little girl said: "mbryu."
And Yermakov chomped, chomped, chomped on cabbages under the fence.
Meanwhile, evening was already setting in.
Mot'ka got tired playing in shit and went to bed.
It was drizzling rain.

The swine ate peas.
Rogozin was peeking into the women's bathhouse.
Sen'ka sat on Man'ka in riding position.
Man'ka, meanwhile, drifted off to sleep.
The sky grew dark. The stars twinkled.
Some rats chewed up a mouse under the floorboards.
Sleep, my little boy, and don't let silly dreams scare you.
Silly dreams come from the stomach.

14.

Shave your beard and your whiskers!
You ain't goats, so don't wear beards!
You ain't cats, so don't wiggle your whiskers!
You ain't mushrooms, so don't stand around in your hats!
Hey, ladies!
Trim down your hatsies!
Hey, little beauties!
Trim down your skirtsies!
Come on you, Man'ka Marusina,
Come and sit on Pet'ka Elabonin.
Cut your braids off, little girls.
You ain't zebras, so don't run around with tails on.
Chubby little girls,
Invite us over for the festivities.

15.

Lead me on with my eyes blindfolded.
I won't go with my eyes blindfolded.
Untie the blindfold from my eyes and I'll go by myself.
Don't hold me by the arms,
I want to give my arms freedom.
Step aside, stupid spectators,
I'm going to start kicking.

I'll walk down one floorboard and I won't lose my balance,
I'll run across the drainpipe and I won't collapse.
Don't get in my way. You'll be sorry.
Your cowardly eyes are unpleasant to the gods.
Your mouths open at the wrong time.
Your noses don't know vibrating smells.
Eat your soup—that's your business.
Sweep your rooms—that's what the age demands of you.
But take those bandages and stomach straps off me,
I live on salt, and you live on sugar.
I have my own flower gardens and vegetable gardens.
In my garden a goat grazes.
In my trunk lies a fur hat.
Don't get in my way, I stand on my own, and you are only
a quart of smoke to me.

January 8, 1937

16.

Today I wrote nothing. Doesn't matter.

January 9

17.

Dmitrii eked out pathetic noises.
Anna was weeping, with her head in a pillow.
Manya cried too.

18.

"Fedya, hey Fedya!"
"What sir?"
"I'll show you what sir!"
(Silence.)

"Fedya, hey Fedya!"

"What's the matter?"

"Now you son of a bitch! And you ask what's the matter."

"What do you want from me?"

"D'you see that? What do I want from him! You know what I could do to you, you scoundrel, for words like that . . . I'm gonna throw you so hard you'll go flying you know where!"

"Where?"

"Into the pot."

(Silence.)

19.

"Fedya, hey Fedya!"

"What now, auntie, have you lost your mind?"

"Oooh! Oooh! Say that again, come on!"

"No, I won't."

"Now that's better! Know your place! Or else! Enough!"

February 23, 1937

20.

I choked on a lamb bone.

I was taken by the arms and brought away from the table.

I lost myself in thought.

A mouse ran by.

Ivan ran after the mouse with a long stick.

A strange old woman watched from a window.

Running by the old woman, Ivan hit her in the face with the stick.

21.

Returning home after my walk,

I suddenly exclaimed: Oh my God!

I've been walking four days in a row!

What will my family think of me now?

22.

We've died on the fields of the everyday.
No hope is left to lead the way.
Our dreams of happiness are naught—
Now poverty is all we've got.

Apr. 3, 1937

23.

To have only intelligence and talent is too little. One must also have energy, real interest, clarity of thought and a sense of obligation.

24.

Here I write down the events of the day, for they are incredible. In truth: One of the events is particularly incredible, I will underline it.

1) Yesterday we had nothing to eat. 2) In the morning I took 10 rubles out of the savings bank, leaving 5 in the passbook, so as not to close the account. 3) Stopped by Zhitkov's place and borrowed 60 rubles. 4) Went home, buying food on the way. 5) The weather is wonderful, spring. 6) Went with Marina to the Buddhist pagoda, taking a bag of sandwiches and a flask of wine mixed with water. 7) On the way back we stopped at the pawn shop and there <u>we saw a pump organ, a Jadmeyer double-manual, a copy of the philharmonic's. The price was only 900 rubles! But half an hour ago it was sold!</u> 7a) At Alexander's we saw an excellent pipe. 85 rubles. 8) Went to Zhitkov's. 9) With Zhitkov we found out who bought the pump organ and drove to the address: Pesochnaya 31, apt. 46, Levinsky. 10) Couldn't buy it off him. 11) Spent the evening at Zhitkov's.

April 4

25.

Enough of laziness and doing nothing! Open this notebook every day and write down half a page at the very least. If you have nothing to write down, then at least, following Gogol's advice, write down that today there's nothing to write. Always write with attention and look on writing as a holiday.

April 11, 1937

27.

This is how hunger begins:
In the morning you wake lively,
Then weakness,
Then boredom,
Then comes the loss
Of quick reason's strength—
Then comes calm,
And then horror.

28.

Daydreams will be the end of you.
Your interest in this harsh life
will vanish like smoke. At that time
The herald of the sky will not descend.

Your desires and your lusts will wilt and then
Youth's ardent thoughts will, racing, pass you by . . .
Abandon them! Leave off your dreams my friend,
Make free of death your mind.

October 4, 1937

29.

DAY

(Amphibrach)

And a little fish flashes in the river's cool wave,
And a little house stands far far away,
And a barking dog barks at a herd of cows,
And Petrov rides a barrow straight down a hill,
And a little flag flutters on top of the house,
And nourishing grain grows ripe in the field,
And the dust shines like silver on every leaf,
And the flies with a whistle fly everywhere,
And young girls stretch out in the sun to get warm,
And the bees in the garden buzz over the flowers,
And the geese are diving in shadowy ponds,
And the day passes by in its usual labors.

October 25/26, 1937

OTHER
WRITINGS

(AN INCIDENT ON THE RAILROAD)

Grandma waved her hand
and a steam train right away
rolled up to the children, saying:
drink your kasha and your trunk.
In the morning they turned back
and the children sat down on the fence
and they were saying: stallion,
go to work, i won't do it,
Masha's not that type of girl
as you wish, maybe you're right
we'll lap up even all the sand
that the sky expectorated
disembarking at the station
greeting, greetings Georgia

how can we get out of here
just past that big thing
not the fence—oh my children—
the paleandra grew and grew and
swooping down upon the train-cars
washed up the wrong guy, not the one
who was frightened by the eel
and surrounded it with seven oxen
who from his pocket took the money
drab gray money in his face.

That's how it went, and decay followed
"all is soup," auntie said
"all is sparrows," said the dead man
even the body's gone down hill

chirping in a friendly way,
but also looking slightly bored
and seeming to go backwards.

The children heard the morning mass
as they put it on their backs
through the apron ran a mouse
tearing shoulders both apart

while the Georgian woman on the stoop
harangued. And the Georgian
stooping down under the mountain
with his fingers combed the dirt.

(1926)

THE AVIATION OF
TRANSFORMATIONS

Wingless flying is cruel amusement
try it, clumsy, you'll fall over backwards
she chose no other form of torture
they hit her over the head with a tightrope.
Oh, how she fell over the swamp!
Her skirts all raised! The boys all stared
meanwhile she called for the pilot in confusion
but the pilot's soft mustache quickly ripped.
A youth, he peers
and laughs and steers
stopping the flies' incessant buzz
he slowly lands upon the moss.
SHE: I lie here in agony
HE: Madam, you can lean on me
SHE: I'm dying, bring me a snack!
TOGETHER: We die of the axe!
Our little faces are getting colder
the beating is gone.
We're lying down. The windows are open
and we're breathing hard.
Here come the guards.
A maiden's daydreams are weightless.
Women eat their grandkids.
Fish swim in the river.
Fir trees rush around in the forest.
Across the seas the warlock moans
while words unfurl above the town:
The Management of Things.
To them their uncle is a bird's eye

or else their heart is resonant ice
suddenly away the airplane flies
quietly getting all the geese at once.
There, puffed up, it disappeared.
Who is left upon the sand?
We don't know. But grandpa dug
his stately holes so sad.
And tossing the roots
down carefree chutes
he mixes powders into pills
for the horses that are ill.
The reckless reins neigh
pointing fingers at the fool
stop, friends, he's a wizard
knows his stuff
he spins the cloud of closets
he pours the oven-dregs
three hundred dunce caps in the sky
using bricks to build towers so high.
Where a greyhound warms the sun
gnawing on the goddamn dark
where a plane soars into Europe
carrying a beautiful trollop.
SHE: I'm flying to my suitors.
PILOT: The engine broke.
She shouts at the pilot: jerk!
The airplane sank right there and then.
She shouts: father, father,
I lived here. I was born here.
And that was all she wrote
she has turned into a candleholder.
Madeleine, you've grown too cold
to lie alone beneath a bush
a youth bows down over you
with a face as hot as Tibet.
The pilot has grown old along the way.

He waves his hands—but doesn't fly
he moves his legs—but doesn't go
waves once or twice and falls
then lies for years without decay
Poor Madeleine grieves
a braid she weaves.
and chases idle dreams away.

    enough

(January 1927)

                                     [Translated with Ilya Bernstein]

FIRE

A room. The room's on fire.
A child juts out of his cradle.
Eats his kasha. Up above,
just below the ceiling now,
the nanny's napping upside-down.
The wall is burning. Dishes clatter.
The father's running. Father: "Fire!
There's my boy, my little Petya,
thrashing like an air balloon.
Where can I find myself a monkey
in place of a son?" In place of walls
sharp stoves blow out smoke
through the chimney to the sky.
The sleepy nanny chatters on.
Nanny: "Where am I? What's happened?
The world is getting shorter,
Petya's flying like a phantom."
Like a she-wolf Nanny prowls,
eats a carrot on the way
has a coffee and keeps going
tries to get out through the doors.
Quickly darting through the doorway
cracking some delicious nuts
like a cardigan she gallops
through the yard, along the metal fence.
Then she runs around in fright
in search of Petya and a hammock.
"Where are you. Petya, my dear boy?
You forgot to eat your kasha."
"Nanny, Nanny, I'm burning up!"

Nanny looks into the cradle—
he's gone. She peers into the keyhole
and she sees: The room is empty.
Curls of smoke attack the windows
the walls are thin as feathers now
atop the cornice the fire nests
sudden thunder drizzling downpour
and the soul quakes in the chest.

enough

February 20, 1927

[SERENADE]

Enter Maria taking a bow
in sorrow Maria comes out on the stoop
while off to the balcony high up we go
singing a song, with our face in the soup.
Maria looks on
and stretches her arm
and pushes the leaves with her beautiful foot
meanwhile, we grab a guitar and we sing
into the ear of the unyielding wife.
Above us golden smokes rise free
Behind our back a cat runs through
Here on the balcony singing are we
But there past the tree staring sadly are you.
Later a shawl and a shoe were left
and the round balcony soaring so
and the ceiling piercing the stormy sky.
Enter Maria taking a bow
Maria steps softly into the grass
and seeing a flower, graceful and new,
she says: "I won't pick you, but will only pass,
will only pass by, bowing to you."
But we run around on the balcony high
shouting: "Bow down!"—as we shake our guitar
Maria looks on
and stretches her arm
and suddenly bowing runs back to the stoop
and pushes the leaves with her beautiful foot.
Meanwhile, we grab a guitar and we sing
into the ear of the unyielding wife
and into the sky we toss up our eyes.

                    enough

October 12, 1927

                                    [Translated with Ilya Bernstein]

VISITING ZABOLOTSKY

And so I walked up to the house
that stood in the midst of the field
and flung its doors open to me.

Onto the steps I jump! I run.
And then for the fourth time.
And the house stands on the shore,
the shore is right nearby.

And so I knock with fists upon the door:
"Open up and put me in!"
But the oak door doesn't say a word
into the master's ribs.
The master of the house lies in the room
and in the room he lives.

Into this room I cast my glance,
and then into this room I prance,
where smoke from cigarettes
will grab you by the shoulder,
and Zabolotsky's hand
runs around the room,
picks up a winged trumpet
and pipes on it everywhere.
The music dances. I enter
in an expensive top hat.

I sit down to the right of me,
laughing for the master,
my eyes on him I fix and read
my crafty poems.

And the house on the river,
the one that's in the fields,
(and in the distance) stands there
looking like a pea.

enough

December 14, 1927

All all the trees go piff
all all the rocks go paff
all all of nature poof.

All all the girls go piff
all all the guys go paff
all all the marriage poof.

All all the slavs go piff
all all the jews go paff
all all of Russia poof.

(early October 1929)

A fly struck the forehead of a gentleman who was running by; it passed through his frontal lobe and came out the back. The gentleman, whose name was Dernyatin, was extremely surprised; it seemed to him that something whistled through his brain, and on the back of his head a thin layer of skin burst and started to tickle. Dernyatin stopped in his tracks and thought for awhile. "What would such a thing mean? After all, it's perfectly clear I heard a whistle in my brain. Nothing comes to mind that would allow me to understand what's going on here. In any case, this rare sensation resembles some kind of mental disease. I'll continue my run, instead of thinking any more about it." With these words Mr. Dernyatin ran on, but no matter how he ran, it just wouldn't turn out that way. On the sky-blue path, Dernyatin stumbled and just barely avoided falling; he even had to flail his arms around in the air. "It's a good thing I didn't fall," thought Dernyatin, "or else I would have broken my glasses and would no longer have been able to make out the direction of the paths." Dernyatin continued at a walk, leaning on his cane. But one danger followed another. Dernyatin began to sing a song in order to dispel his unhappy thoughts. The song was joyful and resonant, such that Dernyatin lost himself in it and even forgot that he was on the sky-blue path, where at this time of day automobiles flew by at dizzying speeds. The sky-blue path was very narrow, and to dodge cars by jumping to the side was rather difficult. Thus it was considered a dangerous path. Mindful people always walked along the sky-blue path with caution, so as not to die. Here death awaited a pedestrian at every step either in the form of an automobile or in the form of a bandit; or if neither of those, then in the form of a wagon with bituminous coal. Before he could even blow his nose, an enormous automobile bore down on Dernyatin. Dernyatin cried, "I am dying!" and leaped to the side. The grass parted before him and he fell into a damp trench. The automobile rumbled by, having raised the distress flag over its roof. The people in the automobile were sure that Dernyatin had died, so they took off their head-wear and now continued bareheaded. "Did anybody notice which wheels ran over that wanderer? Was it the front or the back?" asked the gentleman in the muff, rather, not in the muff, but in the *bashlyk*. "My cheeks and ear lobes," the gentleman went on, "have been terribly exposed, that's why I always wear my *bashlyk*." Next to the gentleman, there was a lady with a remarkable mouth. "I'm worried," said the lady, "and what if we are somehow blamed for the murder of that wayfarer." "What? What?" asked the gentleman, pulling the *bashlyk* away from his ear. The lady restated her fears. "No," said the gentleman in the bash-lyk, "murder is punished only in those cases where the murdered resem-bles a pumpkin. But not we. But not we. We are not to blame for the death of the wayfarer. The man himself shouted: 'I am dying!' We are but witnesses to his sudden death." Madam Annette smiled with her remarkable mouth and said to herself, "Anton Antonovich, you're so clever at getting out of trouble." Meanwhile, Mr. Dernyatin lay in the damp trench, having stretched out his arms and legs. And the automo-bile had already sped away. Already, Dernyatin understood that he was not dead. Death in the form of an automobile had passed him by. He stood up, brushed his suit off with his sleeve, spit on his fingers and went down the sky-blue path to make up for lost time.

―――――

The Rundadar family lived in a house on the quiet river Svirechka. The father of the Rundadars, Platon Ilyich, loved knowledge of lofty matters: Mathematics, Tripartite Philosophy, the Geography of Eden, the books of Vintviveq, teachings on mortal tremors and the celestial hierarchy of Dionysius the Areopagite were Platon Ilyich's most beloved sciences. The doors of the Rundadar house were open to all strangers who had visited the holy places of our planet. In the Rundadar home, sto-ries about flying hills, brought by ragamuffins from the Nikitinsky settle-ment, were met with lively and acute attention. Platon Ilyich kept long lists with the details of the flights of large and small hills. Especially exceptional among all other flights was the flight of Kapustinsky Hill. As is well known, Kapustinksy Hill took off at night, at around 5, uprooting a cedar. From the point of its takeoff the hill rose not in a serpent-like trajectory like all the other hills, but in a straight line, making little vibra-tions only when it had reached the elevation of 15 to 16 kilometers. And the wind, blowing against the hill, flew through it, not driving it from its course, as if the hill of flint rock had lost its property of impermeability.

Through the hill, for example, flew a seagull. It flew, as though through a cloud. This has been confirmed by a few eyewitnesses. It contradicted the laws of flying hills, but the fact remained a fact, and Platon Ilyich included it in the log of details on Kapustinsky Hill. Every day at the Rundadar's there gathered esteemed guests, and visible signs of the laws of the alogical chain were discussed. Among the guests of honor were: Professor of Railroads Michael Ivanovich Dundukov, Father Superior Mirinos II, and Loogieologist Stefan Dernyatin. The guests gathered in the lower living room and sat at a long table, on which was placed a common washtub filled with water. The guests, conversing, spat into the washtub—such was the custom of the Rundadar family. Platon Ilyich himself sat with a whip. From time to time he wet it in the water and lashed it on an empty chair. This was called "making a racket with an instrument." At nine o'clock the wife of Platon Ilyich, Anna Malyaevna, would appear and lead the guests to the table. The guests ate liquid and solid dishes, then crawled up on all fours to Anna Malyaevna, kissed her hand and sat down for tea. During tea, Mirinos II would narrate an incident that had occurred 14 years prior. It went that he, Father Superior, was one day sitting on the steps of his porch, feeding the ducks. All of a sudden a fly flew out of the house, circled around and around, and struck Father Superior in the forehead. It struck him in the forehead and passed straight through his head and came out the back and flew back into the house. Father Superior was left sitting on the steps with a smile of delight because he had finally seen a miracle with his own eyes. The rest of the guests, having heard out Mirinos II, would beat themselves with teaspoons on the lips and on their Adam's apples as a sign that the party was over. Afterwards the discussion would take on a frivolous character. Anna Malyaevna would leave the room, while the gentleman Loogieologist Dernyatin spoke on the subject of "Women and Flowers." At times it happened that certain guests would stay overnight. Then they would push a few wardrobes together and make a bed for Mironos II on top of the wardrobes. Professor Dundukov slept in the dining room on the grand piano, and Mr. Dernyatin got in bed with the Rundadar's servant girl, Masha. But, in most cases, the guests went to their separate homes. Platon Ilyich himself would lock the door after them and go back to Anna Malyaevna. Nikitinsky fishermen floated down the Svirechka River singing songs. And the Rundadar family would fall asleep to the tune of fishermen's songs.

————

Mr. Dernyatin crawled out of the ditch and went along the sky-blue path in pursuit of lost time. There was less and less danger of death in the sense that at this hour there was less traffic. Mr. Dernyatin was on his way to visit a certain Rundadar. Everyone was already gathered in Rundadar's living room. A paper boat floated in a washtub full of water. A blue cap was on Mirinos II's head. Professor Dundukov sat with his sleeves rolled up. Platon Ilyich was waving a kerchief like a whip. Mr. Dernyatin sat down at the table, having spat into the washtub . . .

————

"Today I will report to you on my collection of material about the tri-fold structure of the world and of all things," said Platon Ilyich. Of Rundadar's gathered guests only the Loogieologist Dernyatin was lacking. But Mikhail Ivanovich Dundukov was sitting with his cheeks puffed up.

"I know," said Father Superior Mirinos II. "All things resemble a three-story house, and the world is three steps in the shelter of God."

"And go ahead, tell me where there are three divisions in a chair? In a table? or in this washtub?"

Chapter II

Platon Ilyich Rundadar got stuck in the doorway of his dining room. He locked his elbows into the jamb, sprouted his legs into the wooden threshold, rolled his eyes into his head and stood like that.

————

Mr. Dernyatin, a well-known Loogieologist, decided to erect a real pyramid in the middle of the city of Petersburg. In the first place, to sit on it is better than sitting on a roof, and in the second place, in the pyramid one can arrange a room and sleep there.

(1929-1930)

[Translated with Simona Schneider]

THEME FOR A STORY

A certain engineer made up his mind to build a giant brick wall across all of Petersburg. He thinks over how this is to be accomplished, he doesn't sleep nights reasoning it out. Gradually a club of thinker-engineers forms and a plan for building the wall is produced. It is decided that the wall will be built during the night and in such a way that the whole thing is put up in one night, so that it would appear as a surprise to all. Workers are rounded up. The job is divided up. The city authorities are lured away, and finally the night comes when the wall is to be built. Only four people know of the building of the wall. The engineers and workers are given exact orders as to where each should go and what each should do there. Thanks to exacting calculations, they're able to build the wall in one night. The next day Petersburg is all commotion. The inventor of the wall himself is despondent. What this wall was good for, he himself never knew.

(1930)

There lived a
miller. His daughter Agnes
played with animals all day
scaring cattle from the depths of forests
her pupils shine with fire flames.
The miller fierce and wicked was
beat Agnes with a whip
drove barley from far villages
and after went to sleep.
One morning, inside the miller's
adam's apple, Agnes plants a bean.
Agnes growls. The miller springs.
But the priest comes walking in.
Long Agnes takes her seat
the winged miller seats the priest
nearby. He is embarrassed.
Oh would there blow a sudden wind
and then the windmill's wings would spin
the cleric, Agnes and the chatterling in flight
would then upon the roof alight.
The miller's happy. He's a magician.

January 3, 1930

AN EVIL GATHERING OF INFIDELS

Not I, Lord, is it?—thought the apostles.
Here are the signs:
a face like a mouse,
a wing like a knife,
a little steamship foot,
a house like a family,
a rope-ladder bridge,
a robe like atlas' brow.
And only one's a genius. Yes, but which?
One's smart, another is a dullard, the third is a dolt.
But who's the genius? Oh Lordy, Lordy!
All people are poor. I am a sheepskin coat.

January 17, 1930

I.

We were lying in bed. She, facing the wall on an incline, and I was lying by the bedside table. Only two words can be said about me: Big ears. She knew everything.

II.

Is this a fork? Or an angel? Or a hundred rubles? This is Nona. A fork is too small. An angel is too tall. The money ran out long ago. So Nona—she is she. She alone is Nona. There were six Nonas and she is one of them.

III.

A dog in a small hat came up. Footsteps sounded and splashed. A fly was throwing the windows open. Let's look out the window!

IV.

There's nothing to see out the window. Do you see anything? I don't see anything, do you? I see skis. And who is on the skis? A soldier is on the skis and he has a belt over his shoulder, though he's not wearing a belt.

1930

[Translated with Simona Schneider]

NOTNOW

This is This.
That is That.
This is not That.
This is not This.
What's left is either this, or not this.
It's all either that, or not that.
What's not that and not this, that is not this and not that.
What is this and also that, that is itself Itself.
What is itself Itself, that might be that but not this, or else this
      but not that.
This went into that, and that went into this. We say: God
      has puffed.
This went into this, and that went into that, and we have no
      place to leave and nowhere to come to.
This went into this. We asked: Where? They sung in answer: Here.
This left That. What is this? It's That.
This is that.
That is this.
Here are this and that.
Here went into this, this went into that, and that went into here.
We watched, but did not see.
And there stood this and that.
There is not here.
That's there.
This is here.
But now both this and that are there.
But now this and that are here, too.
We long and mope and ponder.
But where is now?
Now is here, and now there, and now here, and now here
      and there.

This be that.
Here be there.
This, that, here, there, be, I, We, God.

May 29, 1930
Daniil Kharms

THE WERLD

I told myself that I see the world. But the whole world was not accessible to my gaze, and I saw only parts of the world. And everything that I saw I called parts of the world. And I examined the properties of these parts and, examining these properties, I wrought science. I understood that the parts have intelligent properties and that the same parts have unintelligent properties. I distinguished them and gave them names. And, depending on their properties, the parts of the world were intelligent or unintelligent.

And there were such parts of the world which could think. And these parts looked upon me and upon the other parts. And all these parts resembled one another, and I resembled them. And I spoke with these parts.

I said: parts thunder.

The parts said: a clump of time.

I said: I am also part of the three turns.

The parts answered: And we are little dots.

And suddenly I ceased seeing them and, soon after, the other parts as well. And I was frightened that the world would collapse.

But then I understood that I do not see the parts independently, but I see it all at once. At first I thought that it was NOTHING. But then I understood that this was the world and what I had seen before was NOT the world.

And I had always known what the world was, but what I had seen before I do not know even now.

And when the parts disappeared their intelligent properties ceased being intelligent, and their unintelligent properties ceased being unintelligent. And the whole world ceased to be intelligent and unintelligent.

But as soon as I understood that I saw the world, I ceased seeing it. I became frightened, thinking that the world had collapsed. But while I was thinking this, I realized that had the world collapsed then I would already not be thinking this. And I watched, looking for the world, but not finding it.

And soon after there wasn't anywhere to look.

Then I realized that since before there was somewhere to look—there had been a world around me. And now it's gone. There's only me.

And then I realized that I am the world.

But the world—is not me.

Although at the same time I am the world.

But the world's not me.

And I'm the world.

But the world's not me.

And I'm the world.

But the world's not me.

And I'm the world.

And after that I didn't think anything more.

May 30, 1930
Daniil Kharms

1. One day Andrei Vasilyevich was walking down the street when he lost his wrist watch. He died soon after. His father, a hunchback who was getting on in years, sat around in a top hat all night clenching in his left hand a walking stick with a hook-like handle. His head was visited by various thoughts, including the following: Life is a smithy.

2. Andrei Vasilyevich's father, whose name was Grigory Antonovich, or—in truth—Vasily Antonovich, hugged Maria Mikhailovna and called her his sovereign queen. She, meanwhile, stared straight ahead and upwards, silently and hopefully. And it was then that Vasily Antonovich, that wretched hunchback, decided to destroy his hump.

3. To achieve this goal Vasily Antonovich got into his saddle and arrived at Professor Mamayev's. Professor Mamayev sat in his garden reading a book. Mamayev answered all Vasily Antonovich's pleas with one simple phrase: "Time will come." Then Vasily Antonovich went and signed himself into the surgical ward.

4. The nurses and sisters of mercy spread Vasily Antonovich on a table and covered him with a sheet. Then Professor Mamayev himself came into the room. "A shave," asked the professor. "No, just cut off my hump," said Vasily Antonovich.

The operation began. But ended unsuccessfully, in part because one of the sisters of mercy covered her face with a plaid rag and couldn't see a thing and therefore didn't pass the correct instruments. And one male nurse tied up his mouth and nose in such a way that he couldn't breathe, and by the end of the operation he gasped for breath and fell nearly dead on the floor. But the most unpleasant thing was that, in all the excitement, Professor Mamayev forgot to remove the sheet from the patient, so he cut off something entirely other than the hump—the back of the head, perhaps. The hump was all poked through with surgical instruments.

5. At home, Vasily Antonovich could not get hold of himself until some Spaniards broke into the house and chopped off the cook Andrushka's scalp.

6. Having calmed down, Vasily Antonovich went to another doctor who quickly amputated his hump.

7. From there everything went smoothly. Maria Mikhailovna divorced Vasily Antonovich and married Bubnov.

8. Bubnov did not love his new wife. Whenever she left the house, Bubnov would buy himself a new hat and spent his time exchanging greetings with his neighbor, Anna Moiseyevna. But once one of Anna Moiseyevna's teeth broke and she opened her mouth real wide in pain. Bubnov began to ponder deeply his biography.

9. Bubnov's father, who had the surname of Phy, fell in love with Bubnov's mother, by the name of Hnyu. One day Hnyu was sitting on the stove, gathering the mushrooms that grew next to her. But, unexpectedly, Phy spoke thus: "Hnyu, I want us to have a Bubnov."
Hnyu asked: "Bubnov? Yes, yes?"
"Exactly, your excellency," answered Phy.

10. Hnyu and Phy sat close together and thought of various funny things and laughed a very long time.

11. Finally, Hnyu gave birth to Bubnov.

(1931)

PRAYER BEFORE SLEEP
MARCH 28, 1931 AT 7 O'CLOCK
IN THE EVENING

Lord, smack in the middle of the day
a laziness came over me.
Permit me to lie down and go to sleep, Lord,
and while I sleep, oh Lord, pump me full of Your Strength.
There is much I wish to know
but neither books nor people will tell me.
Only You can enlighten me, Lord,
by way of my poems.
Wake me up strong for the battle with meanings
and quick to the governance of words
and assiduous in praising the name of God
        for all time.

At two o'clock on Nevsky Prospect, or rather on the Avenue of October 25th, nothing of note occurred. No, no, that man who stopped nearby the "Coliseum" was there purely by accident. Maybe his boot came untied, or maybe he wanted to light a cigarette. Or something else entirely! He's just a visitor and doesn't know where to go. But where are his things? Wait, he's lifting his head for some reason, as if to look into the third floor, or even the fourth, maybe even the fifth. No, look, he simply sneezed and now he's on his way again. He slouches a little and his shoulders are raised. His green overcoat flaps in the wind. Just now he turned onto Nadezhdenskaya and disappeared around the corner.

A shoeshine man of eastern features stared after him and smoothed down his fluffy mustache with his hand.

His overcoat was long and thick, of a purple hue, either plaid or maybe striped, or maybe, damn it all, polka-dot.

(1931)

THE WINDOW

SCHOOLGIRL:
>   I stare out the window
>   and see bird battalions.

TEACHER:
>   You should be staring at the bottom of the mortar
>   and grinding the grains with your pestle.

SCHOOLGIRL:
>   I can no more grind these little pebbles:
>   Teacher, they are so hard
>   and my hand so tender.

TEACHER:
>   Who would have thought, a princess!
>   You must study the hidden warmth
>   of vaporization.

SCHOOLGIRL:
>   Teacher, I am worn out with exhaustion
>   by this unending chain of experiments.
>   Five days and nights I grind. And the result?
>   My hands have gone numb,
>   gone dry my chest,
>   O God, o God!

TEACHER:
>   Soon your torments will be done.
>   Your mind will become clear.

SCHOOLGIRL:

> Oh how my spine does creak!

TEACHER:

> Make sure the mortar keeps chiming
> and the grains cracking under the pestle . . .
> I see: You've turned green
> and crossed your legs.
> I recollect eleven cases
> similar to this. What a parable!
> The poor girl strains to make a final effort—
> and there she lies, a cold little corpse.
> How heavily this weighs on me!
> While I had clambered up the chair
> to still the pendulum and set
> the clock correctly,
> she expired, the poor wretch,
> before she could finish up her education.

SCHOOLGIRL:

> Oh, my dear teacher,
> I have grasped the hidden warmth of vaporization.

TEACHER:

> I'm sorry, but I can't hear you anymore,
> though I'd listen gladly!
> You, my girl, have become incorporeal,
> and are mum, sadly.

WINDOW:

> I opened suddenly.
> I'm a hole in walls of buildings.
> The soul spills out through me.
> I'm the air-vent of enlightened minds.

(March 15, 1931)

HNYU AND THE WATER

HNYU:
Oh where, oh where
are you rushing, water?

WATER:
To the left.
There, around the bend
stands a gazebo.
In the gazebo sits a damsel.
The black net of her hair
shrouds her soft body.
A swallow has landed on the bridge of her nose.
Now the damsel gets up and leaves the garden.
She walks straight for the gate.

HNYU:
Where?

WATER:
There, around the bend,
Lady Katya treads on the grasses
with her round heels.
On her left eye is a bluebell,
and on the right
shines a lunar hill
and with her pheels . . .

HNYU:
With what?

WATER:

That I said in the water tongue.

HNYU:

Oh no, someone's coming our way.

WATER:

Where?

HNYU:

There.

WATER:

That's the fisherman Foma.
His daughter drowned in me,
he's coming to beat me with a stone.
Let us better loudly speak
of the recent week.

FISHERMAN:

Alone am I.
Branches stretch from inside me.
Calloused hands can't pick up pine needles.
When I look out into the sea
my eyes quickly fill with tears.
I get in the boat,
but the boat sinks.
I jump onto the shore,
the shore shakes.
I climb onto the stove,
where my grandfathers dwelled,
but the stove crumbles.
Hey, comrade fishermen,
what am I to do?

(noticing Hnyu)

It couldn't be—Hnyu?

HNYU *(silently)*:

>   Yes it's me.
>   And here's my fiancé, Nikandr.

NIKANDR:

>   Your daughter, I must say, I love
>   and in this matter seek your help
>   to conquer her virginity.
>   I am myself from far away Buturlinsk,
>   I force myself on girls,
>   while we play backwards-checkers.
>   And, little fisherman, in reward
>   I'll grant you floats of cork
>   and a fishing net of steel.

FISHERMAN:

>   Sshankyou, Sshankyou!

NIKANDR:

>   A half-dollar—catch!

WATER:

>   What a disgusting scene
>   I observe.
>   The old man caught the coin in his teeth.
>   Faster, faster, around the bend
>   I'll steer my sounding streams.

HNYU:

>   Farewell, water.
>   You don't love me?

WATER:

>   So it is, your legs are much too skinny.
>   I'm leaving. Where's my walking stick?

HNYU:

Do you like black-braided girls?

WATER:

Zhyrk zhyrk
liu liu liu
zhurch zhurch
glub
glub
glub.

THAT'S ALL

March 29, 1931

HNYU—FRIEND OF THE LAMP

I

A short lightning flash of white snow
flew into the woods frightening the animals
there a hare hops around the bird-cherry
there a bobcat lies in wait for an underwater mouse
puffed out its muzzle
raised its tasseled tail
mangy beast of prey
to you woodpeckers and rabbits are as scrambled eggs to us
only the oak stands paying no attention to anyone
itself just recently fallen from the sky
the pain not yet abated
the branches had not drawn apart
not a reproach nor an answer
did I deserve
oh my spurs
seize me chop me and beat me
right in the back
right in the back
oh he's fast
I thought I see before me the torah
but no the lun a tic
the lunatic of my words
one thing I won't repeat
will not repeat my whole life through
this is ladies and gentlemen
ladies and gentlemen my attentive audience
that leap
the leap from the heights of treesongers
down on to the boards of stone

the tables of stone
tables of oh giant Numbers.

II

Again it started small
a soul in a green wreath
began to sing
here we listened and the water
flowed through us
we hugged the wall
and there came a knock upon our wall
this beat us on the spine
and narrow little lamps
narrow little lamplettes
rascalettes that they are
narrow little icon lamps
I saw above the heads of each.
—Do you know—said one of—
sin sin—of those present—
it grates upon my ears
grates upon my ears.
—Do you know—said the third—
Faran I've gone blind
oh come now
oh how it socked me
over into my little soul.
—Griffon!—the soul called out—
makander
up high we brethren
on high griffons darandasy.

III

The two put on fresh tunics
and the lunatics came out toward us.
—Hey where are your faces?—we shouted

then they then they can you imagine
shook our dwellings with their hands
trying to scare us away.
—In vain—said we
turning the meanings of speech with tender tongues —
in vain.
—But no—said one—
two—he said—
three—he whispered—
four—he begged—
eight eight—he repeated—
after us you girls
will do the same.
—Well what then what then?—we asked
we asked for explanation
a year went by and we found out
it happened so:
one gardener
loved a saw
the saw did answer him in silence
the gardener asked her to forget
forget his rudeness
the saw then turned away
it cherished and gave drink
to its own honor.
—Why did you stupid gardener
pursue me with your speeches
from you I tried to run
but by dark nights of summer
you counted stars and placed into a bag
your different notes
while your thoughts about me
gardener were filthy
now you are full of rubbish
darling gardener denied by me
the falsity of your thoughts

will not fool me
I will lash out my whip if need be
your world will not give you shelter
in your expulsion
know this: The more simplicity
the higher the quality.
THE GARDENER:
This is all foolery
all hope has left me
I've abandoned the clarity of klir
come along soul. Though I'm an ignoramus
still you are my favorite lyre
how quickly you come closer
toward me my soul
I'm very glad how soon
there will be no more argument between us.

IIII

That's where the fish first started swimming
don't tell me you didn't see the bee fly out
you saved yourself perhaps from wasps
or from the lashes of her strong plaits
or having upon her legs leaned back your head
were tender
were all of a sudden ardent
were again tender
now sensitive to caresses
now dull
now a red-muzzled horse
now a corpse
now daydreaming pressed against a fence
now wringing your hands at a distance.

March 31, 1931
at Poret's. Yudina played.

HNYU

Property of P.I. Sokolov

Hnyu went out of the woods on foot,
kneading with her feet both swamp and mud.
Hnyu fed on little roots
of raven's horns, raspberries too,
or Hnyu would pick at the sprouts
of happy hops, the native of the groves.
In a wagon rode the gods.
Their might was clearly felt,
filled high with the juice of liana and the rivers' aloe,
and thought lay petrified in craniums on high.
Chattering their teeth in the moss,
with chests out-thrust against their shirt clasps,
the wanderers were cooking chowder,
some naked fliers flew about,
hanging at times upside-down from little boughs
they rested momentarily, then, belting out their terrifying howls,
they'd make their way into the cauldron for the soup,
grabbing bits of meat into their ruddy jowls,
there were the finches flying into clouds of nothings,
and a bear who, having thrust his claws into the bark so as not to fall,
        sat in a tree
and reasoned about the justice system of the crickets,
there, too, was God, who nursed a butterfly's cocoon deep in the brush,
two wolves played knocker with a deck of cards.
So looked the svidrigal of night
through which Hnyu ran in quite a rush
and thought, counting the tree stumps of her heart's beating.

The ascetic is master in the desert,
the bomb is sovereign mistress of the air,

put both together and you've got the best proof of human genius;
let the comet try and poke the earth,
threatening to throw off course the path of our mother,
and if the foam—girlfriend of fire—were to let loose upon the black crater
the flies with heavenly scrawl on their paws,
then we proudly gaze at the volcano
and in the file folders
of earthly business
and, with an astronomer's hand, check off the event
that could shower the dreadnought with petals of bird cherry.
We turned the world into a national amusement
and we've increased the population density everywhere.
Just recently Jupiter flew with his nose turned up,
celebrating his birthday once in 422 years,
until a playful comet slipped by in the form of a bowl
in the crystal stomach of Glaphira.
The starry discs were quickly lost for good,
fine ethers disappeared,
even in the deserts of arithmetic the Ascetic lost his strength to
        abide in solitude.

Hnyu walked onward and only in part
sliding upwards with her supple figure.
Villages' light, rivers' ring, and forests' rustling
grew more distant with every minute.
Hnyu sang. Clean lakes
lolled, here and there, shimmering a little.
At times a dangerous gadfly zoomed by,
other times a rattling wire squealed between two posts
making seats of the white insulators. At times the lamps
lit up the stony tussocks—
pleasant leg supports along
the fluffy swamp's path,
and often insolent motors moaned their song
into the looming gates of the eternal past.
Once in a while a white hanky would settle on an aspen's tippy-top.

Hnyu applauded.
Bright hills cast their slender arrow shadows.
Hnyu bounded over chasms,
and the shadows of the hills made a tigress out of Hnyu.
Hnyu, brushing a tear off with her sleeve,
tossed butterflies into a woven basket.

Lie quiet, butterflies, and you, colorful ones,
peasant women of the air over wildflower beds,
and you, wingwavers and whistlers,
and you, sorcerettes with burgundy hips,
and you, ligreas, with the springs of your little trunks
suck, my sweet ones, the flowers' porridge,
you, sword-bearers, with your warlike paws,
beat the slavic women,
you, village librarians, with medals of your battles on the plane of wings,
strike up a koorkooroo,
you, tailors with patterns cut from newspaper,
remember professor Chebyshev,
and you, aspen boletes,
make yourself into red keys.
I will lock up the basket with you
so as not to lose my childhood.

Hnyu leaned against
a telegraph pole to rest.
Her cheeks went dim. The bashful window
in her forehead now dissolved.
A snake ran through the grass
sticking out its pliant sting,
in its eyes a marvelous penny glistened.
Hnyu breathed slowly,
accumulating her spent strength
and loosening tight jars of muscle.
She felt her breasts under her sweater.
She was in fact a charming lass.

O, if only people knew this better!

It is so nice to know of what has passed,
so pleasant to believe in that which has been proven,
a thousand times re-reading books accessible to rules of logic,
it's nice avoiding darker corners of the sciences,
and making merry observations,
and to the question Does God exist, a thousand hands are raised,
inclined to postulate that God is make-believe.
We are happy, glad to destroy
the liberated canvas of science.
We thought Galileo an enemy,
he who gave new keys.
And now, five oberiuts,
having once more turned the key in the arithmetics of faith,
are made to wander betwixt homes,
in punishment for disturbing customary rules of reasoning
          about meanings.
See that your hat remains whole,
that from your forehead no tree grows—
here the dead lion is stronger than the dog,
and, truly, I should say, my hut's not visited by guests.
Having rested, Hnyu heaved her strong bones upward
and started forward.
Obedient, the water parted.
Fish flickered. It was growing colder.
Gazing into a little hole, Hnyu prayed,
having reached logic's outer limit.
"I am no longer bothered by
the earth, which carries on a conversation
about heat's cancellation,"
Hnyu whispered to her neighbor,
"the paths of the knife-grinder beetle
attack me no longer,
and nails no longer cuckoo
in the large hands of the gravedigger,

and if all the bees, flying out of the suitcase, at me directed their
        blunt stingers,
even then, take my word, from fear I would not quiver."
"You are right, my little darling,"
her companion answers her,
"but the earth's muffled pipe
is truly full of noises, I'm sure."
Hnyu answered: "I was born
a fool only to sit in a haystack,
the noises of a full day's keyboard
I cannot bear to hear.
And if the butterflies can hear the crackling of sparks
in the roots of burdock,
and if beetles carry in their tiny knapsacks the notes of
        vegetable voices,
and if water spiders know the name and patronymic of the
        gun the hunter lost,
then I must confess, that I am just a stupid little girl."
"That's how it is," said her companion,
"the highest purity of categories
exists in the complete ignorance of the surroundings.
And that, I confess, I find terribly pleasing."

   April 23, 1931

I know the reason that the roads
breaking away from the earth
play with the birds,
tumbledown boughs of wind
sway the tiny baskets sewn by woodpeckers.
The woodpeckers run about the tree trunks
holding little pencils in their hands.
There, a bottle flies out of a hollow,
directing its flight toward the lake
in order to fill itself up with water—
won't the oak be ecstatic
when a heart of water
is placed in its center.
I was walking past two doves.
The doves knocked their wings together
in an attempt to frighten a fox
that was eating the doves' chicks
with its sharpened paws.
I lifted my notebook, opened it
and read seventeen words
I had come up with the night before—
in a moment the doves flew away
and the fox turned into a little match box.
And I was incredibly happy.

(1931)

How strange, how indescribably strange, that behind the wall, this very wall, there's a man with an angry face sitting on the floor with his legs stretched out and wearing red boots.

If one could only punch a hole in the wall and look inside, one could see right away that this angry man is sitting there.

But it's better not to think about him. What is he? Is he not a particle of a dead life that has drifted in from the imaginary void? Whoever he may be, God be with him.

June 22, 1931

I raised my gaze higher and higher
There are the windows of the second story,
There's a mast
There just the sky,
There, heaven,
and god in heaven with a face like mine
Yes I resemble man
And man resembles god
And god resembles the world
And the tree, the grass, the flower and the leaf
are the beginning of life.
The grass resembles a stone
But the stone crumbles into sand
Sand resembles earth
And into the earth all that is dead seeks to go
The earth lets out a sprout
And gathering moisture
As green clay
Lies on the banks of a river
We collect this clay
And sculpt little people
And man was created by god
From earth and clay
Yes, man resembles the world
And the world resembles god.
And I
lift my gaze still higher and higher
I see that I am created in the image and likeness of god.
And I wander in heaven,
And there is no one there
and I shout: But where is god?
And god says to me:
God is I.

November 14, 1931

Man is made of three parts,
of three parts,
of three parts.
Hey-la-la,
drum-drum-tu-tu!
Made of three parts is man.

A beard and an eye, and fifteen hands,
and fifteen hands,
and fifteen hands.
Hey-la-la,
drum-drum-tu-tu!
Fifteen hands and a rib.

But really, not fifteen items of hands,
fifteen items,
fifteen items.
Hey-la-la,
drum-drum-tu-tu!
Fifteen items, but not hands!

(1931)

I am alone. Every evening Alexander Ivanovich goes off some-place and I remain alone. The landlady goes to sleep early and locks up her room. The neighbors sleep four doors away and only I alone sit in my little room burning the kerosene lamp.

I do nothing: I'm coming down with a bad case of fear. These days I stay at home because caught a cold that turned into the flu. For a week already I've had a slightly high temperature and a pain in my lower back.

But why does my lower back hurt, why has my temperature been the same for a week—what am I sick with, and what should I do? I think about all this, listening to my body, and I get scared. Fear caus-es my heart to quake, and my legs to grow cold, and the fear takes hold of the back of my head. The back of my head gets squeezed from below, and it seems—a little more and they'll squish my whole head from above; then you lose the capacity to recognize your states of mind, and you go mad. A weakness begins to take over the whole body, and it begins with your legs. And suddenly the thought comes to you in a flash: What if this is not because of the fear, but the fear is because of this. Then it gets even more frightening. I can't distract my thoughts at all. I try to read. But whatever I read suddenly turns transparent and I see my fear again. If only Alexander Ivanovich would get home soon! But he won't be back for at least another two hours. He's out strolling with Elena Petrovna, explaining to her his views on love.

(1932)

[Translated with Eugene Ostashevsky]

We lived in two rooms. My friend had the smaller room, while I had a rather large room, three windows across. My friend would be out all day and would come back only to spend the night. As for me, I was in my room all of the time, and if I went out it was either to the post office, or to buy something for dinner. In addition, I had a case of dry pleurisy, which gave me all the more reason to stay put.

I like being alone. But then a month went by, and I got sick of my solitariness. Books didn't entertain me, and I would often sit at my desk for long stretches of time without writing a line. I would pick up my book again leaving the page blank. And then that sickly state on top of it! In short, I started to sulk.

The city I lived in at that time was loathsome to me. It stood on a hill and everywhere you looked was like a picture postcard. I became so disgusted with those views that I was happier to stay at home. And really, other than the post office, the market and the store, there was nowhere to go.

And so I sat at home like a hermit.

There were days when I ate nothing. On those days I would try to manufacture a joyous mood for myself. I would lie down on my bed and smile. I would smile for twenty minutes at a time, but then the smile would turn into a yawn. That was not at all pleasant. I would open my mouth just enough to make a smile, but it opened wider and I yawned. I'd start daydreaming.

I saw before me an earthen jug full of milk and pieces of fresh bread. And myself sitting at a desk and writing quickly. On the desk, the chairs, and the bed were sheets of paper covered in writing. And I write more and more, winking and smiling at my ideas. And how nice that nearby is the bread and the milk and a walnut snuff box full of tobacco!

I opened the window and looked out on the garden. Violet and yellow flowers grew right against the house. Tobacco was growing and a big military chestnut tree stood farther away. And over there, the beginning of an orchard.

It was very quiet. Only trains whistled under the mountain.

Today I couldn't do anything. I paced the room then sat down at the desk, but soon after I'd rise and switch over to the rocking chair. I'd pick up a book and, right away, discard it and pace the room again.

I suddenly had the impression that I had forgotten something, some incident or important word.

I would painstakingly try to remember this word, and it even seemed to me that the word began with the letter "M." No, no! Not with an M at all, but with an R.

Reason? Rapture? Rectangle? Rib? Or: Mind? Misery? Matter?

I was making coffee and singing to myself all the words starting with R. Oh, what a tremendous number of words I made up starting with the letter R! Perhaps among them was that one word, but I didn't recognize it, taking it to be the same as all the others.

And yet again, perhaps that word didn't come up.

(1932-1933)

[Translated with Eugene Ostashevsky]

AN UNEXPECTED DRINKING PARTY

Antonina Alexeyevna once hit her husband with an official seal and marred his forehead with ink.

Feeling tremendously insulted, Petr Leonidovich, the husband of Antonina Alexeyevna, locked himself in the bathroom and wouldn't let anybody in.

However, the tenants of the communal apartment, having a strong need to get in to where Petr Leonidovich was sitting, decided to break down the locked door by force.

Seeing that his case was lost, Petr Leonidovich got out of the bathroom and went to his room where he lay down on the bed.

But Antonina Alexeyevna decided to pursue her husband to the very end. She tore a bunch of paper into fine shreds and sprinkled them over Petr Leonidovich who was lying on the bed.

Enraged, Petr Leonidovich lunged into the hallway and started tearing off the wallpaper.

At that point, all the tenants ran out and, seeing what Petr Leonidovich was up to, threw themselves upon him and ripped apart the vest he was wearing.

Petr Leonidovich made a dash for the co-op office.

Meanwhile, Antonina Alexeyevna undressed and hid in a trunk completely naked.

Ten minutes later, Petr Leonidovich returned with the building super in tow.

Not finding his wife in the room, the super and Petr Leonidovich decided to make use of the vacant room and drink a little vodka. Petr Leonidovich took on the task of running out to the corner for this beverage.

As soon as Petr Leonidovich left, Antonina Alexeyevna crawled out of the trunk and stood in the nude before the super.

The stupefied super jumped up from his chair and ran over to the window, but seeing the powerful build of the young twenty-six-year-old woman he suddenly became wildly excited.

Just then Petr Leonidovich came back with a liter of vodka.

Petr Leonidovich furrowed his brow upon seeing what was going on in his room.

But his spouse Antonina Alexeyevna showed him the official seal and Petr Leonidovich mellowed.

Antonina Alexeyevna expressed her desire to partake in the drinking party but only in the nude and, moreover, on the table where it was supposed the chasers to go with the vodka would be spread.

The men sat down on their chairs, Antonina Alexeyevna sat on the table, and the drinking party began.

It would be wrong to call it hygienic if a naked young woman sits on the same table where others are eating. In addition, Antonina Alexeyevna was a rather full-figured woman and not especially clean, so it was really God knows what.

Soon, however, they were all drunk and fell asleep. The men slept on the floor and Antonina Alexeyevna on the table.

And quiet reigned in the communal apartment.

D. Kh.
January 22, 1933

A FFAIRY TALE

There once was a man by the name of Semyonov. Once Semyonov went out for a walk and lost his handkerchief. Semyonov started looking for the handkerchief and lost his hat. He started looking for his hat and lost his jacket. He started looking for his jacket and lost his boots.

"Well," said Semyonov, "at this rate I'll lose everything. I'd better go home."

On the way home Semyonov got lost.

"No," Semyonov said, "I'd better sit down awhile."

Semyonov sat down on a rock and fell asleep.

(1933)

[Translated with Simona Schneider]

F.L.F.

The forest sways its tippy-tops,
people walk around with pots,
catching water from air with them.
In the sea, water bends.
But fire will not bend to the very end.
Fire loves airy freedom.

D. Kharms
(August 21/22) 1933

I understood while walking in the woods:
A wheel looks like the water should.
So listen up: Some time ago
I was dying of thirst almost,
my stomach longed to be filled with H_2O
I stood,
my legs would go no longer.
I sat,
and light flooded the window.
I lay down,
and my thought was a goner.

September 2, 1933

Dear
Nikandr Andreyevich,

I received your letter and understood right away that it was from you. First I thought, what if it's not from you, but as soon as I opened it I knew it was from you, but I almost thought that it wasn't from you. I am glad that you have long been married because when a person marries the one whom he wanted to marry that means he has achieved that which he wanted. And so I am very glad that you got married because when a man marries someone he wanted to marry that means that he got what he wanted. Yesterday I received your letter and right away I thought that this letter was from you, but then I thought it seemed that it wasn't from you, but I unsealed it and saw it was certainly from you. You did very well to write me. At first you didn't write to me and then suddenly you did write, although earlier, before you didn't write me for some time you also wrote to me. As soon as I received your letter I decided right away that it was from you and that's why I'm very glad that you had already married. Because if a man wants to get married then he must get married no matter what. That's why I am so very glad that you finally married precisely the one you wanted to marry. And you did very well to write me. I was overjoyed when I saw your letter and right away I thought it was from you. Although, to tell the truth, while I was opening it a thought flashed through my mind that it was not from you, but then in the end I decided that it was from you. Thanks for writing. I am grateful to you for this and very happy for you. Perhaps you can't imagine why I am so happy for you, but I'll tell you straight away that I am happy for you because, because you got married and married precisely the person you wanted to marry. And, you know, it is very good to marry precisely the person you want to marry because precisely then you get what you wanted. And that is precisely the reason that I am so happy for you. And I am also happy that you wrote me a letter. Even from afar I knew that the letter was from you, but when I took it in my hands I thought: And what if it's not from you? And then I thought: No, of course it is from you. I myself am opening the letter and at the same thinking: From you or not from you? From you or not from you? And then, when I opened it I could clearly see that it was from you. I was overjoyed and decided I would also write you a letter. I have lots to tell you, but I literally don't have the time. What I had time to tell you, I have told you in this letter, and the rest I will write you later because now I have no time left at all. At the least it's good that you wrote me a letter. Now I know that you've long been married. I knew, too, from previous letters, that you got married, and now I see it again: It's completely true, you got married. And I am very happy that you got married and wrote me a letter. As soon as I saw your letter, I knew that you had got married again. Well, I thought, it's good that you got married again and wrote me a letter about it. Now write to me and tell me, who is your new wife and how did it all happen. Relay my greetings to your new wife.

Daniil Kharms
September and October 25, 1933

ON THE ILLS OF SMOKING

You should quit smoking in order to boast of your will power.

It would be nice, not having smoked for a week and having acquired confidence in yourself that you will be able to hold back from smoking, to come into the company of Lipavsky, Oleinikov, and Zabolotsky, so that they would notice on their own that all evening you haven't been smoking.

And when they ask, "Why aren't you smoking?" you would answer, concealing the frightful boasting inside you, "I quit smoking."

A great man must not smoke.

It is good and useful to employ the fault of boastfulness to rid yourself of the fault of smoking.

The love of wine, gluttony, and boastfulness are lesser faults than smoking.

A man who smokes is never at the height of his circumstance, and a smoking woman is capable of just about anything. And so, comrades, let us quit smoking.

1933

In America there lived two Americans, Mister Pick and Mister Pack. Mister Pick worked in an office and Mister Pack worked at a bank. But once Mister Pick came to his office and they said to him: "You are no longer working here." And on the next day, Mister Pack was told the same thing at the bank. So Mister Pick and Mister Pack were left without jobs. Mister Pick came over to Mister Pack's and said:

"Mister Pack!"

"What? What? What-what? You're asking: What are we going to do? What are we going to do! You're asking: What can we do?"

"Yes," said Mister Pick.

"Well now, well now, well now, well now! Well now, see what's happened? You see? You see, what a pickle we're in!"

"Yes," said Mister Pick and sat in a chair while Mister Pack started running around the room.

"What we have here now, right here . . . I'm saying, right here in the United States, the American United States, in the United States of America, right here, in the . . . Do you understand?"

(1933)

[Translated with Simona Schneider]

GIRLFRIEND

On your face, my dear girlfriend,
two bark beetles neatly etched
the letter K and number seven,
and circles, one-o-two of them.

Years pass over you, and your cold
mouth has turned a little green.
The weather's made your eye explode,
and in your nose the loud winds ring.

What's going on inside your soul,
I have no clue. But the trunk
of your thought might suddenly dissolve
with a thunderous thunk.

Your sweet dream from the very start
will be understood by everyone.
Your soul will rush from your chest
like gas propellant, gone.

What are you waiting for? The stars'
crowded movement or the jumbling of the planets?
or do you wait, leaning on a pillar
in your reach, for the weaving of fates?

Are you waiting for desire
to descend to you from heaven,
and words to come from your ideas
with the breathing of your bosom?

We're not living at full speed,
aren't counting all our days,
but with every year the minutes
get longer as we turn away.

And then we'll tune the lyre,
run our fingers o'er the strings
and sing out in reply
as the world dreams our song.

Faster the rivers will flow.
You will watch from their high banks
with a cold unfeeling eye
from under a lifted lash

through centuries without end
every day of our glory.
No shadow ever will fall
on your lofty forehead.

(1933)

[Translated with Eugene Ostashevsky]

THE CONSTANCY OF DIRT AND JOY

Cool water gurgles in the river,
mountain shadows lie down in a field,
and in the sky the light fades, while
birds have flown into our dreams,
and the janitor with black mustaches
stands all night long by the rusty gate
and with his dirty hands he scratches
under his dirty hat his itching pate;
through windows hear the joyous din,
the stomp of feet and bottles' ring.

A day goes by, and then a week,
and then the years are passing by,
and one by one in single file
the people vanish in their graves,
while the janitor with black mustaches
year after year by the rusty gate
and with his dirty hands he scratches
under his dirty hat his itching pate;
through windows hear the joyous din,
the stomp of feet and bottles' ring.

The moon and sun have paled together,
the constellations change their shape,
and motion turns to sticky syrup,
and time becomes a lot like sand.
But the janitor with black mustaches
stands once again by the rusty gate
and with his dirty hands he scratches
under his dirty hat his itching pate;
through windows hear the joyous din,
the stomp of feet and bottles' ring.
October 14, 1933

The little old man scratched himself with both hands. The places he couldn't reach with both hands, the old man scratched with one, but quick-quick. And the whole time he quickly blinked his eyes.

Steam, or so-called smoke, poured out of the steam train's pipe. And a festive bird, flying into this smoke, flew out of it all greasy and crumpled.

Khvilishchevsky ate cranberries trying not to wrinkle up his face. He was waiting for everyone to say: "What strength of character!" But nobody said anything.

He could hear the dog sniffing at the door. Khvilishchevsky clenched his toothbrush in his fist and opened his eyes wide in order to hear better. "If that dog comes in here," thought Khvilishchevsky, "I'll hit it right in the temple with this ivory handle."

. . . Some sort of bubbles came out of the box. Khvilishchevsky removed himself from the room on tippy-toes and closed the door quietly behind him. "Screw it!" said Khvilishchevsky to himself. "It ain't my business what's in it. Really! Screw it!"

Khvilishchevsky wanted to shout: "I won't let you in!" But his tongue got tangled somehow and it came out: "I ton't wet you in." Khvilishchevsky squinted his right eye and exited the hall with dignity. But still it seemed to him that he heard Zukkerman snigger.

(1933-1934)

THE DIFFERENCE IN HEIGHT
BETWEEN HUSBAND AND WIFE

HUSBAND: I spanked my daughter and now I'm going to spank my wife.

WIFE & DAUGHTER *(from behind the door)*: Bahbahbahbahbahbah! Moomoomoomoomoomooo!

HUSBAND: Ivan! Butler???? Ivan!

Enter Ivan. Ivan has no hands.

IVAN: At your service!

HUSBAND: Where are your hands, Ivan?!

IVAN: In the war years I was bereft of them in the excitement of battle!

(1930-1934)

[BLACK WATER]

Andrei Ivanovich spat into a cup of water. Right away the water turned black. Andrei Ivanovich squinted his eyes and looked intently into the cup. The water was very black. Andrei Ivanovich's heart started beating faster.

Meanwhile, Andrei Ivanovich's dog awoke. Andrei Ivanovich walked over to the window and fell into thought.

Suddenly something big and dark swept past him and flew out the window. It was Andrei Ivanovich's dog flying out and rushing like a crow onto the roof of the opposite house. Andrei Ivanovich knelt down in a squat and began to moan.

Comrade Popugayev ran into the room.

"What's with you? Are you sick?" asked comrade Popugayev.

Andrei Ivanovich was silent and rubbed his face with his hands.

Comrade Popugayev took a look into the cup on the table.

"What is that you have there in the cup?" he asked Andrei Semyonovich.

"Don't know," said Andrei Semyonovich.

Comrade Popugayev instantly vanished. The dog flew back in through the window again, lay down in its former place and fell asleep.

Andrei Semyonovich walked up to the table and drank the cup of black water.

And it became light in Andrei Semyonovich's soul.

August 21 (1934)

A neck stuck out from the collar of the fool's shirt, and on the neck was a head. The head was at one time closely cropped. By now the hair had grown out like a brush. The fool talked about a lot of things. No one listened to him. Everyone thought: when will he shut up and leave? But the fool, noticing nothing, continued talking and laughing.

Finally, Elbov couldn't stand it any longer and came up to the fool and said, curtly and viciously, "Make yourself scarce this very minute." The fool looked around at a loss, without a clue of what was going on. Elbov gave the fool a clout on the ear. The fool flew out of his chair and dropped to the floor. Elbov gave him a kick and the fool went flying through the doorway and rolled down the stairs.

———

So it is in life: a fool through and through and yet he wants to express himself. They need to be punched in the snout. That's right, in the snout!

Wherever I look, everywhere I see this foolish mug of a convict. A boot in the snout is what they all need.

(August 1934)

ON EQUALIBRIUM

Nowadays, everybody knows how dangerous it is to swallow stones.

One of my acquaintances even made up an expression that goes: "Kabeo," which means Keep Boulders Out. And it was a good thing that he did. "Kabeo" is easy to memorize and quickly comes to mind whenever you need it.

This acquaintance of mine served on a steam train as an engine stoker. He'd ride the northern line sometimes, and sometimes he'd ride to Moscow. His name was Nikolai Ivanovich Serpukhov and he smoked Rocket brand cigarettes, 35 kopecks a pack, and always said that they didn't make him cough as much as the five ruble smokes, which, he said, "always make me choke."

And so it happened that Nikolai Ivanovich Serpukhov, by sheer luck, got into the European Hotel, to the restaurant. So Nikolai Ivanovich is sitting at a table and sitting at the table next to him are some foreigners chowing down apples.

And that's when Nikolai Ivanovich said to himself: "Interesting," said Nikolai Ivanovich to himself, "how man is made."

Just as he said that to himself, from out of the blue a fairy appears to him and says:

"What can I do for you, my good man?"

Well, of course, some commotion occurs in the restaurant, like where did this unknown little lady come from. The foreigners even stopped chomping on their apples for a minute.

As for Nikolai Ivanovich, it's no joke, he crapped his pants, and said simply, just to get out of the situation:

"I'm sorry," says he, "nothing special, I don't really need anything."

"No," says the unknown little lady, "I'm what they call a fairy," she says. "In an instant I can cook up anything you desire."

Nikolai Ivanovich noticed that a certain civilian, part of a gray couple, was eavesdropping attentively to their conversation. And the maître d' was running through the open doors pursued by another persona with a cigarette between his lips.

"What the devil!" thought Nikolai Ivanovich, "you can't tell what's going on!"

And, truly, you really couldn't tell what was going on. The maître d'hotel was jumping on the tables, the foreigners were rolling the rugs up into tubes, and the devil knows what! Each according to his abilities!

Nikolai Ivanovich ran out onto the street, even forgot to get his hat out of safe-keeping at the coat check, and ran out onto LaSalle Street and said to himself, "Kabeo! Keep Boulders Out! And what doesn't go on in this world!"

Coming home, Nikolai Ivanovich told his wife this: "Don't be alarmed, Ekaterina Petrovna, don't worry! But there's no equalibrium in the world, none whatsoever. And the thing is, the mistake is only some one-and-a-half kilograms off for the whole universe, and yet it's amazing, Ekaterina Petrovna, completely amazing!"

THAT'S ALL

Daniil Dandan
September 18, 1934

ON PHENOMENA AND EXISTENCES
#1

The artist Michael Angelo sits down on a heap of bricks and, propping his head up on his hands, starts to think. Here comes a rooster walking by. The rooster looks at the artist Michael Angelo with its round, golden eyes. It stares and does not blink. Now the artist Michael Angelo lifts his head and sees the rooster. The rooster does not look away, it does not blink and does not shake its tail. The artist Michael Angelo lets down his gaze and notices that something is stinging his eyes. The artist Michael Angelo rubs his eyes with his hands. And the rooster is no longer standing there, it's not standing there but going away, it's going away past the shack, past the shack to the bird pen, to the bird pen to its hens.

And the artist Michael Angelo rises from the heap of bricks, shakes the red brick dust off his pants, throws his belt aside and goes to see his wife.

But the artist Michael Angelo's wife is very-very long, the length of two rooms.

On the way, the artist Michael Angelo runs into Komarov, grabs him by the arm and screams: "Look!"

Komarov looks and sees a sphere.

"What is that?" whispers Komarov.

And from the sky rumbles: "It's a sphere!"

"What sort of a sphere?" whispers Komarov.

And the sky again rumbles: "A smooth-surfaced sphere!"

Komarov and the artist Michael Angelo sit down in the grass and they sit there, in the grass, like mushrooms. They hold each other's hands and gaze at the sky. And in the sky appear the outlines of a gigantic spoon. What can it be? No one knows. People run away and lock themselves in their houses. And they lock their doors and their windows. But can this really help? Come on! That won't help at all.

I remember how in 1884 an average comet appeared in the sky the size of a steamship. It was really frightening. But here—a spoon! What's a comet compared to such a phenomenon.

Lock the doors and windows!

Can this really help? You can't guard against a heavenly phenomenon with a wooden board.

In our building lives Nikolai Ivanovich Stupin; he has a theory that everything is smoke. But, if you ask me, not everything is smoke. Maybe there's no smoke at all. And maybe there's nothing. There's only the difference. And maybe there's not even any difference. It's hard to say.

They say one famous artist once examined a rooster. He examined it and examined it and came to the conclusion that the rooster didn't exist.

The artist told his friend about it and his friend burst out laughing. "What do you mean," he said, "it doesn't exist when," he said, "it's standing right there and I," he said, "am observing it quite clearly."

And the great artist then lowered his head and sat down, right where he was standing, on a heap of bricks.

THAT'S ALL

Daniil Dandan
September 18, 1934

ON PHENOMENA AND EXISTENCES
#2

Here's a bottle of vodka, so called spirits. And next to it you see Nikolai Ivanovich Serpukhov.

Now, from the bottle rise the vapors of the spirits. See how Nikolai Ivanovich Serpukhov breathes through his nose. Have a look at how he squints, licking his lips. You can see how very pleasant this is for him and mainly because it's spirits.

But direct your attention to the fact that behind Nikolai Ivanovich's back there's nothing. It's not that there isn't a wardrobe standing there, or a dresser, or anything like that, but that there's nothing there at all, not even any air. You can believe it or not, but behind Nikolai Ivanovich's back there isn't even any air-less space or, as they say, universal ether. Frankly speaking, there's nothing there.

Of course, it's impossible to even imagine it.

But we couldn't give a shit. We're only interested in the spirits and Nikolai Ivanovich Serpukhov. Now Nikolai Ivanovich takes the bottle of spirits and brings it close to his nose. Nikolai Ivanovich sniffs and moves his mouth around like a rabbit.

And now the time has come to say that not only behind the back of Nikolai Ivanovich but in front—that is to say, in front of his chest—and all around him there is nothing. The complete lack of any sort of being, or, as they used to joke: the absence of any presence.

However, let us interest ourselves only with the spirits and Nikolai Ivanovich.

Let's imagine Nikolai Ivanovich peers into the bottle of spirits, then brings it to his lips, overturns the bottle bottoms up and drinks, if you can imagine it, all the spirits.

How clever! Nikolai Ivanovich drank the spirits and blinked several times. How clever! How'd he do that?

And now we must say this: Plainly speaking, not only was there nothing behind the back of Nikolai Ivanovich or in front and around only but also inside Nikolai Ivanovich nothing existed.

It, of course, could have been as we just said and Nikolai Ivanovich himself could still exist quite splendidly. This is, of course, true enough. But, frankly speaking, the crux of the matter is that Nikolai Ivanovich did not and does not exist. Now that's the crux of it.

You may ask: And what about the bottle of spirits? And particularly, where the heck did the spirits go if it was drunk by the non-existent Nikolai Ivanovich. The bottle, for instance, is left. But where's the spirits? Just here and suddenly it's gone. And you say Nikolai Ivanovich doesn't exist, you say. So how's that possible?

At this point we ourselves get lost in these guessing games.

And yet, what's this we're saying? Haven't we already said that just as nothing exists inside Nikolai Ivanovich, so nothing exists on the outside. And since nothing exists neither inside nor outside then that means the bottle doesn't exist either. Isn't that so?

But, on the other hand, direct your attention to the following: If we're saying that nothing exists neither inside nor outside then the question comes up: inside or outside what? Something exists then, doesn't it? But maybe it doesn't. Then why are we saying "inside" and "outside."

No, this is clearly a dead end. And we don't know what to say. Goodbye.

THAT'S ALL

Daniil Dandan
September 18, 1934

THE FALL FROM GRACE, OR THE KNOWLEDGE OF GOOD AND EVIL
Didascalia

An alley lined with beautifully groomed trees represents the garden of paradise. In the middle stands the Tree of Life and the Tree of the Knowledge of Good and Evil. In back and to the right is a church.

FIGURA *(pointing with his hand at a tree, speaks):* Here is the Tree of the Knowledge of Good and Evil. You can eat the fruit from other trees, but from this tree do not eat the fruit.

ADAM *(pointing at the tree):* Here is the Tree of the Knowledge of Good and Evil. We will eat the fruit from other trees, but from this tree we will not eat the fruit. You, Eve, wait for me, while I go pick raspberries. *(Leaves.)*

EVE: This is the Tree of the Knowledge of Good and Evil. Adam forbade me to eat the fruit from this tree. But how does it taste, I wonder?

Master Leonardo appears from behind the tree.

MASTER LEONARDO: Eve! Here I come to you.

EVE: Tell me, Master Leonardo, why?

MASTER LEONARDO: You are so beautiful, white-skinned and full-bosomed. I am busying myself for your benefit.

EVE: You better be.

MASTER LEONARDO: You know, Eve, I love you.

EVE: How do I know what that is?

MASTER LEONARDO: Don't you know?

EVE: How would I know?

MASTER LEONARDO: Are you trying to surprise me?

EVE: Oh, look, how funny—the he-pheasant is riding the she-pheasant!

MASTER LEONARDO: That's exactly it.

EVE: What is it exactly?

MASTER LEONARDO: It's love.

EVE: Then it's funny. And you? You want to ride me too?

MASTER LEONARDO: Yes. I do. But don't tell Adam.

EVE: Ok, I won't.

MASTER LEONARDO: I see you're a good girl.

EVE: Yeah, I'm a tough broad.

MASTER LEONARDO: And do you love me?

EVE: I wouldn't mind if you gave me a ride around the garden.

MASTER LEONARDO: Climb up on my shoulders.

Eve mounts Master Leonardo, and he gallops with her around the garden. Enter Adam with a cap full of raspberries in his hands.

ADAM: Eve! Where are you? Want some raspberries? Eve! Where did she go? I'll go look for her. (*Leaves.*)

Enter Eve riding Master Leonardo.

EVE (*jumping off onto the ground*): Well thanks. That was real good.

MASTER LEONARDO: Now try this apple.

EVE: What, are you crazy? You can't eat fruit from this tree.

MASTER LEONARDO: Listen, Eve! I learned all the mysteries of paradise long ago. I can tell you something.

EVE: Ok, talk. I'll listen.

MASTER LEONARDO: Will you listen to me?

EVE: I won't disappoint you.

MASTER LEONARDO: You won't betray me?

EVE: No, believe me.

MASTER LEONARDO: What if it comes to light.

EVE: Not through me.

MASTER LEONARDO: Alright. I believe you. You went to a good school. I've seen Adam, he's a dummy.

EVE: He's a bit crude.

MASTER LEONARDO: He doesn't know anything. He hasn't traveled much and he hasn't seen a thing. He was fooled. And now he's fooling you.

EVE: In what way?

MASTER LEONARDO: He forbids you to eat the fruit of this tree. But these are the tastiest fruits. And when you eat this fruit you'll know right away what's good and what's bad. Right away you'll know a lot, and you'll even be smarter than God.

EVE: Is that possible?

MASTER LEONARDO: I'm telling you it is.

EVE: Well, frankly, I don't know what I should do.

MASTER LEONARDO: Eat this apple! Eat it, eat it!

Enter Adam with a cap in his hands.

ADAM: Here you are, Eve! And who's that?

Master Leonardo hides behind the bushes.

ADAM: Who was that?

EVE: That was my friend, Master Leonardo.

ADAM: What did he want?

EVE: He let me climb up onto his shoulders and ran with me around the garden. I laughed like mad.

ADAM: Was that all you did?

EVE: Yes.

ADAM: What's that in your hands?

EVE: It's an apple.

ADAM: What tree is it from?

EVE: That one.

ADAM: No, you liar, it's from this one.

EVE: No, that one.

ADAM: I bet you're lying.

EVE: Take my word for it, I'm not.

ADAM: Alright, I believe you.

SERPENT (*sitting in the Tree of the Knowledge of Good and Evil*): She is lying. Don't believe her. That apple is from this tree!

ADAM: Drop that apple. Liar.

EVE: No. You're a dummy. You've got to try what it tastes like.

ADAM: Eve! Watch it!

EVE: There's nothing to see!

ADAM: Well, it's your own business.

Eve bites off a piece of the apple. The Serpent claps his hands in joy.

EVE: Oh, this tastes so good! Wait, but what's going on? You keep disappearing and then reappearing again. Wow! Everything disappears and then everything comes back again out of nowhere. Oh, this is so interesting! A-ah! I'm naked! Adam, come closer to me, I want to mount you.

ADAM: What's wrong?

EVE: Here, you eat this apple too!

ADAM: I'm scared.

EVE: Eat it! Eat it!

Adam eats a piece of the apple and immediately covers himself with his cap.

ADAM: I am ashamed.

Figura comes out of the church.

FIGURA: You, he-person, and you, she-person, you have eaten the forbidden fruit. Therefore, get out of my garden!

Figura goes back into the church.

ADAM: Where are we supposed to go?

EVE: We're not going anywhere.

Enter Angel with a sword of fire and chases them out of paradise.

ANGEL: Get out of here! Get out of here! Get the hell out of here!

MASTER LEONARDO *(emerging from behind the bushes):* Get out! Get out! *(Waves his hands.)* Curtains!

CURTAIN.

Dandan
September 27, 1934

WHAT ARE WE TO DO?

While the dolphin and the sea-horse
Played silly games together,
The ocean beat against the cliffs
And washed the cliffs with its water.
The scary water moaned and cried.
The stars shone. Years went by.
Then the horrid hour came:
I am no more, and so are you,
The sea is gone, the cliffs, the mountains,
And the stars gone, too;
Only the choir sounds out of the dead void.
And for simplicity's sake, our wrathful God
Sprung up and blew away the dust of centuries,
And now, freed from the shackles of time
He flies alone, his own and only dearest friend.
Cold everywhere and darkness blind.

Dandan
October 15, 1934

Would you like me to tell you a story about the crichen? No, not a crichen, but a chickrichen. Or no, not chickrichen, but chuckroochen. Phooey! Not a chuckroochen, a charckoochen. Of course it's not a charckoochen but a coochoockrichen. No, that's not it! Chickyckraten? No, not chickyckraten! Coocheecoockitchen? No, wrong again!

So I've forgotten what this bird's called. But if I hadn't forgotten, I would tell you the story about this choockoockurookochen.

(1934-35)

[Translated with Simona Schneider]

There's a rumor that soon all the broads will have their rears cut off and sent strolling down Volodarskaya Street.

———————

That's not true! The broads will not have their rears cut off.

———————

SONG

We will close our eyes,
    People! People!
We will open our eyes,
    Warriors! Warriors!

Raise us above the water,
    Angels! Angels!
Drown the enemy under the water,
    Demons! Demons!

We closed our eyes,
    People! People!
We opened our eyes,
    Warrriors! Warriors!

Give us the strength to fly over the water,
    Birds! Birds!
Give us the courage to die under the water,
    Fish! Fish!

(1934-1935)

A HOLIDAY

On the roof of a certain building two draughtsmen sat eating buckwheat kasha.

Suddenly one of the draughtsmen shrieked with joy and took a long handkerchief out of his pocket. He had a brilliant idea—he would tie a twenty-kopeck coin into one end of the handkerchief and toss the whole thing off the roof down into the street and see what would come of it.

The second draughtsman quickly caught on to the first one's idea. He finished his buckwheat kasha, blew his nose and, having licked his fingers, got ready to watch the first draughtsman.

As it happened, both draughtsmen were distracted from the experiment with the handkerchief and twenty-kopeck coin. On the roof where both draughtsmen sat an event occurred which could not have gone unnoticed.

The janitor Ibrahim was hammering a long stick with a faded flag into a chimney.

The draughtsmen asked Ibrahim what it meant, to which Ibrahim answered: "This means that there's a holiday in the city."

"And what holiday would that be, Ibrahim?" asked the draughtsmen.

"It's a holiday because our favorite poet composed a new poem," said Ibrahim.

And the draughtsmen, shamed by their ignorance, dissolved into the air.

(January 9, 1935)

AN INCIDENT ON THE STREET

A man once jumped off a tram, but he did it so badly that a car hit him.

The traffic stopped and the policeman set about determining the cause of the accident.

The driver was explaining something for a long time and pointing to the front wheels of his car.

The policeman felt the wheels and wrote something down in his little book.

A fairly numerous crowd gathered.

A certain citizen with dull eyes kept falling off a concrete traffic divider.

Some lady repeatedly glanced at another lady who, in turn, repeatedly glanced at the former lady.

Then the crowd dispersed and the traffic started moving.

But the citizen with dull eyes still kept falling off the traffic divider until, finally, he too put a stop to his activity.

At this time someone carrying what appeared to be a brand new chair hit a tram straight on and smack got run over.

Again the policeman came, again the crowd gathered, and the citizen with dull eyes again started falling off the traffic divider.

Later everything was alright again, and Ivan Semyonovich Karpov even dropped into a self-service cafeteria.

Daniil Kharms
January 10, 1935

[Translated with Eugene Ostashevsky]

TO OLEINIKOV

Train conductor of digits, friendship's mean mocker,
what are you thinking? Finding fault once again with the world?
In your book Homer is a pervert and Goethe a stupid sinner,
you've made a mockery of Dante. Your only idol—Bunin's word.

Your poetry is sometimes funny and sometimes stirs the heart,
it hurts at times the ear or is not funny oft at all,
at times it even maddens, it is depraved in art;
into the chasm of petty thoughts it rushes fast to fall.

Hold on! Come back! Where do your cold thoughts take you,
have you forgotten of the law of visions bringing on the hordes?
Whose breast has your dim arrow struck a road through?
Who is your foe and who your friend? Where waits your fatal
    sword?

January 23, 1935

FIRST EPISTLE TO MARINA

I will not love you for the silence
that you keep, my dearest friend.
And, having lost love, I'll forget you
and never suddenly recall.

Whether silence, trickery or malice
has spilt the chalice of our love,
the talisman of keeping silent
will never fill the cup.

But if you can but say a word,
utter even the smallest sound,
my love for you will be ignited,
and with new strength it will rebound.

August 19, 1935

A KNIGHT

Alexei Alexeyevich Alexeyev was a real knight. So, for example, once, seeing from the tram how a lady had tripped on a post and dropped a glass shade for a table lamp out of her shopping bag, which of course immediately shattered, Alexei Alexeyevich, wishing to help the lady, decided to sacrifice himself and, jumping out of the tram at full speed, fell and completely split open his mug against a stone. Another time, seeing that a lady had gotten her skirt caught on a nail while climbing over a fence, and in such a way that, straddling the fence, she was able to move neither backward nor forward, Alexei Alexeyevich got so worried that he pushed his two front teeth out with his tongue out of agitation. In short, Alexei Alexeyevich was truly a knight, and not just in regard to the ladies. With unprecedented ease Alexei Alexeyevich could give his life for Faith, Czar and Fatherland, which he proved in 1914, at the beginning of WWI, by throwing himself onto the street from a third floor window shouting "For the Homeland!" By some miracle Alexei Alexeyevich survived, getting off with a few minor bruises, and soon, as a patriot of rare zeal, was sent to the front.

On the front Alexei Alexeyevich was remarkable for his uncommonly lofty emotions. Any time he uttered the words "banner," "bugle," or even simply "epaulets," a tear of tenderness ran down his cheek.

In 1916 Alexei Alexeyevich was wounded in the loins and removed from the front. As a an invalid of the 1st Category, Alexei Alexeyevich no longer worked, and, making use of the free time, he set his patriotic feelings down on paper.

Once, chatting with Konstantin Lebedev, Alexei Alexeyevich said his favorite phrase: "I gave myself for my Homeland with my shattered loins, but I persist by the strength of the convictions of my hind subconscious."

"And what a fool!" Konstantin Lebedev told him. "The highest service to the motherland can be rendered only by a LIBERAL."

For some reason these words struck a chord deep in his soul, and so in 1917 he was already calling himself a liberal, who gave his loins for the Fatherland.

Alexei Alexeyevich greeted the revolution with enthusiasm, even in spite of the fact that he had been denied his pension. For some time K. L. supplied him with cane sugar, chocolate, canned suet and millet. But when Konstantin Lebedev disappeared no one knows where, Alexei Alexeyevich had to go out on the street and ask for handouts. In the beginning Alexei Alexeyevich held out his hand and said: "Give a little, for the sake of Christ, to one who has suffered with his loins for the homeland." But this brought no success. Then Alexei Alexeyevich replaced the word "homeland" with the word "revolution." But this didn't have any success either. Then Alexei Alexeyevich composed a revolutionary song and, catching sight of a person on the street who in Alexei Alexeyevich's opinion could give charity, he would take a step forward and, proudly, with dignity, with his head thrown back, began to sing:

> To the barricades
> we will go, you and I!
> In the name of freedom
> we will all be crippled and die!

And, clicking his heels in the Polish fashion, Alexei Alexeyevich would extend his hat and say, "Give to the poor, for the sake of Christ." This helped, and Alexei Alexeevich rarely remained without a bite to eat.

Everything was going well, but then in 1922, Alexei Alexeyevich made the acquaintance of a certain Ivan Ivanovich Puzyryov, who sold sunflower oil at the Haymarket. Puzyryov invited Alexei Alexeyevich to a cafe, treated him to a real coffee and, munching on pastries, laid out some kind of complicated endeavor of which Alexei Alexeyevich understood only that he too had to do something, for which he would receive from Puzyryov the most valuable consumable products. Alexei

Alexeyevich agreed, and right away Puzyryov, in a gesture of encouragement, handed him two boxes of tea and a pack of Raja cigarettes under the table.

From that day on, Alexei Alexeyevich came to Puzyryov at the market every morning and, having received some papers with crooked signatures and myriad seals, took a sleigh if it was winter, or, if it happened to be summer, a cart, and following Puzyryov's orders went to various offices, where, after presenting the papers, he received some crates, which he loaded onto his sleigh or cart and in the evening delivered to Puzyryov's apartment. But once, when Alexei Alexeyevich rolled up with his sleigh to Puzyryov's apartment he was approached by two men, one of whom was in a military overcoat, and asked him, "Is your name Alexeyev?" Then they put Alexei Alexeyevich in a car and took him away to prison.

During the cross-examination Alexei Alexeyevich didn't understand a thing and only repeated that he had suffered for the revolutionary homeland. Despite this, however, he was sentenced to ten years of exile to the northern climes of his Fatherland. Returning to Leningrad in 1928, Alexei Alexeyevich took up his former craft and, positioning himself on the corner of Volodarsky Prospect, he tossed his head back with dignity, stomped his heel and began to sing:

> To the barricades
> we will go, you and I!
> In the name of freedom
> we will all be crippled and die!

But, before he could even sing it a second time, he was taken away in a covered car somewhere in the direction of the Admiralty. And that was the last anyone saw of him.

That is the short plot of the life of the valiant knight and patriot Alex Alexeyevich Alexeyev.

(1934-1936)

[Translated with Simona Schneider]

A monk walked into a mausoleum full of dead people and said, "Christ hath risen!" And they answered in unison: "Verily risen!"

[Translated with Eugene Ostashevsky]

I was born in the reeds. Like a mouse. My mother gave birth to me and put me in the water. And I swam away. Some kind of fish with four whiskers on its nose circled around me. I started crying. And the fish started crying. Suddenly we noticed that some porridge was floating atop the water. We ate the porridge and began to laugh. We were very happy, and we swam along with the current until we met a crayfish. It was an ancient, great crayfish; it held an ax in its claws. A naked frog followed swimming behind the crayfish. "Why are you always naked," asked the crayfish, "aren't you ashamed?"—"There's nothing shameful in it," answered the frog. "Why should we be ashamed of our fine bodies, given us by nature, when we are not ashamed of the vile acts that we ourselves perpetrate."—"Your words are true," said the crayfish. "And I do not know how to answer you. I suggest we ask a human, because humans are smarter than we. We are only smart in the fables that man writes about us, i.e. it means once more that it is the human that is smart and not us." But then the crayfish noticed me and said: "And we don't even have to swim anywhere to find him—because here he is, a human." The crayfish swam over to me and asked: "Should one be embarrassed of one's own body? You, human, answer us!"—"I am a human and I will answer you: One should not be embarrassed of one's own body."

(1934-1937)

Now I will tell you how I was born, how I grew up and how the first signs of genius manifested themselves in me. I was born twice. It happened like this.

My dad was wed to my mom in 1902, but only at the end of 1905 did my parents bring me into this world because dad wished for his child to be born on new year's day without fail. Dad calculated that the conception must take place on April 1st and only on that day rolled up to mom with the proposition to conceive a child.

The first time dad rolled up to my mom was April 1st, 1903. Mom had been waiting for this moment for a long time and was awfully happy. But dad, evidently, was in a joking mood and couldn't help but say, "April Fool's!"

Mom got awfully upset and didn't let dad near her that day. There was nothing to do but wait until the following year.

In 1904, on April 1st, dad weaseled up to mom with the same proposition. But, remembering the previous year's incident, mom said that she didn't want to be made a fool of once more, and again didn't let dad near her. No matter how much dad raged, it couldn't be helped.

And only a year later my dad was able to talk my mom into conceiving me.

And that's how my conception occurred on April 1st, 1905.

Yet, all of dad's calculations were foiled because I ended up being born prematurely, four months before I was due.

Dad threw such a fit that the midwife who had taken me out was flustered and started shoving me back into the place I'd just crawled out of.

Witness to all this was a student we knew from the Military Medical Academy who proclaimed that shoving me back in wouldn't work. Despite the words of the student they shoved me in after all. But, as it turned out, though they really did shove me back in, they shoved me into the wrong place.

Here began a terrible commotion. The birth-mother crying

"Bring me my baby!" And the reply: "Your child," they say, "is inside of you." "What!" says the birth-mother, "how can the child be inside me when I just gave birth to it!"

"But," they say to the birth-mother, "perhaps you're mistaken?"

"What do you mean, mistaken!" shouts the birth-mother. "How can I be mistaken! I saw it with my own two eyes. Just a second ago the child was lying right here on the sheet."

"This is true," comes the reply, "but maybe he crawled in somewhere." In short, they just don't know what to say.

And the birth-mother keeps making a ruckus and demanding her baby.

They had to call an experienced doctor. The experienced doctor examined the birth-mother and threw up his hands. But then he thought of something and gave the birth-mother a good-sized helping of English salts. The birth-mother made a bowel movement, and that's how I came into the world for the second time.

At that point my dad flew into another fit of rage, saying something like, what, you call this a birth?, and he went on to say it's not even a person yet, more like half-way to a fetus, and that it should either be shoved back in or else put in an incubator.

And so they put me in an incubator.

September 25, 1935

[Translated with Simona Schneider]

MY TIME IN THE INCUBATOR

I spent four months in the incubator. I remember only that the incubator was made of glass, was transparent and had a thermometer. I sat inside the incubator on cotton-wool. I don't remember anything more.

After four months they took me out of the incubator. This was done exactly on the First of January, 1906. That's how I was born for the third time, if you like. Since then the day of my birth has been said to be January 1st.

(September 1935)

[Translated with Simona Schneider]

A FABLE

One short man said: "I would give anything if only I were even a tiny bit taller."

He barely said it when he saw a lady medegician standing in front of him.

"What do you want?" says the medegician.

But the short man just stands there so frightened he can't even speak.

"Well?" says the medegician.

The short man just stands there and says nothing. The medegician vanishes.

Then the short man started crying and biting his nails. First he chewed off all the nails on his fingers, and then on his toes.

————

Reader! Think this fable over and it will make you somewhat uncomfortable.

(1935)

[Translated with Eugene Ostashevsky]

There lived a man called Kuznetsov. One time his stool broke. He left his house and went to the store to buy carpenter's glue in order to glue the stool back together.

When Kuznetsov was walking past a house under construction, a brick fell from high up and hit Kuznetsov on the head.

Kuznetsov fell, but hopped right back on his feet and groped his head. An enormous lump had popped out.

Kuznetsov rubbed the lump and said:

"I am citizen Kuznetsov, I emerged from my house and set out for the store in order to . . . in order to . . . in order to . . . Ack! What's this! I forgot why I was on my way to the store!"

At the same time a second brick fell from the roof and again Kuznetsov was struck on the head.

"Ack!" Kuznetsov cried out, he grasped his head in his hands and discovered a second lump.

"What a story!" said Kuznetsov. "I, citizen Kuznetsov, emerged from my house and set out for the . . . for the . . . Where was I going? I forgot where I was going!"

At this point, a third brick fell from above onto Kuznetsov and on Kuznetsov's head a third lump appeared.

"Ow! Ow! Ow!" Kuznetsov shouted, seizing his head. "I, citizen Kuznetsov, emerged from . . . emerged from . . . the cellar? No. Emerged from an all night bender? No! Where did I emerge from?"

A fourth brick fell from the roof, hit Kuznetsov across the back of his head, and on the back of his head appeared a fourth lump.

"So and so!" said Kuznetsov, scratching his forehead. "I . . . I . . . I . . . Who am I? It sounds like I forgot what my name is. What a story! What's my name? Vasily Petukhov? No. Nikolai Shumaker? No. Panteley Sumpter? No, so who am I?"

But now a fifth brick fell from the roof and hit Kuznetsov's occiput so hard that Kuznetsov definitively forgot everything in the universe and, crying "Uga-gu," ran down the street.

———

Please! If someone meets a person on the street with five lumps on his head, remind him that his name is Kuznetsov, and that he needs to buy carpenter's glue to fix the broken stool.

November 1, 1935

[Translated with Simona Schneider]

A window with a drawn curtain was getting brighter and brighter because the day was beginning. The floors squeaked, the doors creaked, chairs were being moved around in apartments. Climbing out of bed, Ruzhetsky fell on the floor and smashed his face. He was in a rush to get to work so he went outside covering his face with just his hands. His hands made it hard for him to see where he was going. Twice he bumped into an advertising kiosk, then shoved some old man in a vinyl hat with fur earflaps, which sent the old man into such a fury that a janitor, happening to be in proximity because he was trying to catch a cat with a shovel, said to the increasingly agitated old man: "Shame on you, gramps, making so much trouble at your age."

(1935)

[Translated with Simona Schneider]

A Frenchman was given a couch, four chairs and an armchair. The Frenchman sits down on the chair by the window, but then he wants to lie around on the couch. The Frenchman sat on the couch, but he'd like to sit a while in the armchair. The Frenchman got up from the couch and sat down in the armchair like a king, but in his own head he's already got thoughts like, it's a bit too opulent in the armchair. Better to be a little plainer, on the chair. The Frenchman switched to the chair by the window, but he's restless in this chair because there's kind of a draft coming from the window. The Frenchman switched to the chair near the stove and realized that he was tired. Then the Frenchman decided to lie down on the couch and rest, but before he made it to the couch, he veered off to the side and sat down in the armchair.

"Now that's good!" said the Frenchman, but right away he added, "Yes, it's probably better on the couch."

THE INTIMATE SUFFERINGS
OF A MUSICIAN

They called me a cruel monster.
And isn't that the case?
No, it's not the case. But I won't offer any proof.

———

I heard my wife talking into the telephone receiver, telling some Mikhusya that I was dumb.
At the time I was sitting under the bed and could not be seen.
O! What suffering I experienced in that moment!
I wanted to jump out and shout: "No, I'm not dumb!"
I can imagine just what would have happened then!

———

Again I was sitting under the bed and was not visible.
But I sure could see what that same Mikhusya was doing with my wife.

———

Today my wife received this Mikhusya again.
I'm beginning to think that, in my wife's eyes, I'm receding into the background.
Mikhusya even searched around in the drawers of my writing desk.
I myself sat under the bed and was not to be seen.

———

I was sitting under the bed again and was not visible.
My wife and Mikhusya were talking about me in the most unpleasant tones.
I couldn't take it any longer and shouted to them that they were all lying.

———

It's already the fifth day after I was beaten up, but my bones still whimper.

D. Kh.

THE DEATH OF A LITTLE OLD MAN

A little sphere sprung out of a little old man's nose and fell to the ground. The little old man bent over to lift up the little sphere and that's when a little stick sprung from his eye and also fell to the ground. The little old man was frightened and, not knowing what to do, moved his lips. At that moment, out of the little old man's mouth sprung a little square. The little old man grabbed his mouth, but then a little mouse sprung out of the little old man's sleeve. The little old man became ill with fear and, so as not to fall, he squatted down. But then something snapped inside the little old man and, like a soft plush coat, he toppled to the ground. That's when a longish little reed sprang from the torn hole, and on its very end sat a thin little bird. The little old man wanted to scream out but one of his jaws got stuck behind the other and he only hiccuped weakly and closed one eye. The little old man's other eye remained open. It ceased moving and glistening and became motionless and murky, like that of a dead person. In this way cunning death caught up to the little old man who did not know his hour.

Marina told me that one Sharik had visited her in bed. Who, or what, was this Sharik, I couldn't for the life of me determine.

———

A few days later this Sharik visited again. Then he started coming quite often, about every three days.

———

I was not at home. When I came home, Marina told me that Cinderyushkin had called on the phone asking for me. Apparently, if you can believe it, some Cinderyushkin wanted me!

———

Marina bought some apples. We ate a few after dinner and left maybe two apples for later that evening. But in the evening when I wanted to claim my apple, the apple was not to be found. Marina said that Misha the waiter had come by and took the apples away for a salad. He didn't need the apple cores, so he cleaned the apples right there in our room and threw the cores away in the waste paper basket.

———

I found out that Sharik, Cinderyushkin and Misha usually live in our stove. It's hard for me to comprehend how they got settled in there.

———

I was asking Marina about Sharik, Cinderyushkin and Misha. Marina tried to get out of giving me any straight answers. When I let her know of my misgivings that this company was possibly not completely goodnatured, Marina assured me that in any case they were "Golden Hearts." I could get nothing more out of Marina.

———

With time, I learned that the "Golden Hearts" did not all get the same education. To be honest, Sharik received a high school education, and Cinderyushkin and Misha received none at all. Sharik has even written some scholarly works. And for that reason his attitude toward the rest of the "Golden Hearts" is somewhat haughty.

I was very curious, what sort of scholarly works these were. But that remained unknown. Marina says that he was born with pen in hand, but doesn't divulge any further details of his scholarly activities. I began to suss it out and, finally, I learned that he was more in the cobbler's line of work. Whether this has anything to do with his scholarly activity, I was unable to determine.

———

Once I learned that the "Golden Hearts" had a party. They pooled their money and bought a marinated eel. And Misha even brought a jar of vodka. It should be said: Misha likes to drink.

———

Sharik's boots are made out of cork.

———

One evening Marina told me that Cinderyushkin called me a troublemaker because I stepped on his foot. I also got angry and asked Marina to pass on to Cinderyushkin that he should stay out of my way.

(1935-1936)

[THE COPPER LOOK]

"You see," he said, "I saw you riding with them, three days ago, in a boat. One of them was sitting at the rudder, two rowed, and the fourth was sitting next to you and was talking. For a long time I stood on the bank and watched those two rowing. Yes, I can boldly affirm that they wanted to drown you. People only row like that before a murder."

The lady with the yellow gloves looked up at Klopov.

"What does that mean?" said she. "How can one row a special way before a murder? And then, what would they get from drowning me?"

Klopov turned abruptly towards the woman and said, "Do you know what the copper look is?"

"No," said the woman, involuntarily moving away from Klopov.

"Aha," Klopov said, "When a fine porcelain teacup falls out of a cupboard and flies downward, in that moment, while it is still flying in the air, you already know that it will touch the ground and shatter to pieces. And I know that if one person gives another the copper look then, sooner or later, he will inevitably kill him."

"They looked at me with the copper look?" asked the lady with the yellow gloves.

"Yes, Madame," said Klopov and put on his hat.

For some time both were silent. Klopov sat with his head bowed low.

"Forgive me," he said quietly, all of a sudden.

The lady with the yellow gloves looked at Klopov in wonder and was silent.

"None of that is true," said Klopov. "I made up the thing about the copper look just now, right here, sitting with you on this bench. You see, I broke my watch today, and everything appears to me in a gloomy light."

Klopov took a handkerchief out of his pocket, unrolled it, and extended his smashed watch to the woman.

"I wore it for 16 years. Do you understand what that means? To break a watch that, for 16 years, ticked right here under my heart. Do you have a watch?"

(1935-1936)

[Translated with Simona Schneider]

THE FATE OF THE PROFESSOR'S WIFE

Once one professor ate something not quite right and he started to vomit.

His wife comes and says, "What's with you?"

And the professor says, "Nothing." The wife goes away again.

The professor lay down on the couch, lay around a while, rested and went to work.

At work a surprise awaited him: They'd docked his pay—in place of 650 rubles, only 500 was left. The professor made a fuss, but nothing helped. He goes to the director, and the director throws him out. He goes to the bookkeeper, and the bookkeeper says, "See the director." The professor got on a train and went to Moscow.

On the way the professor caught the flu. He arrived in Moscow but couldn't get out onto the platform.

They put the professor on a stretcher and carried him off to the hospital.

The professor lay in the hospital no more than four days and died.

The body of the professor was incinerated in a crematorium. His ashes were placed in a jar and sent to his wife.

So, the wife of the professor is sitting and drinking coffee. Suddenly there's the doorbell. What is it? "You have a package."

The wife gets excited, smiles with all her teeth, presses a half-ruble into the postman's hand and hurries to open the package.

She looks inside and in the package there is a jar of ash and a note: "This is all that is left of your spouse."

The wife can't understand a thing. She shakes the jar, holds it up to the light. She read the note six times, and finally understood what was going on and got terribly upset.

The wife of the professor was very upset and cried for about three hours and then went to bury the jar of ash. She wrapped the jar up in newspaper and took it to the Park of the First Five Year Plan, previously the Tavrichesky Garden. The wife of the professor chose the most desolate path and just when she was about to bury the jar—here comes a watchman.

"Hey!" shouted the watchman. "What do you think you're doing here?"

The wife of the professor got frightened and said, "Well, I just wanted to catch some frogs in this jar."

"Alright," said the watchman, "that's fine, just watch out—walking on the grass is forbidden."

When the watchman went away, the wife of the professor buried the jar, patted down the dirt around it with her foot and went for a walk in the park.

In the park some sailor started hitting on her. Come on, let's go, he says, to sleep, and the like. She says: "Why sleep during the day?" And he goes on again talking about sleep, sleep.

And really the professor's wife was getting kind of sleepy.

She walks the streets, but she's sleepy. All sorts of people are running around, blue ones and green ones, and she's still sleepy.

She's walking along asleep. And she has a dream that Leo Tolstoy is coming towards her, holding a bedpan in his hands. She asks him, "What is that?" And he points to the bedpan and says:

"There," he says, "I've done something in here, and now I'm taking it to show the whole world. Let everyone look at it!"

The professor's wife starts looking too, and sees that it's as if it's no longer Tolstoy, but a shed, and in the shed there sits a chicken.

The professor's wife started after the chicken, but the chicken stuffed itself under the couch and now was already peeking out as a bunny rabbit.

The professor's wife crawled under the couch after the bunny and woke up.

She wakes up and looks around: She really is lying under the couch.

She crawled out from under the couch and saw that she was in her own room. And there's the table with the unfinished coffee. And on the table is a note: "This is all that is left of your spouse."

Once more the professor's wife let out a sob and sat down to finish drinking the cold coffee.

Suddenly, there's a doorbell. What is it? Some people come in saying, "Let's go for a ride."

"Where to?" the professor's wife asks.

"To the madhouse," the people answer.

The professor's wife kicked and screamed and dug her heels in, but the people grabbed her and drove her away to the madhouse.

And so here sits a perfectly normal wife of a professor on a cot in the madhouse, holding a fishing rod and catching invisible fish on the floor.

This professor's wife is only a sorry example of just how many unfortunate people there are in life, who occupy a place in life they are not meant to occupy.

Daniil Kharms
August 21, 1936

[Translated with Simona Schneider]

HOW ONE MAN FELL TO PIECES

"They say all the good babes are wide-bottomed. Oh, I just love big-bosomed babes. I like the way they smell." Saying this he began to grow taller and, reaching the ceiling, he fell apart into a thousand little spheres.

Panteley the janitor came by and swept up all these spheres into the dustpan, which he usually used to gather horse manure, and took the spheres away to some distant part of the yard.

All the while the sun continued to shine as before, and puffy ladies continued, as before, to smell enchantingly.

Aug 23, 1936

There once was a mechanic who decided to take turns at work standing on one leg and then on the other in order not to tire.

But no good came of this: He started getting even more tired than before and his work wasn't coming together the way it used to.

The mechanic was called into the office where he was reprimanded and given a warning.

But the mechanic decided to overcome his nature and continued to stand on one leg while on the job.

The mechanic fought against his nature a long time and, finally, sensing a pain in his spine that grew with every day, he was forced to seek medical attention.

Aug 27, 1936

FATHER AND DAUGHTER

Natasha had two candies. Then she ate one candy and one candy was left. Natasha placed the candy in front of her on the table and started to cry. She looked up, and suddenly there were two candies again in front of her on the table. Natasha ate one candy and started crying again. Natasha kept crying, but all the while she watched the table out of the corner of one eye to see whether the second candy had appeared. But the second candy did not appear. Natasha stopped crying and started singing. She sang and sang and suddenly she died. Natasha's dad came in, picked up Natasha and carried her over to the building superintendent. "Here," said Natasha's dad, "certify this death." The super breathed on his stamp and pressed it against Natasha's forehead. "Thank you," said Natasha's dad and carried Natasha to the cemetery. The watchman Matvei was at the cemetery as usual. He sat at the gate and let no one into the cemetery, so the dead had to be buried right on the street. So dad buried Natasha in the street, took off his hat, put it on the spot where he had dug Natasha under, and went home. He comes home and Natasha's already there. How's that? Easy: She just crawled out from underground and ran home. What do you know! Dad was at such a loss that that he fell over and died. Natasha calls over the super and says: "Certify this death." The super breathed on his stamp and pressed it against a little slip of paper, and then on the same slip of paper he wrote: "Hereby it is certified that so-and-so actually died." Natasha took the slip of paper and carried it over to the cemetery to bury it. But the watchman Matvei says to Natasha, "No way I'll let you in." Natasha says, "I just need to bury this slip of paper." But the watchman says, "Don't waste your breath." So Natasha buried the slip of paper in the street, put her socks on the same spot where she had dug in the slip of paper and went home. She came home and her dad was already there playing billiards by himself with little metal balls on a miniature pool table.

Natasha was surprised, but said nothing and went to her room to grow up.

She grew and grew and in four years became a mature young lady. Natasha's dad, meanwhile, had grown old and bent. But whenever they remember how they took each other for dead, they fall down laughing on the couch. Sometimes they laugh for twenty minutes straight.

And the neighbors, hearing their laughter, get dressed and go out to the movies. One time, they went out and never came back again. I think they got run over.

(September 1, 1936)

SOMETHING ABOUT PUSHKIN

It's hard to say something about Pushkin to a person who doesn't know anything about him. Pushkin is a great poet. Napoleon is not as great as Pushkin. Bismarck compared to Pushkin is a nobody. And the Alexanders, First, Second and Third, are just little kids compared to Pushkin. In fact, compared to Pushkin, all people are little kids, except Gogol. Compared to him, Pushkin is a little kid.

And so, instead of writing about Pushkin, I would rather write about Gogol.

Although, Gogol is so great that not a thing can be written about him, so I'll write about Pushkin after all.

Yet, after Gogol, it's a shame to have to write about Pushkin. But you can't write anything about Gogol. So I'd rather not write anything about anyone.

Kharms
December 15, 1936

[Translated with Eugene Ostashevsky]

Into the woods Petrov walked on.
He walked and walked and then was gone.
"Well," Bergson expressed his thought,
"Could I be dreaming? No, I'm not."
He looked and there a ditch he saw,
And in the ditch Petrov he saw.
Bergson climbed and clambered down
And was nowhere to be found.
Said Petrov surprised as hell:
"Perhaps I am not feeling well.
Bergson vanished, so I thought . . .
Could I be dreaming? No, I'm not."

(1936-1937?)

"Is there anything on earth that might have meaning and might even change the chain of events not only here on earth, but in other worlds as well?" I asked my teacher.

"There is," my teacher answered.

"What is it?" I asked

"It's . . ." began my teacher and suddenly became silent.

I stood there and waited tensely for his answer. And he was silent.

And I stood and was silent.

And he was silent.

And I stood and was silent.

And he was silent.

We both stand and keep silent.

O-la-la!

We both stand and keep silent.

O-le-le!

Yes, yes, we both stand and keep silent.

July 16-17, 1937

A man had left his home one day
With bag in hand and metal bar
And off he went
And off he went
A stroll that took him very far.

He walked on straight and forward
And always looked ahead
He never slept
He never drank
He never stopped to eat or drink nor even rest his head.

And once upon a morning dawn
In darker woods he fared
And from that time
And from that time
He vanished in thin air.

But if perhaps your path with his
Just happens to be crossed
Then quick as you can
Then quick as you can
Run quickly telling us.

(1937)

I looked long at the green trees.
Peace filled my soul.
Still, as before, big and united thoughts elude me.
Just the same shreds, clumps, tatters and tails.
Then an earthly desire might flare up.
Or my arm reaches out toward an entertaining book,
Or suddenly I might grab a sheet of paper,
But right then a sweet dream knocks on the mind's door.
I sit down by the window in the deepest armchair,
I look at my watch, I light my pipe,
But then I jump up and across over to the table,
I sit down on a hard chair and roll myself a cigarette.
I see: a spider running across the wall,
I watch him closely, I cannot tear myself away.
He keeps me from picking up the pen.
Kill the spider!
Too lazy to get up.
Now I look within myself,
But inside I'm empty, monotonous, boring,
The beating of intense living is nowhere to be found,
Everything is limp and drowsy, like damp straw.
Now I've been inside myself
And now I stand before you.
You expect me to tell you of my travels,
But I am silent, for I have seen nothing.
Leave me be and let me look calmly—upon the green trees.
And then, perhaps, peace will fill my soul,
And then, perhaps, my soul will wake,
And I will wake, and intense living will beat again inside me.

August 2, 1937

HOW I WAS VISITED BY MESSENGERS

There was a knocking noise in the clock and the messengers came to me. It took me a while to realize that the messengers had come to me. First I thought something had gone bad in the clock. But then I saw that the clock continued ticking and, in all probability, showed the right time. Then I thought there was a draft in the room. And suddenly I was surprised: What kind of phenomenon can this be for which both the flawed ticking of the clock and a draft in the room can serve as the cause. Thinking this over I sat in the chair next to the sofa and gazed at the clock. The minute hand stood at nine, and the hour hand near four, therefore it was a quarter to four. Under the clock hung a tear-off calendar and the calendar's pages fluttered as if a strong wind was blowing in the room. My heart pounded and I was afraid I would lose consciousness.

"I've got to drink some water," I said. On the table next to me stood a pitcher of water. I reached out my hand and took the pitcher.

"Water might help," I said and started to examine the water.

It was then I realized that the messengers had come to me, but I could not distinguish them from the water. I was afraid to drink the water because I might by accident drink up a messenger. What does this mean? This doesn't mean anything. One can only drink liquid. And can messengers really be liquid? So that means I can drink the water, there's nothing to fear. But I couldn't find the water. I walked about the room looking for it. I tried sticking a belt in my mouth, but it was not water. I stuck the calendar in my mouth—this was also not water. I forgot about the water and began looking for the messengers. But how is one to find them? What do they look like? I recalled that I could not distinguish them from water, so that meant they must look like water. But what does water look like? I stood and thought.

I don't know how long I stood there and thought, but suddenly I quivered.

"Here's the water!" I said to myself. But it was not water, it was just that my ear had begun to itch.

I started groping under the wardrobe and under the bed, thinking that there I would surely find water or a messenger. But under the wardrobe, among the dust, I found only a ball chewed up by a dog, and under the bed some pieces of broken glass.

Under a chair I found a partly eaten meatball. I ate it and felt better. The wind was already hardly blowing, and the clock ticked calmly, showing the correct time: a quarter to four.

"Well, so the messengers have already gone," I said to myself and started to change clothes in order to go visit some friends.

Daniil Kharms
August 22, 1937

[Translated with Eugene Ostashevsky]

THE CONNECTION

Philosopher!

1. I am writing to you in answer to your letter, which you are planning to write to me in answer to my letter, which I wrote to you. 2. A violinist bought himself a magnet and was carrying it home. On the way, a bunch of hooligans ambushed the violinist and knocked his hat off. The wind picked up the hat and carried it down the street. 3. The violinist put down the magnet and ran after the hat. The hat had fallen into a puddle of nitric acid and disintegrated. 4. Meanwhile, the hooligans had grabbed the magnet and disappeared. 5. The violinist returned home without his hat and coat, because the hat had disintegrated in the nitric acid and the violinist, upset over the loss of his hat, had forgotten his coat on the tram. 6. The conductor of that tram took the coat to the flea market and exchanged it there for sour cream, grain, and tomatoes. 7. The conductor's father-in-law gorged himself on the tomatoes and died. The corpse of the father-in-law of the conductor was placed in the morgue, but then got mixed up and instead of the father-in-law they buried some old woman. 8. A white post was placed at the old woman's grave with a sign that read "Anton Sergeyevich Kondratyev." 9. Eleven years later, worms had eaten holes through the entire post and it fell to the ground. The cemetery watchman sawed the post in four and burned it in his stove. And the cemetery watchman's wife made cabbage soup on the fire. 10. But when the soup was ready, a clock fell from the wall right into the pot the soup was in. They took the clock out of the soup, but there had been bedbugs in the clock, and now they were in the soup. They gave the soup away to Timothy the pauper. 11. Timothy the pauper ate the soup with the bedbugs and told Nikolai the pauper of the cemetery watchman's kindness. 12. The next day Nikolai the pauper came to the cemetery watchman begging for alms. But the cemetery watchman gave nothing to Nikolai the pauper and chased him away. 13. Nikolai the pauper

became very angry and set fire to the cemetery watchman's house. 14. The fire spread from the house over to the church and the church burned down. 15. A lengthy investigation got underway but the reason for the fire was not discovered. 16. In the place where the church had stood, they built a club, and for the day of the club's opening a concert was organized at which performed the violinist who fourteen years prior had lost his coat. 17. And in the audience sat the son of one of the hooligans that had knocked the violinist's hat off fourteen years before. 18. After the concert they went home on the same tram. Yet, in the tram behind them the driver was that same conductor who had once long ago sold the violinist's coat at the flea market. 19. So here they are, riding through the city late at night: the violinist and the hooligan's son in front, and behind them the tram-driver, previously the conductor. 20. They ride along not knowing what connects them, and they will not know it until death.

September 14, 1937

(1) Do not wave the wheel around, do not whittle away the wheel, do not look in the water, do not intimidate others with the stone. (2) Do not strike with the wheel, do not turn the wheel, do not lie down in the water, do not break stones. (3) Do not befriend the wheel, do not tease the wheel, lower it into the water, tie the stone to the wheel. (4)

(1937)

PASSACAGLIA #1

The quiet water swayed at my feet. I stared into the dark water and saw the sky.

Here, at this very spot, Ligudim will tell me the formula for the construction of nonexistent objects.

I will wait until five o'clock, and if Ligudim does not appear among those trees by then, I will leave. The wait has started to feel insulting. I've been standing here for two and a half hours already and the quiet water sways at my feet.

I stuck a stick in the water. Suddenly someone under the water grabbed my stick and jerked on it. I let it out of my hands. The wooden stick disappeared into the water so fast that it even whistled.

I stood by the water feeling frightened and perplexed.

———

Ligudim arrived exactly at five. It was exactly at five because just then a train sped by across the river: Every day exactly at five it flies by that little house.

Ligudim asked me why I looked pale. I told him. Four minutes passed, which Ligudim spent staring into the dark water. Then he said, "This has no formula. You can frighten children with such things but to us it is of no interest. We are not collectors of the fantastic. Only meaningless actions please our hearts. We detest folk art and Hoffmann. A palisade stands between us and mysterious events like these."

Ligudim turned his head in all directions and backed out of my field of vision.

November 10, 1937

[Translated with Eugene Ostashevsky]

THE FOUR-LEGGED CROW

Once upon a time there lived a four-legged crow. Strictly speaking, it had five legs, but that's not worth talking about.

One time the four-legged crow bought itself some coffee beans and thought, "So, I've bought coffee—now what do I do with it?"

Then, to make matters worse, a fox ran by. It spotted the crow and hollered to it. "Hey!" it yelled. "You, crow!"

And the crow yelled back at the fox:

"Crow yourself!"

And the fox yelled at the crow:

"You're a pig, crow, that's what you are!"

The crow was so insulted that it spilled the coffee. And the fox ran off. And the crow climbed down to the ground and went home on its four, or to be precise, on its five legs to its lousy house.

February 13, 1938

[Translated with Eugene Ostashevsky and Simona Schneider]

When sleep is running away from a man, and the man lies on his bed, dumbly stretching out his legs, while nearby a clock ticks on the bed stand and sleep is running from the clock, then it seems to the man that an immense black window opens wide before him and that his thin little gray human soul is going to fly out through this window and his lifeless body will stay lying on the bed, dumbly stretching out its legs, and the clock will ring its quiet bell: "yet another man has fallen asleep"; at that moment the immense and utterly black window will swing shut with a bang.

A man by the last name of Oknov was lying on his bed, dumbly stretching out his legs, trying to fall asleep. But sleep was running away from Oknov. Oknov lay with his eyes open and frightening thoughts knocked inside his increasingly wooden head.

March 8, 1938

THE DEATH OF THE WILD WARRIOR

The clocks tick-tock,
the clocks tick-tock
and dust flies over the world.

They sing in the cities,
they sing in the cities,
the sand is ringing in the plains.

To cross the river,
to cross the river
a whistling spear takes flight.

The savage falls,
the savage falls,
he sleeps while his amulet shines.

And light as steam,
and light as steam,
his soul takes off and flies.

Into the sun,
into the sun
it pierces, rustling its braids.

Four hundred warriors,
four hundred warriors
raise their swords at the sky.

The fallen man's wife,
the fallen man's wife
crawls to the riverside,

the fallen man's wife,
the fallen man's wife
breaks off a chunk of stone

and hides the dead warrior,
and hides the dead warrior
beneath the stone in the sand.

Four hundred warriors,
four hundred warriors
keep silent four hundred nights,

for four hundred days
and four hundred nights
the clocks stop over the world.

June 27, 1938

THE ARTIST AND HIS WATCH

Serov, an artist, went to the Obvodny Canal. Why did he go there? To buy rubber. What does he need rubber for? To make himself a rubber band. And what does he need a rubber band for? To stretch it, that's what for. There you have it. What else? This is what else: The artist Serov broke his watch. The watch worked really well, but he went and broke it. And what else? There's nothing else. Nothing, and that's it! And don't stick your ugly snout where it's not wanted! Lord have mercy!

There once lived an old woman. She lived and lived and burned up in a stove. And she deserved it! At least that's what Serov, the artist, figured . . .

Wow! I'd write some more but the inkwell's gone missing somewhere.

October 22, 1938

A NEW TALENTED WRITER

Andrei Andreyevich thought up this story: In an old castle lived a prince, an awful drunk. And the wife of this prince was the other way around—she didn't even drink tea, only water and milk. But her husband drank vodka and wine, and never drank milk. Actually, his wife drank vodka too, but on the sly. And the husband was shameless and concealed nothing. "I don't drink milk, but I do drink vodka!" he used to say. So the wife would quietly get the little jar out from under her apron, and bam, she was drinking. Her husband, the prince, he says: "Why don't you give me some of that." And his wife, the princess, she says: "No way, there's barely enough for me. Yhu!" "Oh, you lay-dee!" says the prince. And with those very words he smashed her on the floor! The wife's busted up her whole face and she's lying there on the floor, crying. The prince meanwhile wrapped himself in his mantle and went up to his tower, where he had a cage. He had chickens, you see. So he gets to the tower and the chickens are screaming, asking for food. One of the chickens started neighing even. "So you're a chanticleer now, are you?" said the prince to the chicken. "Shut up before you get whacked in the teeth!" The chicken doesn't get it and keeps on neighing. So, check out this scene: The chicken's whooping it up in the tower, the prince is, basically, yelling and cussing, and the wife is downstairs sprawled on the floor. There's only one word for it— utter Sodom.

What a story Andrei Andreyevich thought up. Just by this one story one can judge that Andrei Andreyevich has serious talent. Andrei Andreyevich is a really smart guy, very smart and very good!

Daniil Kharms
October 12–30, 1938

I hate children, old men and old women, and reasonable older individuals.

––––––––

Poisoning children is cruel. But something has to be done about them!

––––––––

I respect only young, healthy, plump women. Other representatives of humanity I treat with suspicion.

––––––––

Old women who go around thinking sensible thoughts should really be apprehended with bear traps.

––––––––

Any face that is of reasonable fashion brings out in me the most unpleasant sensations.

––––––––

What's all the fuss about flowers? It smells way better between a woman's legs. That's nature for you, and that's why no one dares find my words distasteful.

(late 1930s)

[Translated with Eugene Ostashevsky]

A TREATISE MORE OR LESS
FOLLOWING EMERSEN

I. On Gifts

The following kinds of gifts are imperfect gifts: For example, we give the birthday boy the lid for an inkwell. But where is the inkwell itself? Or we give the inkwell together with its lid. But where is the desk on which the inkwell must sit? If the birthday boy already has a desk, then the inkwell would be the perfect gift. Then, if the birthday boy has an inkwell, then one may give him only the lid and that would be a perfect gift, as well. Decorations of the naked body, such as rings, bracelets, necklaces, etc. are always perfect gifts (if, of course, the birthday boy is not a cripple), or such presents as a stick, for instance, to the end of which has been attached a wooden ball and to the other end a wooden cube. Such a stick can be held in the hand, or, if one puts it down, then it doesn't matter at all where. Such a stick is no use for anything else.

II. The Correct Way of Surrounding Oneself With Objects

Let us suppose that one completely naked authorized apartment resident decides to settle in and surround himself with objects. If he starts with a chair then he'll need a desk to go with the chair, and a lamp for the desk, then a bed, a blanket, bed sheets, a dresser, under-clothes, outer dress, an armoire, then a room to put it all in, etc. Here, at every point in this system an unusual little system-branch might manifest itself: The desire might arise to place a doily on the small round table, then to place a vase on the doily, then to shove a flower into the vase. Such a system of surrounding oneself with objects, in which one object snags another—this is an incorrect system, because, if the flower vase has no flowers in it, then this vase is made meaning-less, and if the vase is taken away, then the small round table is made meaningless; of course the vase can be replaced with a decanter of

water, but if some water is not poured into the decanter, the discourse
on the flower vase remains in force. The annihilation of one object
disrupts the whole system. And if the naked authorized resident were
to put on rings and bracelets and to surround himself with spheres
and celluloid lizards, then the loss of one or twenty-seven objects
wouldn't make any essential difference. Such a system of surrounding
oneself with objects is the correct system.

III. The Correct Way of Annihilating Surrounding Objects

One (as usual) mediocre French writer, namely Alphonse Daudet,
expounded an uninteresting thought: that objects do not attach them-
selves to us, rather we attach ourselves to objects. Even the most self-
less person, having lost watch, raincoat and buffet, will regret these
losses. But even if one quits one's attachment to objects then any per-
son having lost bed and pillow, ceiling and floor, and even more or less
comfortable stones, and having become acquainted with insomnia,
will begin to complain about the loss of objects and the comforts asso-
ciated with them. Therefore, the annihilation of objects collected
according to an incorrect system of surrounding them around oneself
is also the incorrect method of annihilation of objects around oneself.
But the annihilation of gifts around oneself which are forever per-
fect—of wooden spheres, celluloid lizards, etc.—will not present the
more or less unselfish person with even the slightest feeling of regret.
Annihilating correctly the objects around ourselves, we lose our taste
for acquisition.

IV. On Approaching Immortality

Every person has a striving for pleasure, which always takes the
form of either the satisfaction of sexual desire, or gastronomical satia-
tion, or acquisition. But only that which does not lie on the path
toward pleasure will lead us to immortality. Each and every system
leading to immortality converges upon one rule: *Do continually that
which you don't want to do*, because every person wants continuously
either to eat or to satisfy his sexual feelings or to acquire something,
or all of these more or less at once. It is interesting that immortality is
always connected with mortality and is interpreted by various religious

systems either as eternal pleasure or eternal suffering, or as the eternal absence of pleasure and suffering.

V. On Immorality
Righteous is he to whom God has given life as a perfect gift.

Daniil Kharms
February 14, 1939

I thought about eagles for a long time
And understood a lot:
Eagles fly on heights sublime,
Disturbing people not.
I saw that eagles live on mountains hard to climb,
And make friends with spirits of the skies.
I thought about eagles for a long time,
But confused them, I think, with flies.

March 15, 1939

[Translated with Ilya Bernstein]

When I see a man, I want to smack him in the face. It's so much pleasure to pound on a man's face.

I sit in my room doing nothing.

Then—someone's come over to see me; he's knocking on my door. I say, "Come in!" He comes in and says: "Greetings! It's great that I've caught you at home." And that's when I knock in his face, and then I let my boot fly into his crotch, too. My guest falls over from the terrible pain. And I give him a heel to the eyes! Like, don't be whoring around when you're not invited!

Or else, there's also another way: I offer my guest to take a cup of tea with me. The guest accepts, sits down at the table, drinks his tea and starts telling me some story. I make it seem like I'm listening to him with fascination—I nod my head, sigh, make my eyes wide with surprise, and laugh. The guest, flattered by my attentions, gets more and more animated.

I calmly pour myself a whole cup of boiling water and throw the boiling water in the guest's face. My guest springs to his feet grasping his face. Then I tell him: "There is no more benevolence in my soul. Get out!" And I push my guest out the door.

THE LECTURE

Pushkov said, "What is woman? The workbench of love." And immediately got punched in the face.

"What for?" asked Pushkov but, receiving no answer, continued:

"This is what I think: You roll up to women from below. Women love that, they only pretend they don't."

Here they socked him again.

"What's going on, comrades? Fine then, if that's the case, I won't speak!" said Pushkov but, after waiting a quarter of a minute, continued:

"Woman is arranged in such a way that she is all soft and moist."

Here they again socked Pushkov. Pushkov pretended he didn't notice and continued:

"If you olfactorate a woman . . ."

But at this point Pushkov got whacked so hard in the face that he grabbed onto his cheek and said:

"Comrades, it is completely impossible to conduct a lecture under such conditions. If it happens again, I will cease!"

Pushkov waited a quarter of a minute and continued:

"Where were we? Oh . . . yes! So: Woman loves to look at herself. She sits down in front of the mirror completely naked . . ."

As the word came out of his mouth, he got punched in the face again.

"Naked," repeated Pushkov.

"Pow!" they laid another one on him.

"Naked!" shouted Pushkov.

"Pow!" they got him yet again.

"Naked! Naked all over! Tits and ass!" Pushkov was shouting.

"Pow! Pow! Pow!" Punch after punch landed on his face.

"Tits and ass with a washtub!" Pushkov was shouting.

"Pow! Pow!" the punches rained down.

"Tits and ass with a tail!" shouted Pushkov, spinning to avoid the punches. "Bare-naked nun!"

But then they hit Pushkov with such force that he lost conscious-
ness and fell to the floor like a mown-down flower.

Saturday, August 12, 1940

[Translated with Eugene Ostashevsky]

THE INTERFERENCE

Pronin said:

"You have very pretty stockings."

Irina Mozer said:

"You like my stockings?"

Pronin said:

"O, yes. Very much." And he groped them with his hand.

Irina said:

"And why do you like my stockings?"

Pronin said:

"They are very smooth."

Irina raised her skirt up and said:

"And see how tall they are."

Pronin said:

"O, yes, yes."

Irina said:

"But right here they end. From here on up it's bare leg.

"And what a leg!" said Pronin.

"I have very fat legs," said Irina. "And I'm very wide in the hips."

"Show me," said Pronin.

"I can't," said Irina. "I don't have panties on."

Pronin went down on his knees in front of her.

Irina said:

"Why are you standing on your knees?"

Pronin kissed her leg just above the stocking and said:

"That's why."

Irina said:

"Why are you lifting up my skirt still higher? I already told you that I don't have panties on."

But Pronin lifted her skirt anyway and said:

"It's okay, it's okay."

"Just what do you mean, it's okay?" said Irina.

But just then someone knocked on the door. Irina quickly fixed her skirt and Pronin stood up and went over to the window.

"Who's there?" asked Irina through the door.

"Open the door," said a harsh voice.

Irina opened the door and a man in a long black coat and tall boots walked into the room. Two military men of low rank with rifles in their hands followed him in, and they were followed by the janitor. The lower ranks stood by the door, while the man in the black coat walked up to Irina Mozer and said:

"Your name?"

"Mozer," said Irina.

"Your name," asked the man in the black coat, addressing Pronin.

"My name is Pronin."

"Do you have any weapons?" asked the man in the black coat.

"No," said Pronin.

"Sit down over there," said the man in the black coat, pointing Pronin to a chair.

Pronin sat down.

"And you," said the man in the black coat, turning to Irina, "put on your coat. You'll have to take a ride with us."

"Where? Why?" asked Irina.

The man in the black coat did not answer.

"I have to change clothes," said Irina.

"No," said the man in the black coat.

Irina silently put on her fur coat.

"Farewell," she said to Pronin.

"Conversations are not allowed," said the man in the black coat.

"And should I go with you as well?" asked Pronin.

"Yes," said the man in the black coat. "Get dressed."

Pronin stood up, took his coat and hat off the rack, got dressed, and said:

"Well, I'm ready."

"Let's go," said the man in the black coat.

The lower ranks and the janitor rapped their soles against the floor.

Everyone went out into the hallway.

The man in the black coat locked the door to Irina's room and sealed it with two brown seals.

"Now out on the street," he said.

And everyone left the apartment, loudly slamming the outside door.

August 12, 1940

How easy it is for a person to get tangled up in insignificant things. You can walk for hours from the table to the wardrobe and from the wardrobe to the couch and never find a way out. You can even forget where you are and shoot arrows into some small cabinet on the wall. "Beware, cabinet!" you can yell at it. "I'll get you!" Or you can lie down on the floor and examine the dust. There is inspiration in this, too. It's best to do it on a schedule, in conformity with time. Although it's difficult to determine the time limit, for what are the time limits of dust?

It's even better to gaze into a tub of water. To look at water is always good for you and edifying. Even if you can't see anything in it, it's still good. We looked at the water and saw nothing in it, and soon we got bored. But we comforted ourselves that still we had done a good deed. We counted on our fingers. But what were we counting— we didn't know; for is water in any way countable?

(August 17, 1940)

[Translated with Simona Schneider]

POWER

Faol said, "We sin and do good blindly. A certain legal aide was riding his bicycle and, having reached the Kazan Cathedral, suddenly disappeared. Does he know what he was destined to do—good or evil? Or consider this case: An actor bought himself a fur coat and supposedly did good for the old woman who was selling the fur coat out of desperation; but at the same time it would appear that he did evil to another old woman, more precisely to his own mother, who lived with the actor and who usually slept in the foyer, where the artist kept his new fur coat. For the new fur coat smelled so intolerably of some sort of formalin and naphthaline, that one time the old woman, the mother of that actor, could not wake up and died. Or this: A graphologist got trashed on vodka and perpetrated such a thing that here, I dare say, even Colonel Dibich couldn't have picked apart the good from the bad. It is very difficult to distinguish between sins and good deeds."

Deep in thought over Faol's words, Myshin fell off his chair.

"Ho-ho," he said, lying on the floor, "cha-cha."

Faol went on: "Let's take love. It seems like it's good, and at the same time, it's bad. On the one hand it is said: Love; and on the other hand it is said: Don't fool around. Maybe the best thing to do is not to love at all? And yet it is said: Love. And if you do love—you'll spoil it. What is one to do? Perhaps one should love, but not too much? Then why is the same word used by all nations to represent the right and the wrong way of love. For example, one actor loved his mother and a plump young girl. And he loved them in different ways. To the girl he gave the better part of his earnings. Quite often, the mother went hungry while the girl drank and ate for three. The actor's mother lived in the foyer where she slept on the floor, while the girl had at her disposal two good rooms. The girl had four coats, and the mother had one. The actor took that one coat from his mother and had a skirt made from it for the girl. And finally, the actor fooled around with the girl, but he didn't fool around with his mother—he loved her with a pure love. The actor feared the death of his mother, but the thought of the girl dying did not scare the actor. So when the mother died, the actor wept, but when the girl fell out of a window and also died, the actor didn't cry and found himself another girl. So it turns out the mother is valued as unique article, like a rare postal stamp that can't be replaced by another."

"Sho-sho," said Myshin, lying on the floor, "ho-ho."

Faol went on: "And this is called pure love! Can such love be good? And if not, then how is one to love? A certain mother loved her child. This child was two-and-a-half years old. The mother used to take him to the park to play in the sand. Other mothers brought their children to that same place. Sometimes there accumulated on the sand up to forty children. And then one time a mad dog broke into the park, ran straight for the children and started biting them. The mothers rushed screaming to their children, our mother included. Ready to sacrifice herself, she sprang toward the dog and ripped from its jaws what she thought to be her child. But, having torn the child away, she saw that it was not her child, and the mother threw it back to the dog in order to snatch up and save from its death her own child who who was lying right there on the ground. Who will answer me: Did she sin or did she do good?"

"Su-su," said Myshin, tossing and turning on the floor.

Faol went on: "Does a rock sin? Does a tree sin? Does an animal sin? Or does man alone sin?"

"Mlyam-mlyam," said Myshin, listening carefully to Faol's words, "Shoop-shoop."

Faol went on: "If man alone sins, that means that all the sins in the world are located in the human proper. Sin does not go into a human, but only comes out of him. Similar to food: A person eats up good food and expels bad. Nothing bad exists in the world, only that which passes through a person can become bad."

"Umnyaf," said Myshin, trying to pick himself up from the floor.

Faol went on: "I was just talking of love, I was speaking of those of our states which are called by the same name: 'love.' Is this a mistake in the language or are all of these states the same? The love of a mother for a child, the love of a son for a mother, and the love of a man for a woman—can it be that this is all one love?"

"Definitely," said Myshin, nodding his head.

Faol said, "Yes, I think that the essence of love doesn't change depending on who loves whom. Every person is given a certain amount of love. And every person is looking for where he can apply it without taking off his fuselage. The discovery of the secret shifts and the insignificant qualities of our soul, like a bag of sawdust . . ."

"Enough!" cried Myshin, jumping up from the floor. "Get lost!"

And Faol disintegrated, like bad sugar.

Sunday, September 29, 1940

[Translated with Simona Schneider]

Perechin sat on a thumbtack, and from that moment his life changed drastically. Ordinarily a thoughtful, quiet person, Perechin was transformed into a typical scoundrel. He grew out his mustache and from that point onward trimmed it with exceptional clumsiness, so that one of his mustaches was always longer than the other. And, generally speaking, his mustache grew a bit crooked. It became impossible to even look at Perechin. Adding to that, he got in the habit of winking and jerking his jowl in the most loathsome manner. For a while, Perechin limited himself to petty baseness: He gossiped, he ratted, and he cheated tram conductors by paying them in the smallest copper coins and always underpaying by two or even three kopecks.

Wednesday, October 14, 1940

A half-transparent youth tossed in his bed. In a chair, her face in her hands, sat a woman, presumably his mother. A gentleman in a starched collar, presumably a doctor, stood beside the night table. The yellow curtains were lowered over the windows. The door creaked and a cat stuck his head into the room. The gentleman in the starched collar kicked the cat in the face with his boot. The cat disappeared. The youth moaned.

The youth said something. The gentleman, who looked like a doctor, strained to listen. The youth said: "Boats float." The gentleman bent over the youth.

"What's the matter, my dear friend?" The gentleman asked, leaning in toward the youth. The youth was lying on his back silently, but his face was turned toward the wall.

"Alright," said the gentleman, straightening up." You don't wish to answer your friend. Alright."

The gentleman shrugged his shoulders and walked toward the window.

"Get me a boat," the youth pronounced.

Standing by the window, the gentleman chuckled.

———————

About eight minutes passed. The youth located the gentleman in the starched collar with his eyes and said:

"Doctor, tell me the truth—am I dying?"

"You see," said the doctor, playing with his watch chain. "I would rather not answer your question. I don't even have the right to answer it."

"What you said is quite enough," said the youth. "Now I know that there is no hope."

"Well now, that's just your own invention," said the doctor. "I didn't say a word to you about hope."

"Doctor, you take me for a fool. But rest assured that I am not so foolish as that, and I understand my predicament perfectly."

The doctor chuckled and shrugged his shoulders.

"Your predicament is such," he said, "that it is impossible for you to understand."

(1940)

[Translated with Simona Schneider]

SINFONIA #2

Anton Mikhailovich spat and said "eh," spat again, again said "eh," spat again, said "eh" again, and left. God bless. I'd better tell you about Ilya Pavlovich.

Ilya Pavlovich was born in 1893 in Constantinople. When he was still a little boy he was taken to Petersburg, and that's where he went to the German school on Kirochnaya Street. After that he worked at some kind of store, went on to do something else, and at the start of the revolution he moved abroad. And God bless him. I'd better tell you about Anna Ignatyevna.

But it's not that easy to tell you about Anna Ignatyevna. First of all, I know nothing about her, and second of all, I fell off my chair just now and forgot what I was going to tell you about. Better, I'll tell you about myself.

I'm tall, rather bright, and dress elegantly and with considerable taste. I don't drink, don't attend the races, but I am drawn to the ladies. And the ladies don't try to shirk me. They even like it when I stroll with them. Seraphima Izmaylovna has invited me over many a time, and Zinaida Yakovlevna also said that she's always glad to see me. But with Marina Petrovna I had a curious incident, which is what I want to tell you about. The incident was really quite typical, but still curious, for thanks to me Marina Petrovna went completely bald, like the palm of your hand. It happened like this: One day I came over to see Marina Petrovna and—bang!—she went bald. And that's all.

Daniil Kharms
The night of Monday to Tuesday, June 9th–10th, 1941

REHABILITATION

Not to toot my own horn, but when Volodya hit me in the ear and spat at my forehead I grabbed him in such a way that he won't likely forget it. Only later did I beat him with the primus stove, and it was already evening when I beat him with the clothes iron. Therefore his death was not at all sudden. The fact that I had already cut off his leg in the daytime is no evidence at all. He was still alive then. I only killed Andryusha out of inertia and I can't blame myself one bit for that. Why did Andryusha and Elizaveta Antonovna get in my way? There was no reason for them to jump out from behind the door. I am accused of being bloodthirsty. They say I drank blood. But this is not true: I did indeed lap up the spots and puddles of blood—it's a natural human urge to destroy the traces of one's crime, however petty. While we're on it, I did not rape Elizaveta Antonovna. First of all, she was not a virgin anymore, and secondly, I was dealing with a corpse, so she has no cause for complaint. What of it if she was just about to give birth? Didn't I drag out the child? It's not my fault he wasn't long for this world. It wasn't me that tore his head off—the cause of that was his skinny neck. He was created not for this life. It's true that I smeared their doggie all over the floor with my boot. But isn't it cynical to accuse me of the murder of a dog when, one could say, three human lives were annihilated. Well, alright: In all of this (I do agree) a certain cruelty on my part can be discerned. But to consider a crime the fact that I squatted and defecated on my victims—that is, if you'll excuse me, absurd. Defecation is a natural urge, and for that reason not a criminal act. Thus, I understand the apprehensions of my defense, but still have hope for a complete acquittal.

Daniil Kharms
Tuesday, June 10, 1941

NOTES

EVENTS

In the late 1930s, Kharms copied a number of short prose pieces and miniature plays into a fairly plain notebook. On the cover he wrote his name and the title, *Sluchai*, in black pen, filling in the letters with a blue pencil. Underneath the title he dedicated the collection to his wife, Marina Malich. Kharms had also written "1933-1938" on the cover, but had crossed it out so that it is barely visible. The works collected in this notebook were mostly copied (in black ink) from other notebooks and drafts, often incorporating minor edits. (The notebook itself and many of the draft versions exist in Yakov Druskin's archive at the Russian National Library in St. Petersburg.) The notebook begins with a table of contents which lists thirty-one pieces. However, one of the texts in the notebook, "An Incident on the Street"—which I have included separately in the fourth section of this book—is crossed out, leaving exactly thirty pieces. The last five pieces may have been written directly into the notebook; the last three are written in blue ink, in a less consistent hand, and contain edits within the texts. Kharms signed dates (but only the year—1939) to only two pieces towards the end of the series ("An Episode from History" and "Fedya Davidovich," which is also written rather crookedly in a slightly different ink). There are no other dates written in the rest of the collection, but many of them are known, some exactly, others approximately. I provide a list of dates here, following the order of the 30 texts, in the hopes that they shed light on the deliberate nature of Kharms's method of assemblage: (1) January 6, 1937; (2) August 22, 1936; (3) 1936-1937; (4) November 12, 1935; (5) Date Unknown; (6) 1934; (7) 1934; (8) 1935; (9) January 30, 1937; (10) August 21, 1936; (11) March 15, 1936; (12) August 22, 1936; (13) April 11, 1933; (14) Date Unknown; (15) April 13, 1933; (16) Date Unknown; (17) Date Unknown; (18) Date Unknown; (19) Date Unknown; (20) 1934; (21) 1933; (22) August 19, 1936; (23) Date Unknown; (24) 1936-1938; (25) 1933; (26) 1939; (27) February 10, 1939; (28) 1939; (29) 1939; (30) 1939.

The title of the notebook and therefore the cycle—*Sluchai*—is problematic for translation, because the Russian word has a range of meanings that are not encompassed by a single English word. *Sluchai* is a plural noun that, in its singular form, can mean "case," "incident," "occurrence," "lucky opportunity," or, simply, "event," as in something that has happened. It is etymologically connected to the words for chance, accident and coincidence. The word appears in the title and the body of several Kharms texts. In those cases I have translated the word as "incident"—as in "An Incident Involving Petrakov"—foregrounding its more apparent and everyday meaning. However, in order to emphasize the more theoretical or even philosophical facet of the word's meaning for Kharms, I have translated the title of the whole cycle as *Events*. My hope is that this choice will invoke another dimension of the meanings hidden in this simple word and suggest a less mundane reading of the unique genre Kharms invented.

SONNET (pg. 48)

"An Incident on the Street" preceded this story in the *Events* notebook, but was crossed out with an "X" in gray pencil and (later?) one in red pencil as well, although the story remained listed in the table of contents. (It appears in this collection in the section of *Other Writings.*) The draft of "Sonnet," from November 12, 1935, contains a different ending, which Kharms changed when he copied it into the *Events* notebook.

PETROV AND MOSKITOV (pg. 49)

The name Kamarov is a deliberate variation on the name Komarov—*komar* being the Russian word for "mosquito." I translate it here as Moskitov to maintain both the joke and the orthographic shift. *Note: Commentary on character names and references to historical figures can be found in the Glossary following this section of notes.*

THE MATHEMATICIAN AND ANDREI SEMYONOVICH (pp. 59-61)

In the *Events* notebook, Kharms drew a simple, even primitive, curtain shape at the bottom of the page under the final word of this play—"Curtain."

FOUR ILLUSTRATIONS (pg. 64)

In the draft version of "Four Illustrations," Kharms wrote out in full the word *govno* ("shit") all four times that it appears. However, when copying it into the *Events* notebook, Kharms felt inclined to censor himself, perhaps because the cycle was dedicated to his wife. In the first two instances he spelled the word using just the first and last letters, with dashes in place of each omitted letter. In the second two instances, Kharms covered the word completely with a rectangle of black ink.

MAKAROV AND PETERSEN #3 (pp. 66-67)

MAKAROV—See Glossary.

MALGIL—Kharms makes up "magic" words that mimic the sounds of ancient languages. *Malgil* sounds like it may be fashioned after biblical Hebrew (Kharms apparently owned an old Hebrew Bible). The first syllable may be seen as cognate to the French *mal* or the English "malevolent."

ANEGDOTES FROM THE LIFE OF PUSHKIN (pg. 82)

"Anegdote" and "erpigarm" in this piece are intentionally misspelled. Kharms deliberately played with the spelling of certain words. In a diary entry dated November 22, 1937, Kharms wrote that when confronted with a "mistake" in one's writing, one should always answer, "That's how it always looks in my spelling." Alexander Kobrinskii has written an article that attempts to sort out Kharms's "intentional" mistakes and the problems of "correcting" Kharms for purposes of publication. See: Alexander Kobrinskii, *O Kharmse i ne tol'ko: Stat'i o russkoj literature XX veka. [Not Just About Kharms: Articles on 20th Century Russian Literature]* (St. Petersburg: SPGUTD, 2007), pp. 58-84.

PAKIN AND RAKUKIN (pg. 85)

In the manuscript, Kharms originally titled this story "Ossa #2," but then crossed it out and added the new title. "Ossa" is the title of Kharms's poem from August 6, 1928, and is a reference to Greek mythology: Mount Ossa, near Pelion, figures in the war between the Gods and the Titans; Ossa is also the name of Zeus's messenger, the goddess of rumor.

THE OLD WOMAN

The epigraph is taken from Knut Hamsun's novel *Mysteries*. The clock without hands that appears on the first page of Kharms's story is borrowed from another of Kharms's favorite writers, Gustav Meyerink (1868-1932), from his novel, *The Golem*. Kharms's story is an inversion of the plot of Dostoevsky's *Crime and Punishment*. The number of other literary allusions in this minimalist yet all-encompassing meta-fiction is too large to list in this short note. However, there are a number of scholarly works that tackle the problem of intertextuality in *The Old Women* and chronicle numerous literary references. Here are a few I can recommend: Robin Aizlewood's English-language introduction and notes to the text for the student edition of *The Old Woman* (London: Bristol Classics Press, Duckworth, 1995, 2001); and Ellen Chances, "Daniil Kharms' 'Old Woman' Climbs Her Family Tree: *Starukha* and the Russian Literary Past," *Russian Literature* (Netherlands), vol.XVII (1985), pp. 353-366; also, in Russian, Jussi Heinonen's disseration (University of Helsinki, 2003), *Eto i to v povesti Staruha Daniila Harmsa* [*This and That in The Old Woman, a Story by Daniil Kharms*] (http://ethesis.helsinki.fi/julkaisut/hum/slavi/vk/heinonen/); and Jean-Philippe Jaccard, "Nakazanie bez prestupleniia: Kharms i Dostoevsky" ["Punishment without the crime: Kharms and Dostoevsky"] in *Stoletie Daniila Kharmsa*, Alexander Kobrinskii (ed.) (St. Petersburg: IPC SPGUTD, 2005), pp. 49-64.

THE BLUE NOTEBOOK

A slender, hardcover blue notebook with yellow-gold endleaves and plain, unlined paper was found posthumously amid Kharms's papers (in the trunk which Yakov Druskin dragged away from Kharms's apartment after his friend's arrest). A small square slip of paper containing a kind of preface ("For the scrapbook"), dated August 23, 1936, seems to have been placed by the author at the front of the notebook. Kharms filled approximately one-third of the notebook with twenty-nine numbered texts, the twenty-sixth of which—a story about Fonaryov—he crossed out. The entries are written close together, and only on the right-hand side of the page, and are untitled save the final entry. The numbers at the beginning of each entry are circled.

BLUE NOTEBOOK #2 (pg. 115)

PEARLMAN—Most likely Kharms is invoking I.A. Perelman (1882-1942), author of a popular physics text book.

BLUE NOTEBOOK #10 (pg. 117)

On the blank page to the left of this entry in *The Blue Notebook*, Kharms wrote: "Against Kant." He drew an arrow from the marginal comment pointing to the text of #10.

BLUE NOTEBOOK #24 (pg. 122)

MARINA—Marina Malich, Kharms's second wife, to whom he dedicated the *Events* cycle. See the short biography of Malich in the Glossary.

ZHITKOV—Boris Zhitkov (1882-1938), a children's author, and a close friend of Kharms. See the short biography of Zhitkov in the Glossary.

BLUE NOTEBOOK #27 (pg. 123)

The poem with the first line "This is how hunger begins:" seems to have been written on the same day as the next poem, which is dated October 4, 1937. The numbering of this poem and the ones that follow was not changed in spite of the exclusion of entry #26.

OTHER WRITINGS

Arranged chronologically, this section is devoted to shorter, individual works, which were not compiled by their author into a coherent group or collection. My selection of the pieces was based on personal taste and a desire to present to the reader the widest possible variety of approach, form, and genre. The selection was also determined in part by whether or not I felt I could actually translate the works at all, as well as the physical and practical limitations of this book. In those instances that a particular piece was not dated by the author but evidence exists as to the time of its writing, I give the date in parentheses. When the date-range is too wide or evidence is not conclusive, I have chosen to include no approximate date, but have placed the piece in a position in the chronology that seems to make the most sense. Starting in the 1930s, Kharms often used astrological symbols and his own cypher-language to write short entries in his diaries, and also in the marginalia around his artistic texts; the dates of the following pieces in this collection were written in astrological symbols: "The Lecture," "The Interference," "How easy it is . . . ," "Power," "Perechin sat on a thumbtack . . . ," "Sinfonia #2," and "Rehabilitation."

(AN INCIDENT ON THE RAILROAD) (pp. 127-128)

This is one of the only poems Kharms published during his life in a literary journal (Leningrad Writer's Union, 1926) that was not intended for children. The parentheses around the title are in Kharms's original, but the first draft is untitled.

THE AVIATION OF TRANSFORMATIONS (pp. 129-131)

In the manuscript, two lines of this poem (second page, line 2 and line 16) contain words that are indecipherable. I have chosen to make some sense of these lines by making an imaginative leap.

ENOUGH—Kharms used the three-letter Russian word *vse* (pronounced *vsyo*)—sometimes written in all lowercase, other times in all caps—as a kind of sign-off at the end of many of his earlier poems and even prose pieces dating to the mid-thirties (for example, both of the "Phenomena and Existences" texts). This little word—a kind of flippant version of "The End," which has no easy equivalent in English—has, in Russia, become an immediately recognizable reference to a specifically Kharmsian whimsy. To translate *vsyo* literally (as "end" or "all") won't do, so I have decided to maintain two translations—"enough" for the earlier works and "that's all" for the later ones—to relay the tonal ambiguity.

"A FLY STRUCK THE FOREHEAD . . ." (pp. 138-141)

It is unclear from the remaining manuscript draft whether or not Kharms meant to rearrange the parts of this prose piece at a later time. I have chosen to present all the parts of this seemingly unfinished story, as it is an early example of Kharms's evolving prose style. Kharms crossed out two short passages in the first part of the text with a blue pencil: from "'No,' said the gentleman in the bashlyk . . ." to "We are but witnesses to his sudden death"; and the sentence "He stood up, brushed his suit off with his sleeve, spit on his fingers and went down the sky-blue path to make up for lost time."

BASHLYK—Traditional Georgian headwear: a hood with long flaps that wrap around the neck.

THE WERLD (pp. 148-149)

The title of this piece in Russian is *MYR*: a neologism formed from the combination of "*my*" ("we") and "*mir*" ("world"). I have approximated Kharms's neologism by combining the two English words. The M and R of *MYR* return in the text that begins "We lived in two rooms . . ." (pg. 174).

PARTS OF THE WORLD WERE INTELLIGENT AND UNINTELLIGENT—Kharms may be referencing Descartes' *cogitant res*, i.e. "thinking things."

"AT TWO O'CLOCK ON NEVSKY PROSPECT . . ." (pg. 153)

In the manuscript, this story is crossed out in blue pencil with one vertical line.

NADEZHDENSKAYA—Kharms lived on Nadezhdenskaya Street. See the note in the Glossary below.

HNYU AND THE WATER (pp. 156-159)

This poem is the first in a series of works that contain the character named Hnyu. For explanation of the name, see the Glossary below.

HNYU—FRIEND OF THE LAMP (pp. 160-163)

Written at a friend's apartment during a piano recital by Maria Yudina as a seemingly impromptu exercise in automatic writing, this poem has several obscure references, Khlebnikovian neologisms (such as "treesongers"), as well as made-up words that seem like occult references, but are actually of Kharms's own creation ("Faran," "darandasy," "makander").

LUNATIC—In several published versions of the Russian poems, this word is printed in syllabic breakdown: "lun a tic." It's possible that Kharms separated the syllables in an act of "making strange," thus adding percussive rhythm to the line.

TABLES OF STONE; TABLES OF GIANT NUMBERS—A reference to Velimir Khlebnikov's work on chronological rhythms, "Tables of Destiny."

PORET; YUDINA—Alisa Poret and Maria Yudina; see biographical information in the Glossary.

HNYU (pp. 164-168)

The original manuscript is highly inconsistent with regard to punctuation and capitalization (as are many of Kharms's texts) and predominantly lacks either. Some has been added here (as in most Russian editions of the poem) for clarity.

SVIDRIGAL—A neologistic noun formed from the surname of Svidrigailov, one of the main characters of Dostoevsky's *Crime and Punishment*, contaminated with the German word for "nightingale" (*nachtigall*).

O, IF ONLY PEOPLE KNEW . . .—In the manuscript, it is unclear whether Kharms wrote *lyudi* ("people") or *Lyuda* (diminutive form of a woman's name—Lyudmila).

CHEBYSHEV—See the Glossary below.

"I RAISED MY GAZE..." (pg. 171)

This poem was written a month before Kharms was arrested on the grounds of belonging to an "anti-Soviet group of children's writers." The manuscript was confiscated together with other papers upon his arrest, December 10, 1931, as an example of Kharms's anti-Soviet religious attitudes and entered by a detective of the political police into a small "collection" meant for internal use. My translation is based on the detective's typescript version as it appears in the case file. Obviously, some mistakes may have been made in the process of copying the original, probably lost. Particularly suspicious is the inconsistent capitalization, or lack thereof, in the word God. Being a deeply (though idiosyncratically) religious person, Kharms would have most likely capitalized "God" throughout the poem, whereas the Soviet detective's motives for using the lowercase were most likely politically motivated. On the other hand, Kharms's tendency was to write poems devoid of capitalization and punctuation. To stay on the safe side, in my translation I have followed the police edition, so as not to create further confusion.

"I AM ALONE..." (pg. 173)

ALEXANDER IVANOVICH—Alexander Ivanovich Vvedensky (1904-1941). Kharms's close friend and co-founder of the OBERIU. At the time this piece was written, both writers were serving time in internal exile in the small Russian city of Kursk. (See the short biography of Vvedensky in the Glossary.)

"WE LIVED IN TWO ROOMS . . ." (pp. 174-175)

This text, like the preceding one, refers to Kharms's exile in Kursk. The word that Kharms is trying to remember starts with either the letter R or the letter M, both of which, notes Mikhail Iampolski, are part of Kharms's own name. The word I translate here as "rectangle" is the Russian *rama*, meaning "frame," bringing us back to the windows featured prominently in this story. Kharms associates the window with his first wife Ester Rusakova, out of whose first name in its Latin spelling (ESTHER) he created a monogram that doubles as a drawing of a window, and with himself: The first letter of Kharms's name (the Russian "X") has a special place in his personal mythology because of its occult meaning—it appears twice in God's secret name (YHVH) and the Hebrew name of the letter H—"heit"—actually means "window," or something one looks through. (See: Iampolski, 1988, pp. 42-49, 61.) Thus the missing word is the author's name itself—Kharms—made up of a window (an H), an R and an M.

A FFAIRY TALE (pg. 178)

The title is formed through a permutation of misspellings: The correct spelling of the Russian word is *skazka*, but Kharms first wrote it as *Skazska* (adding the extra 's') then changed the original 'z' into another 's' creating the final title of *Skasska*, which is a better approximation of the Russian word's typical pronunciation. (Kharms also has a prose piece called "A Fairy Tale" in which the title is spelled correctly, and a short poem which he titled "*Skavka*," implying a lisp or defect of pronunciation.) As with other of Kharms's genre-parodying works ("Anegdotes [sic] from the Life of Pushkin" for example), the misspelling of the genre's name foreshadows a deformation of the genre itself.

F.L.F. (pg. 179)

The title of the poem in Russian is *O.L.S.*, which is an abbreviation of the poem's last line, using the first letters of three of its four words: "*Ogon' liubit vozdushnuyu svobodu.*"

[BLACK WATER] (pg. 190)

Untitled in the original. In the manuscript Kharms changes the patronymic of the protagonist mid-story so that Andrei Ivanovich becomes Andrei Semyonovich. This is not an uncommon event in Kharms's work, playing around as he does with accepted ideas of narrative and character. However, due to the state of the manuscripts, it's impossible to say whether the change is intentional (possibly motivated by the end of the protagonist's delusional visions) or is an oversight on his part.

ON EQUALIBRIUM (pp. 192-193)

Kharms uses an idiosyncratic spelling of the Russian word for "equilibrium": He writes *rovnovesie* instead of the correct *ravnovesie*, as if to accent the idea of evenness suggested by the word *rovno* (meaning "even," as in "lying flat"). I have translated this new term as "*equa*librium" in order to achieve a similar effect of slippage. The word itself embodies the idea of "slight error" which is taken up by the story.

KABEO—Kharms's humorous acronym is a word play on the Latin *caveo*, i.e. "beware."

ON PHENOMENA AND EXISTENCES #1 (pp. 194-195)

Kharms made notes in his personal occult code (made up of astrological and occult symbols and Hebrew letters) at the bottom of the last page of this story in the manuscript.

WHAT ARE WE TO DO? (pg. 202)

Kharms wrote "No good" in red pencil in the margins of this poem.

"WOULD YOU LIKE ME TO TELL YOU . . ." (pg. 203)

This story is either a continuation or a rewrite of a story at the top of the same manuscript page. Despite the fact that the two pieces have appeared in some Russian editions of Kharms (and, in Neil Cornwell's translation, in *Incidences*) as part of a whole, because of the large gap between the two pieces and the near word-for-word repetition of several lines and the same permutations of the name of the mysterious bird, I have chosen to include this part as a separate text, thinking that it stands just as well on its own. Here is my translation of the piece that appears above it:

> One Englishman couldn't for the life of him remember what this bird was called.
>
> "This," he said, "is a crichen. Oh no, not a crichen, but a chickrichen. Or no, not chick-richen, but chuckroochen. Phooey! Not a chuckroochen, a charckoochen. Of course it's not a charcoochen either, but a coochoockrichen."

PASSACAGLIA #1 (pg. 245)

This piece is from a notebook titled, in Russian, "*Garmonius*," which also contains the story "The Four-Legged Crow" (pg. 246 in this collection).

HOFFMAN—See the entry on E. T. A. Hoffmann in the Glossary.

A TREATISE MORE OR LESS FOLLOWING EMERSEN (pp. 253-255)

Kharms's misspelling of Ralph Waldo Emerson's name could be a simple phonetic mistake, or an intentional deformation. In any case, he is in fact referring to the American philosopher. Iakov Druskin suggested that in the late 1930s Kharms enjoyed discussing the idea of the "perfect gift," and in these discussions seemed to be almost paraphrasing Emmanuel Kant's view of the category of the aesthetic (disinterest, self-sufficiency, lack of functional purpose or usefulness).

In part IV of the tract, Kharms underlined the instruction that is translated here as "do continually that which you don't want to do." At the end of the last manuscript page, under the date, Kharms added a somewhat cryptic note of self-criticism: "*Chel.* The article is stupid." He signed the addendum simply "*Kharms.*" What is meant by "*Chel*" in unclear; most likely it is a strangely abbreviated, archaic-sounding form of the verb *chitat'* in the past tense, which would suggest that Kharms later re-read the "article" before giving his judgment.

POWER (pp. 264-266)

LIGUDIM—See entry on Ligudim in the Glossary.

COLONEL DIBICH—See the entry for I. I. Dibich in the Glossary.

GLOSSARY OF CHARACTERS, SETTINGS, AND HISTORICAL FIGURES

ANDRYUSHA—Short, familiar version of Andrei (the Russian version of Andrew). The name Andrei and its variations are common among Kharms's characters. The murderer-narrator in Kharms's story "Rehabilitation" calls his victims by the diminutives of their names, as if he were their friend.

IGOR BAKHTEREV—Igor Vladimirovich Bakhterev (1908-1989), a poet, was one of the original and youngest members of the OBERIU group, and was part of the Radix theater group as well (he met Kharms and Vvedensky in the early 1920s). In 1928 he made the set for *Elizabeth Bam* and directed the play together with Kharms, its author, for the first public presentation of the OBERIU. Bakhterev worked in the field of children's literature through the 1930s, although he was arrested in 1931 together with Kharms and Vvedensky in the case of the anti-Soviet children's writers. Bakhterev outlived his friends and continued his poetic experiments, though he could not publish any of his poems in Russia until 1987. His memoirs about his friends in the OBERIU circle are included in a book of reminiscences about Nikolai Zabolotsky.

HENRI BERGSON—The French philosopher Henri Bergson (1859-1941) shows up in Kharms's short poem on pg. 232 of this collection. Kharms rhymes the philosopher's last name with the Russian word for "dream" (*son*). Bergson's writing on time and intuition, as well as his essay on laughter, may have had a deep influence on Kharms. According to Eugene Ostashevsky, "OBERIU writers started off by regarding intuition as the tool for obtaining knowledge of things-in-themselves, that is, of the 'true reality' inaccessible to perception and reason." In his explication of neo-Kantian ideas in Russian avant-garde art and in Kharms's milieu in particular, Ostashevsky goes on to describe this kind of intuition as "Bergsonian insight bordering on the sixth sense." (*OBERIU: An Anthology of Russian Absurdism* (Evanston: Northwestern University Press, 2006), pg. xxi.) See also the note on Alexander Vvedensky, below.

BUBNOV—This surname sounds vaguely normal in Russian, but there is something humorous about it because of its false-etymological connection to the verb "to mutter" (*bubnit'*), which is related to the name of a Russian folk instrument, the *buben*, a kind of tambourine. The surname also invokes the Russian name for the diamond suit in a deck of cards. Kharms may be alluding to an important Soviet leader of the early Soviet period with the same surname.

IVAN BUNIN—The Russian writer Ivan Bunin (1870-1953) lived in the West after the Soviet Revolution. He was the first Russian writer to win the Nobel Prize for Literature, in 1933.

P. L. CHEBYSHEV—Pafnuty Lvovich Chebyshev (1821-1894) was an internationally renowned mathematician who taught at the University of St. Peterburg from 1847 to 1882. Chebyshev is known for his work on number theory, particularly on prime numbers, and his findings in the field of probability and interpolation. A reference to "professor Chebyshev" appears in Kharms's poem "Hnyu" (pg. 164).

ALPHONSE DAUDET—A friend of Zola, Flaubert, and the Goncourt brothers, Alphonse Daudet (1840-1897) was a successful and prolific novelist in the Naturalist vein. He died from complications of syphilis.

I. I. DIBICH—Ivan Ivanovich Dibich, a Russian aristocrat of Silesian descent, was a highly ranked military officer in the Napoleonic War of 1812. After his death from cholera during the Polish revolt of 1830-31, Dibich was replaced as commander of the Russian Army by I. F. Paskevich. "Colonel Dibich," in Kharms's story "Power" (pg. 264), is probably a reference to this military commander.

YAKOV DRUSKIN—Yakov Semyonovich Druskin (1905-1980) was a music theorist, gifted pianist, philosopher, mathmatician, and theologian who befriended Kharms in the early 1920s. Druskin seems to have been an important source of information for Kharms, particularly in the area of philosophy. They also had a mutual love of keyboard music, particularly Bach, and shared an interest in number theory. Together they developed some terminology relevant to the philosophical discussions of the *chinari*. Kharms's story about "Messengers" (pg. 240) is in dialogue with Druskin's idea of angelic inhabitants of other dimensions that briefly come into our own. Kharms's story "The Connection" (pg. 242) is addressed to a Philosopher, and that is probably Druskin. During the blockade of Leningrad, Druskin saved a suitcase of Kharms's papers from the apartment on Mayakovsky Street. Later, in the 1960s, he shared them with young scholars interested in Kharms. Finally, when it was safe to do so, Druskin gave his papers to the Leningrad Public Library (now the Russian National Library in St. Petersburg). Selected English translations of Druskin's works can be found in *OBERIU: An Anthology of Russian Absurdism*.

ELABONIN—The name recalls the Russian verb *balabonit'*, meaning to babble or prattle. Elabonin also has a somewhat vulgar ring to it—see the note below for Elbov.

ELBOV—If one were to change the letters around, it would sound like the surname is derived from *eb-*, the most foul of Russian curse-word roots, relating the name to sexual intercourse.

FAOL—This name appears only once in Kharms's works, in the story "Power." Faol could be a variation on the pre-Socratic philosopher Thales of Miletos (*Fales* in Russian). In one scholar's opinion, the name is derived from "phallus," as motivated by the discussion of love in the story (Iampolski, 1998, pp. 218-19).

FARAN—So far scholars have not identified any reference in this name/word. We can only suppose that the name is meant to sound mysterious and magical.

FOMA—A biblical name, the Russian version of Thomas, unusual in urban society in Kharms's time, recalling the names common among 19th century serfs. It appears, according to Evgeniya Ostroukhova, in six different Kharms pieces.

FOXES NOSE—Translation of Lisii Nos, an area north of Petersburg, on the shore of the Gulf of Finland. An oak grove was planted there during Peter the Great's reign.

GLAPHIRA—An old Russian name, it also appears in classical mythology and Roman histories. In the context of Kharms's poem, it sounds mysterious and mythological.

E. T. A. HOFFMANN—Ernst Theodor Wilhelm Hoffmann (1776-1822) was a German Romantic author of fantasy and horror whose stories served as a springboard for Russian Romanticism. Hoffmann's influence is evident in the writings of Pushkin and Gogol. Though only a slight variation on his real initials, E.T.A. was Hoffmann's pen name. (Perhaps the "A" stood for Anselm—the hero of "The Golden Top," a story dense with references to the occult.)

HNYU—In the Cyrillic alphabet, this wholly made-up name begins with the letter "X," just as Kharms's name does. Kharms often identifies himself with characters whose names contain the H-sound in a predominant position, and he gives the letter a special significance because of its likeness to the symbol of the cross. In Kharms's play "Lapa" (*PAJ*, no. 68, May 2001), one of the main characters, Amenhotep (who moves between the land of the living and the dead), has the "X" in the middle of his name, signifying the kind of "crossing" of which he is capable. (See more above, in the note on "We lived in two rooms . . .".) Mikhail Zolotonosov has made a case for interpreting the name Hnyu as a "psychogram" for the Greek word for "art" ("techne") that uses only the Greek letters χν, (cf. *Kharmsidat Predstavliaet: Sbornik mater'ialov [Kharmsizdat Presents: Collected materials]* (St. Petersburg: Kharmsizdat, 1995)). If this is the case, Kharms is adding an extra vowel in a way that is similar to the construction of the word OBERIU, and its extraneous final letter. The addition of sounds that deform the clarity of reference (to the point of making anything potentially meaningful into nonsense) is a technique used in many other Kharms stories. The name is difficult to pronounce, harking back to early Futurist *zaum* poetry that was made up of the most incongruent sounds—Alexei Kruchenykh's famous "*dyr bul shchil*" is the primary example.

KABLUKOV—A surname derived from the word for "heel," as of a shoe or boot.

KALUGIN—This common-sounding surname is derived from the city Kaluga, founded in the 15th century on the Oka River, southwest of Moscow.

KAPUSTINSKY HILL—Kapustinsky comes from the word for "cabbage." It may be a reference to a cave in Buryatia, Siberia.

NIKOLAI KHARDZHIEV—Nikolai Ivanovich Khardzhiev (1903-1996) is best known as an expert on Russian avant-garde art. In the 1920s he served for a short time as an assistant to Victor Shklovsky and was acquainted with many of the Russian Formalist critics, through whom he met Malevich, and also the *oberiuty*. Khardzhiev thanked Kharms in his edition of Velimir Khlebnikov's unpublished writings (1940). Khardzhiev also edited important posthumous collections of Mayakovsky and Mandelstam. It is likely that the character named Nikolai Ivanovich in Kharms's "Phenomena and Existences #2" is a reference to Khardzhiev. Several of Kharms's original manuscripts and typescripts were saved in Khardzhiev's personal collection.

KHVILISHCHEVSKY—This surname suggests something more Polish than Russian in origin, and echoes the rather unwieldy names that Gogol enjoyed giving to his characters. Perhaps surprisingly, it appears more than once in Kharms's manuscript texts.

KLOPOV—*Klop* is the Russian word for "bedbug" (Mayakovsky's famous satiric play is called *Klop*). The surname derived from it occurs only once in Kharms's works—in the untitled story that has come to be called "The Copper Look." However, in the manuscript, Kharms had crossed out several fragments from which it can be ascertained that Klopov was originally called "Kolpakov," which is a name dear to Kharms, and one of his many occasional pseudonyms as a children's writer. (The name is derived from the word for "foolscap," an object that often recurs in Kharms's writings, particularly in poems of the second half of the 1920s—the foolscap is a sign of belonging to a secret society of magician-jesters, or explicitly to the OBERIU.)

KOMAROV—A common Russian surname that appears to come from "mosquito" (*komar*). Kharms also uses a misspelling of the same name—"Kamarov"—in one of the stories in *Events*, translated in this edition as "Petrov and Moskitov."

KOSHKIN—Koshkin can be translated as Catkin; *koshka* is a female cat.

KOVSHEGUB—The etymology of this name could be parsed as "pitcher-killer" or "pitcher-lip" (*kovsh* is a pitcher, or dipper, or other receptacle for liquid; *gub* as a suffix often means "destroyer" or "murderer," but the word *guba* means "lip"). In any case, the name is unusual and has a humorous, archaic, distinctly Slavic ring, which is fitting for the lampooned historic tale, "An Episode from History," in which this character figures.

KOZLOV—A common Russian surname, but in this context its etymology (coming from *kozel*—meaning "goat") is emphasized.

KUROVA—A common Russian surname that suggests a link to chicken (*kura*).

KUZNETSOV—A common Russian surname, equivalent of the English surname Smith (*kuznets* means "blacksmith"). Kharms uses this name in about six different texts.

KRUGLOV—A realistic surname which in a literal reading suggests a round, plump, sphere-like body (*krug* = "circle"). One of Kharms's several pieces about America has a character named Tom Plumpkin, a name analogous to Kruglov.

KRYLOV—A typical Russian surname, it also belonged to Russia's Aesop, the nineteenth century fabulist Ivan Krylov. In the context of *Events* it appears near the character "Orlov," a name that has in its root the word for "eagle." This proximity highlights the etymology of Krylov as coming from "wing" (*krylo*).

LIGUDIM—Mikhail Iampolski (1998, pp. 30-32) decodes this name in two ways: 1) "To the Hebrews," as in Paul's epistle; 2) A derivation from the Hebrew phrase (abbreviated as LGDM) meaning "non-existent things." In light of this, the scholar makes a comparison to another of Kharms's unusual names—Nona (see below).

LEONID LIPAVSKY—The philosopher Leonid Savelyevich Lipavsky (1904-1941) wrote stories for children under the pseudonym Leonid Savelyev. Lipavsky was a schoolmate of Alexander Vvedensky and Yakov Druskin. (Later, Druskin and Lipavsky both studied under the Russian philosopher Nikolai Lossky.) The three of them, along with Kharms, formed an informal group, referred to by scholars as the *chinari*, which also included Nikolai Oleinikov, Nikolai Zabolotsky (for a short time), Lipavsky's wife Tamara Alexandrovna Meier (1903-1982; previously the wife of Vvedensky), and a few others. The *chinari* gathered often at the Lipavsky apartment to drink, converse, and sometimes share their recent writings. During the period of 1933-34, Lipavsky scrupulously recorded on paper what was said at these gatherings, creating a "photographic" record of the group's philosophical dialogues (a work he titled simply "Conversations"). He also wrote several treatises which, taken together with the "Conversations," explore some of the major philosophical ideas shared or at least discussed by the *chinari*. Lipavsky died on the front line during the defense of Leningrad. An English translation of his "Water Tractatus" is published in *OBERIU: An Anthology of Russian Absurdism*.

MAKANDER—One of the names in Kharms's works that is associated with magic and incantations.

MAKAROV—The character name of Makarov may be a comic allusion to Kharms's friend Nikolai Oleinikov, because of the latter's patronymic—Makarovich. A character in the children's magazine that Oleinikov edited was called Makar the Mean (*Makar Svirepy*).

MARINA MALICH—Kharms married his second wife Marina Vladimirovna Malich (1909–2003) in 1934 soon after they had met through her sister Olga, whom Kharms had been courting. In 1942, after finding out that her husband had died in prison, Malich managed to escape the blockade of Leningrad, but was later taken captive by the Germans. Through a series of seemingly miraculous events, she escaped Germany to Paris as the allies were bombing Berlin. Her mother, who had abandoned her as a child, lived in Nice with a man named Wycheslavzoff. When Malich came to see her mother in Nice, Wycheslavzoff took a liking to her, and soon she became pregnant. She moved with him to Paris, and then to Venezuela. After they separated, Malich married Yury Dournovo, a taxi driver of Russian aristocratic lineage living in Caracas in a community of Russians and other displaced emigres. Malich lived more than half of her life in South America. She left a memoir about her life with Daniil Kharms and about her miraculous World War II journey (co-written with Vladimir Glotzer). She died in Atlanta, Georgia, shortly after the millennium.

MALTSEV MARKET—An open-air market near the center of town in St. Petersburg. Renamed the Nekrasovsky Market during the Soviet era (it is situated near the Nekrasovsky Garden), the name has since been changed back to the original.

MAN'KA MARUSINA—The first name is a diminutive of Maria. The last name is derived from another diminutive of the same name (Marusya).

MASHKIN—A surname derived from the common female name Masha, a diminutive of Maria. Because of its proximity to the name Koshkin (derived from "cat") in the story "Mashkin Killed Koshkin" (pg. 74), its similarity to the name Myshkin (derived from "(little) mouse") is emphasized, thus invoking the game of cat and mouse, the expected outcome of which is reversed in Kharms's story. See also the entry for "Myshin" below.

ILYA MECHNIKOV—The Russian microbiologist Ilya Mechnikov (1845–1916) won a Nobel Prize in 1908 for his ground-breaking research of the immune system.

MIRINOS II—Though it sounds convincingly historical, there was apparently no such important man. Kharms also spells this name as Mironos in one part of the same story ("A fly struck the forehead . . .").

MOT'KA—Diminutive of Matvei, the Russian version of Matthew.

MOTYLKOV—Surname derived from the diminutive of the word for "moth."

MYASOV—An average-sounding Russian surname that comes from the word for "meat."

MYSHIN—This surname can be translated as Mousekin; *mysh* is a mouse. Myshin is formed similarly to Levin in *Anna Karenina*, which comes from both Leo Tolstoy's name, indicating an identification of author and protagonist, and the animal (Lev = Leo = Lion). The name is also akin to that of Prince Myshkin, protagonist of Dostoevsky's *The Idiot*.

NADEZHDENSKAYA STREET—Kharms lived at 11 Nadezhdenskaya Street, apartment #8, from late 1925 until his arrest in August 1941. The street was renamed in the 1930s in honor of Mayakovsky and remains such today. In 2006, a plaque in Kharms's honor was placed on the wall of the building where he lived.

NEVSKY PROSPECT—The main street of Petersburg/Leningrad is named after the river, Neva, and Russia's legendary defender against the Teutonic Knights, Alexander Nevsky.

NEW VILLAGE—Translation of Novaya Derevnya. An area on the outskirts of Petersburg near the Gulf of Finland. The way to Novaya Derevnya from Petersburg goes past the Buddhist temple, which Kharms frequented.

NIKANDR—One of the names in Kharms's writings that is associated with secret words belonging to the realm of magic or the occult.

NONA—A name that echoes Indo-European words connoting negation or nothingness; cf. Latin "non," English "none," etc. It may also have something to do with the Latin word for "nine." (Mikhail Iampolski discusses the significance of this name in *Bespamiatstvo kak istok* [*Oblivion as Source*], 1998, pp. 22-23.)

OBVODNY CANAL—The longest of the Petersburg canals, its construction began in the late 18th century, and once marked the city's outer limit. The project was resumed and expanded in the first half of the 19th century. By the late 19th century it had become an open sewer, lined with impressive granite. Its embankments continue to be central thoroughfares of the city, though the canal is now too shallow for heavy navigation.

OKNOV—A surname derived from the word *okno*, meaning "window." The window motif in Kharms's work and its symbolic meaning has been much discussed by scholars. The name Oknov appears in four Kharms texts. (See the entry for the story "'We lived in two rooms . . . ,'" in the Notes section above, for commentary on the significance of the window in Kharms's personal mythology.)

NIKOLAI OLEINIKOV—Although Nikolai Makarovich Oleinikov (1898-1937) was not officially a member of the OBERIU club, he became a friend to Kharms and Vvedensky in the late 1920s. As an editor at the children's magazines *Siskin* and *Hedgehog*, he was instrumental in keeping his poet friends employed. He had a keen interest in mathematics and authored a manuscript on number theory. In the 1930s he became a key player in the philosophical circle of the *chinari* (see the entry on Leonid Lipavsky above). Oleinikov's own poetry, satirical and sad—and often intentionally "bad"—is still held in high regard, despite a very slim oeuvre. He is perhaps most famous for his playful yet frightening poems about insects. He was arrested and killed in 1937 during Stalin's purges. (See also the note for Makarov, above.)

VSEVOLOD PETROV—Vsevolod Nikolayevich Petrov (1912-1978) met Kharms towards the end of the 1930s. Later in his life, Petrov wrote some informative reminiscences about their friendship that shed some light on the writer's last years. Petrov's papers, archived at the Pushkin House in Petersburg, contain copies (in typescript and manuscript) that Petrov made in the late thirties of several of Kharms's poems and stories, including *The Old Woman*, as well as authorial manuscripts of three of Kharms's earliest poems. Kharms's story "An Episode from History" is dedicated to him.

ORLOV—A typical Russian surname of aristocratic origin. (Count Orlov of Catherine the Great's court is one example.) The name comes from *orel*, meaning "eagle," thus connoting something transcendent, which—in the context of Kharms's story "Events"—becomes comical, because the character dies of eating the lowly meal of mashed peas. (Nikolai Gladkikh: http://gladkeeh.boom.ru /Kharms/Glava3.htm.)

PEREKHRYOSTOV—A Gogolian-type surname, which is akin in sound to the word for "intersection."

PET'KA—Pet'ka is a common diminutive of Petya, which is short for Petr (pronounced Pyotr), the Russian version of Peter, one of the most common names in Kharms's writings. Characters with this name and its various diminutives appear in approximately forty Kharms texts.

PHY—Phy, like Hnyu, is Kharms's creation. The name may be, as one scholar has argued, derived from the Greek letter φ, which is also the Cyrillic "ph" and, after the Soviet orthographic reform, used for all "f" sounds. (See the entry for "Hnyu" above.)

POPUGAYEV—This surname is derived from the Russian word *popugay*, meaning "parrot" (carrying the same pejorative connotation that it does in English). Kharms may also have known of the poet and educator Vasily Vasilyevich Popugaev (1778-1816) from the Radishchev circle, an active member of the Free Society of Lovers of Literature, Science, and the Arts (along with more well-known early 19th-century poets such as Bestuzhev, Batiushkov, Delvig, Kukhelbecker, Ryleev and Zhukovsky).

ALISA PORET—A student of Pavel Filonov and member of his workshop, "Masters of Analytic Art," Alisa Ivanovna Poret (1902-1984) was given the job, jointly with fellow Filonov student and Poret's roommate and friend, Tatiana Glebova (1900-1985), of painting murals on the walls of the House of Print, where in 1928 the OBERIU's "Three Left Hours" took place. Poret and Glebova later illustrated children's stories by the *oberiuty*. The note at the end of Kharms's poem "Hnyu—Friend of the Lamp" suggests that Kharms was attending informal salons at Poret's apartment before his arrest at the end of 1931. Kharms and the two artists also collaborated on a series of photographed "scenes" or staged portraits with elaborate costumes, some of which were parodic imitations of well-known paintings. By the early 1930s Kharms had broken up with his first wife Ester Rusakova (1906-1938), and his diaries and letters indicate several love interests, including Alisa Poret. In the diaries, Kharms writes of his emotions for her quite candidly, but seems to have had trouble opening up to Poret, who—after repeated arguments with Kharms that resulted in prolonged periods of silence—married another man. Her own reminiscences about Kharms, published in the Soviet journal *Panorama of Art* in 1980, describe an unusual but purely platonic friendship.

PUSHKOV—A surname derived from the Russian word for "fluff" or "down" (*pukh* and its diminutive *pushok*). It also resembles the word for cannon (*pushka*). It is difficult to ignore the association with Pushkin that this name evokes.

PUZYRYOV—A surname derived from the Russian word for "bubble" (*puzyr*) and its diminutive form, which means "vial" or "small bottle." Characters with this name appear in four of Kharms's texts. Bubbles, along with balloons, due to their spherical nature, figure prominently in Kharms's pantheon of non-utilitarian objects. Vessels are also significant objects for Kharms, at least in part because of their importance in the Kabbalistic myth of creation. (See Kharms's "Treatise" on pg. 253.)

ROGOZIN—This surname is similar to that of the antagonist in Dostoevsky's *The Idiot*, Rogozhin.

RUNDADAR—A made-up surname with a comical foreign and/or ancient ring to it.

SAKERDON—It has been noted by several scholars that the Greek name Sakerdon is identified in Kharms's *The Old Woman* with the sacral, especially since the Latin word *sacerdos* means "priest." The narrator's conversation with Sakerdon about

God, his meditation, and his asceticism are a case in point. Sakerdon's patronymic comes from the typical Russian name, Mikhail.

SEN'KA—A diminutive form of the name Semyon, and possibly also Arseny.

SEROV—A common Russian surname, with affinity to the word for "gray," this was also the name of a Russian painter of the turn of the century—Valentin Alexandrovich Serov (1865-1911), a major Russian Impressionist.

SHARIK—Typically a name for a pet dog (one may recall that it is the name of Bulgakov's dog-man in "The Heart of a Dog"), it literally means "little ball." Keeping in mind Kharms's predilection for all kinds of spherical and circular objects, this literal meaning is not extraneous. (See note on Puzyryov above.)

SHYROKOV—A rather Gogolian surname derived from the Russian word meaning "wide" or "generous."

PETR SOKOLOV—Petr Ivanovich Sokolov (1892-1938), an artist and friend of Kharms and the *oberiuts*. There is indication, in earlier drafts of the poem "Hnyu," which is dedicated to Sokolov, that during the early 1930s Kharms considered him a fellow member of the (already defunct) OBERIU, then consisting of Kharms, Vvedensky, Zabolotsky, Doivber Levin, and Bakhterev. It seems that Sokolov was involved in art-historical or ethnographic research concerning the peoples of northern Russia—tribes related to those of the Aleutian Islands and Alaska. Judging by the mention of "northern people" in Lipavsky's "Conversations," Sokolov's research may have been of interest to the *oberiuty/chinari*.

SPIRIDONOV—An old Russian surname. Spiridon is the name of a Cypriot saint, patron saint of potters. Spiridon was also the name of the leader of the Swedish forces (and Alexander Nevsky's rival) in the Battle of the Neva (1240).

STRUCHKOV—A surname derived from the word for "string bean."

SVIRECHKA—The made-up name of a river, Svirechka contains in it the word *rechka*, meaning "little river."

IVAN SUSANIN—Ivan Susanin, a peasant hero of patriotic Russian folklore, displayed incredible loyalty to the tsar, Mikhail Romanov. Legend has it that in the year 1613, Susanin led a band of Polish invaders into the depth of the forest where they would get lost and freeze or starve, thus facilitating the Tsar's narrow escape. When they figured out what Susanin was up to, the invaders tortured and killed him. Mikhail Glinka's opera, *Life for the Tsar*, which portrayed the Susanin story, was popular in Soviet times for its patriotic themes, though the title was changed to *Ivan Susanin*. Kharms calls him Ivan Ivanovich, though his patronymic is accepted to have been Osipovich. According to Mark Lipovetsky, Kharms's "Historical Episode" is a parody of Soviet imitations of "old style" Russian writing, and puts the "historic" nature of the Susanin tale into question. (See http://xarms.lipetsk.ru/texts/lip1.html.)

VOLODYA—Short for Vladimir. (See discussion of diminutives in the note on Andryusha above.) The full name Vladimir never appears in Kharms's creative works, but characters named Volodya (the diminutive) appear in no fewer than sixteen texts.

ALEXANDER VVEDENSKY—Alexander Vvedensky (1904-1941) was a poet and perhaps the closest friend and associate of Kharms. Together they were the driving force behind the OBERIU and several other short-lived literary movements.

Considered the most radical poet among the *oberiuty*, Vvedensky thought of his own work as the performance of a "poetic critique of reason—more fundamental" than Kant's. He married, for a second time, in 1936 and moved to Kharkov, at which point his friendship with Kharms became somewhat strained, though Kharms continued to hold Vvedensky in the highest regard as a poet. Most of what survives of Vvedensky's writings—he was notorious for his nonchalant attitude toward his own manuscripts—comes from the papers Kharms had kept among his own. He died in cloudy circumstances on an east-bound prison train from Kharkov to Kazan at the beginning of the German invasion.

MARIA YUDINA—The pianist Maria Veniaminovna Yudina (1899-1970) was one of the most famous performers of classical music during the Stalin period. She was acquainted with many artists in Leningrad's bohemian circles, and played for many informal salons, including at least one at the apartment of Alisa Poret (a Filonov school artist and friend of the *oberiuty*) in the early 1930s. While attending one such apartment performance, Kharms wrote the poem "Hnyu—Friend of the Lamp."

NIKOLAI ZABOLOTSKY—Nikolai Alexeyevich Zabolotsky (1903-1958) probably penned most of the OBERIU manifesto. He is the only *oberiut* to have made something of a career as a Soviet poet. In 1938, during Stalin's purges, Zabolotsky was exiled to Siberia for eight years.

ZAKHARIN—The Zakharin hereditary line is a predecessor to the Romanov dynasty. A member of this old family has a role in Pushkin's retelling of the story of Boris Godunov. The famous nineteenth century liberal political thinker Alexander Herzen also belonged to the Zakharin line. (It is possible that his beard is the object of Pushkin's envy in Kharms's "anegdote.")

BORIS ZHITKOV—Boris Stepanovich Zhitkov (1882-1938) was a well-known author of stories for children. Friendly with Kharms, they both belonged to the circle of children's writers working under the editorial stewardship of the well-known translator Samuil Marshak (1887-1964). Zhitkov also wrote books of popular science and adventure stories, as well as a novel about the Russian Revolution of 1905. Zhitkov's writings for children came back into print during the Thaw, and are now classics of Russian children's literature. Visits to Zhitkov's home are mentioned several times in Kharms's diaries, and in entry #24 of *The Blue Notebook*.

VASILY ZHUKOVSKY—Vasily Zhukovsky (1783-1852) is one of Russia's best known poets, famous for his folkloric and sometimes nightmarish ballads. His popularity among the classics of Russian literature is second perhaps only to that of his friend Alexander Pushkin. The joke in "Anegdotes . . ." (pg. 82) is that, as a sign of friendship, Pushkin shortens Zhukovsky's surname, a linguistic act that is impossible in Russian: Zhukov is simply not the same person as Zhukovsky.

ZUBOV—A common Russian surname that appears to come from *zub*, meaning "tooth," i.e. Toothoff.

ZUKKERMAN—A definitely German and/or Jewish surname, spelled idiosyncratically, derived from the word for "sugar."